Isca

Isca

The Fall of Roman Exeter

Derek Gore

THE
MINT
PRESS

First published in Great Britain by
The Mint Press, 2006

ISBN 1-903356-43-1

Cataloguing in Publication Data
CIP record for this title is available from the British Library

The Mint Press
Taddyforde House South
Taddyforde Estate
New North Road
Exeter, Devon
England EX4 4AT

Typeset by Kestrel Data, Exeter
Cover design by Delphine Jones

Printed and bound in Great Britain
by Short Run Press Ltd, Exeter

Note

This book attempts to portray what it was like to live in and around a large town towards the end of Roman rule in Britain. The town chosen is *Isca Dumnoniorum* – Exeter – but similar events must have taken place around other British cities. Its basis is the little we know of this period from archaeological and written sources. Beyond these imagination takes over and the events of that time are re-created through the lives and experiences of the characters in the story.

Several books proved useful in writing this account especially:

Bidwell, P.T. 1980 *Roman Exeter: Fortress and Town*. Exeter.
Birley, A. 1979 *The People of Roman Britain*. London.
Holbrook, N. & Bidwell, P.T. 1991 *Roman Finds from Exeter*. Archaeological Reports 4. Exeter.
Todd, M. 1987 *The South-West to A.D 1000*. London.

Some place-names for the area survive in a medieval copy of a late Roman list, though few can be identified with known Roman settlements. I have taken the liberty of matching some to places in my text and in one case I have invented a name. Out of necessity, since the events described in the book took place over about 18 months only, some developments known through archaeology have been foreshortened.

I have benefited from discussions of this period with many Lifelong Learning students over the past 20 years and I place on record to them my warmest thanks. I would also like to thank Chris Smart for drawing the map of Roman Devon. A very early draft of the manuscript was read by my former tutor Professor Malcolm Todd, then of the University of Exeter, for whose comments I am grateful. In addition the early chapters were read by my friends Peter Kaye and Paul Rainbird, who both offered valuable advice, although they will realise on re-reading that I did not always take it. Nevertheless I thank them for their efforts to put me right. I am grateful also to my colleague Alan Outram for discussing butchery techniques with me.

Finally I dedicate this book to my dear wife, Anne, and Edward and Olivia, all of whom suffered during the period of its writing, not least when the refrigerator was empty and I was to blame.

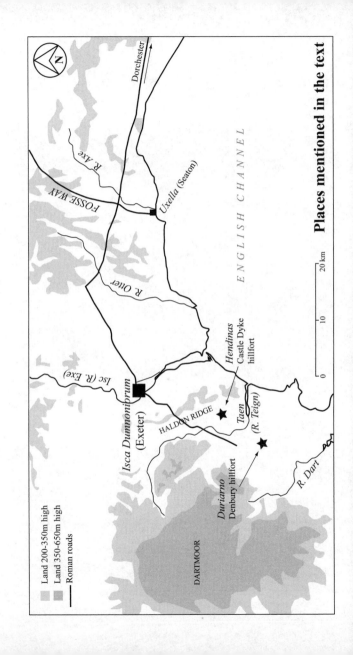

Places mentioned in the text

Isca – Glossary

List of Characters:

Victoricus	orphaned youth
Tadius	his deceased father
Cynan	landlord and would-be tyrant
Gerontius	his son
Bruscius	Cynan's bailiff
Arontius	cobbler and leatherworker
Anicilla	his wife
Viventia	their elder daughter
Armea	their younger daughter
Cinhil	wagoner
Sorio	demolition man
Rufus	retired shopkeeper
Castor	overseer of cattle ranch
Petrus	sick labourer
Attius	workman and friend of Victoricus
Silvius	workman and bailiff
Clemens	neighbour of Tadius

Briginus	guard and boor
Aeternus	farmer
Tullia	his wife
Natalinus	farmer
Marcus	his son
Senacus	official at Uxella
Lucius	retired soldier

List of Places:

Isca Dumnoniorum	Exeter
Corinium Dobunnorum	Cirencester
Augusta	London
Lindinis	Ilchester
Durnovaria	Dorchester
Duriarno	Denbury
Taen	river Teign
Isc	river Exe
Hendinas	Castle Dyke fort
Uxella	Seaton

Terms Used:

civitas	self-governing area
curiales	town councillors
Scotti	Irish

1

Victoricus paused on the brow of the hill and used his hand to shade his eyes against the glare of the early morning sun. Below him in the middle distance the sun was just touching the waters of the Isc as the river approached the sea. Shifting his gaze up river he could make out as a dark blur the walled town of Isca. He knew the town well, having accompanied his father, Tadius, several times to its market in the previous few years. They had usually done well at Isca, he reflected sadly, remembering journeys along this same track with the family's mule cart loaded with produce from their small farm.

Victoricus smiled in spite of himself, thinking of his father bargaining with the ladies and servants from the richer houses behind the forum. He could see him now, a great black-bearded fellow loudly declaring that his were the freshest vegetables on display and worth the best prices. His father's mix of wit, vulgarity and charm had always brought success and though he had begrudged the tolls which the city officials had taken care to collect, they had usually been satisfied with their day's takings.

But that was in the past. With a stab of pain, Victoricus thought of the horror of more recent days. How his father's great frame had been reduced to a hacking heap of bones, spitting blood, after a fever had swept through their household. First to fall ill were his twin sisters. Despite his mother's frantic efforts they had died within hours of each other; exhausted and weak herself his mother had been the next to collapse. Victoricus had helped his father first to nurse her, and then to bury her with her daughters. He had realised at their graveside that his father's weariness was more than grief. Tadius too was infected and died shortly afterwards despite a desperate struggle to survive. With little hope of escaping death himself, Victoricus had stood, numb with shock beside the priest sent by their landlord Cynan, as he performed the burial service. Cynan had attended his father's funeral in person, though hardly from any pious motive as Victoricus was soon to learn!

Cynan was a strict landlord, keeping a careful watch over his tenants and insisting that the customary obligations to work on his own holdings be done on the correct days. Victoricus had known that Cynan in recent years had ended many of his tenancy agreements as tenants had died or become enfeebled. It had been too much to hope that a fifteen-year-old youth, now alone, would be left in charge of the holding. Cynan was descended from an important family, who had ruled over these fertile lands before the Roman Emperor had swallowed them up some 300 years before. Lately he had taken to reminding people of this and Victoricus remembered his father jesting that Cynan was trying to resurrect the ancient kingdom.

The events of the previous day were still vivid in his mind. Cynan had sent his bailiff, Bruscius, to the family's farmstead. Victoricus had known Bruscius all his life and it was clear that the old bailiff did not relish his task. He had been sent to tell Victoricus that his father's holding was to be given in three days' time to Cynan's recently married son, Gerontius. Worse than that Victoricus was required to join the labourers on Cynan's own estate. He was no longer a free man. You'll be treated fairly, Bruscius had said. You'll have regular food, be well shod and when the time comes for you to marry you'll get one of the estate's houses. If you're taken ill, the estate will look after you. It's a hard life, but safe and secure. Victoricus appeared to have no choice. He argued, but finally gave in. But he begged for one more night in his family home and this was allowed.

During that night Victoricus made up his mind to flee. There was nothing now to hold him. He would have stayed, laboured on the farm and done his best to continue his father's work, but he did not relish the thought of working for another. Before it was light, he'd made a pack of a few belongings, transferred the coins from his father's strongbox beneath the floor to his belt purse, and set out. He had few skills, except those learned on

13

the farm, but he was young and strong. Tall for his age and broad across the shoulders, he was used to prolonged hard work in all weathers. A clear sense of right and wrong had been instilled into him from birth by both parents. It made him appear stubborn and opinionated to some and when young had involved him in fights with other farmers' sons, fights which he had invariably won. Thanks to his mother he spoke some Latin and could read and write, though rather hesitantly. He had decided that Isca was the place to make for. He could cover the fifteen miles easily on foot and be safe among Isca's citizens by mid-morning. Cynan might send men in pursuit, but perhaps he could hide in the city.

Rested, having drunk from the leather bottle hung on his pack, Victoricus began to descend the hill as it zigzagged towards Isca, his hob-nailed boots wet with dew from the grass at the side of the track. Two hours later he was crossing the wooden bridge over the Isc, joining a few people passing between the towers of the riverside gateway. The wooden gates looked cracked and worn. Rainwater had dripped from the rusty hinges leaving brown streaks on the timbers. Victoricus noted weeds growing out of the stonework and tried to remember if the walls had appeared this unkempt on his last visit.

He paused on the steep slope of the main street. He was surprised to see shutters, held in place with thick iron bars, closing off the cobbler's shop. The alley running along the side of the shop was strewn with rubbish and the premises were clearly deserted. Victoricus was shocked. His father had occasionally sold hides to this cobbler, Arontius, who had taken them for processing to the tannery downstream from the bridge. The pair of green shoes, bought for his mother's birthday three years ago and treasured by her, had been made by the cobbler.

Victoricus decided to enquire after Arontius at the pie shop next door, where a stout woman sat behind the counter. Sensing a sale, she smiled up at the handsome, well-built youth before her, noting with interest his dark eyes, open features and mass of thick wavy hair, but answering indifferently when he asked his question. Arontius had gone away. She didn't know where and she did not expect him or his family back. But Victoricus was hungry and was tempted by the smell of baking. Extracting a few copper coins from his purse, he handed them over in exchange for a meat pie served on a bay leaf. This small act made the woman more forthcoming and she became talkative.

'Business is slow,' she said. 'Those fellows in charge at the Council put up the rents again at the start of the year. We can hardly make a living. Arontius lost contracts to supply shoes to two estates near the town and couldn't pay his rent. They were evicted two months ago and we've not seen them since. You'll notice other businesses are closed too – several on this street and even some in the forum. We've never known trade this bad before. My man has been a baker for 30 years in different parts of Isca. We had our eyes on a smallholding outside the city for our retirement but our savings have been eaten away and I don't think we can afford it now.'

Victoricus gradually moved away, finally cutting off her outpourings with a brisk farewell. He continued up the street eating his pie. Despite his hunger it took some digesting. There was more gristle than meat and he spat out several small pieces of bone. Clearly times were hard. Wistfully, he remembered meals at home, cooked by his mother. Their own beans, honey and smoke cured ham. But this was no time for reminiscences. He had to look to the future, whatever that brought.

Wiping his mouth with the back of his hand and throwing the leaf onto a heap of rubbish in the gutter he walked through the archway into the forum. There were a few stalls to one side of the forum, but the huge paved area was largely deserted. Walking across to the basilica, Victoricus flung down his pack and sat on the steps. From where he sat he could see the shops and offices on all three sides of the open market place. He was struck by the lack of people and the number of premises locked up. Behind him reared up the aisled hall, which had so astonished him at first sight at the age of five and had continued to amaze him on every visit since. Built entirely of stone with great round columns inside supporting the roof, it was so much larger than any other building of his acquaintance, even Cynan's house, which had stone foundations and was so grand and unlike the timber buildings he was used to. He recalled the cool interior and echoes from footfalls and conversations. His father had told him tales of even larger buildings at places like Corinium and Augusta, but Victoricus had not seen them.

It was warm in the sun and Victoricus, who had been awake most of the night, became pleasantly drowsy and leaning against his pack fell completely asleep. He woke some hours later with sharp pains in his inside. His tunic was wet with sweat and he felt horribly sick. Was this the start of the fever which had carried away the rest of his family? Abandoning his pack, he lurched across the forum to the public latrine in one corner. Retching, he reached the inside, but fetched up against the wall before he could get to one of the stone seats. Sure that death was imminent, he clambered onto one of the seats, pulling down his breeches just in time. Just as he fetched up again into the next hole, his humiliation was completed by the arrival of two men come to ease themselves. Their tasks done, they approached the still heaving youth to offer help and advice. Had he eaten anything lately? The meat pie floated into Victoricus' dulled mind and he was promptly sick again.

The newcomers appeared to support him, while making encouraging and soothing comments. Victoricus eventually waved them away, preferring to be alone in his misery and they departed. Stomach and bowels empty, he made good use of the sponges and running water in the latrine to wipe himself down before staggering out to the doorway. The absence of the weight of his purse at his belt only struck him at that point and he looked round the forum wildly for the helpful thieves. Of course they were nowhere to be seen. Slowly he made his way back to the basilica steps, remembering his abandoned pack. It came as no surprise to find that it too was gone.

This was the nearest Victoricus came to weeping, more out of frustration than self-pity, but he had an optimistic streak, an innate buoyancy which would see him through his present difficulties. Seated on the stone steps, he was just trying to decide what to do, when he was accosted by one of the magistrate's men emerging from the basilica.

'What are you doing idling here?' he demanded. 'Beggars are not welcome in this city. The watchmen have strict instructions to thrust them out of the gates. If they're seen in Isca again the Council has ordered that they be sold to a slave dealer at the port downriver.'

'I am no beggar', protested Victoricus, 'but fit and able and willing to work.'

He started to recount his misfortunes, but was cut short.

'Get work or leave', was the blunt message. 'If we see you hanging around the forum again tomorrow, you'll be put into the watchmen's charge.'

Still feeling weak, the youth trudged across the forum. The stallholders in the corner were packing up. One was wrapping pots in straw and placing them carefully into the panniers of his pack mule.

Business had hardly been brisk, thought Victoricus. He'd seen very few customers. The potter's grim face seemed to confirm that he too had had a bad day.

Out of the forum entrance now, Victoricus turned along the covered way which ran round the side of the building. The shadows of the buildings opposite extended across the street and he was uncomfortably aware that he was cold. He quickened his pace and made in the direction of the east gate, not with any purpose in mind, but merely to keep on the move. Passing through the alleyways off the main street he noticed that servants in some of the house yards were already drawing shutters across the windows. In a few he could make out the glow of oil lamps already lit and heard the voices of diners seated at family meals. But he felt no hunger, despite the smells of cooking and the obvious sounds of eating. The after-effects of that pie were still with him.

The gates were not yet closed for the night, but Victoricus guessed it would not be long before they were swung to. He contemplated the back of the east gate with its great entrance briefly, before deciding to stay within the walls. A heavy wagon pulled by six oxen came slowly under the archway, its driver bawling either at the beasts or at a man walking alongside the leading animals. Mud in great streaks clung to the sides of the empty wagon and the oxen were wet with sweat. The end of a long journey, thought Victoricus. The driver was trying to turn the cart sharp right into the street behind the town wall, but was hardly achieving it. Despite harsh use of a metal tipped goad, his leading man was failing to cajole the beasts round. They were heading for the pavement and the locked up shop on the corner and the wagon was swaying close to the public fountain in the centre of the street.

Victoricus grabbed the harness of the leading beast and tugged. If he could persuade this animal to come round the rest would follow. His fifteen years' upbringing on the farm had given him a knowledge of and respect for animals. The ox was reluctant, but it yielded eventually to his persuasions. Gradually the beasts moved in the right direction and the cart came round without disturbing the basin of the fountain or its ornate inscription. Victoricus walked alongside the ox team as the cart clattered up the street. He remembered the great hill with one of its sides eaten away in this northern corner of the town. Isca had its own quarry inside the walls and stone from it had been used to build the defences and many of the town's buildings. As the wagon turned into a track way going off at a slight angle, Victoricus realised that they were making for the quarry. Gates at the end of the track were opened and the wagon and team passed through.

Out of curiosity, Victoricus accompanied them and watched as the wagon halted outside some wooden sheds and the driver jumped down. An argument started with the driver berating his leading man for his incompetence and the latter criticising the driver's skills. At first Victoricus thought it would come to blows, especially as both flourished whips, jabbing them in each other's direction, but gradually he sensed that these were old arguments well-rehearsed between them. Both appealed to him from time to time over different points, but he wouldn't be drawn in. Eventually the driver, whom Victoricus now knew as Cinhil, since his companion had shouted his name many times, wearied of the argument and spoke directly to Victoricus. His remarks about his companion's incompetence nearly started the arguments again, but he was quick to thank Victoricus for coming to their assistance. He praised his handling of the beasts and enquired where he had picked up the skills. Victoricus explained his own situation briefly, putting stress on the fact that he was looking for work. Cinhil thought there was little possibility of work in the quarry, but suggested he return the following morning, when the manager might be on site.

By now it was dark and Victoricus had to decide where he was going to bed down for the night. He had already had one idea. He had thought of Arontius' old shop, empty and boarded up. He retraced his steps back to the main street and descended the hill. Pausing outside the cobbler's premises, he noted that the pie shop was closed up and only the faintest of glows through a first floor shuttered window suggested the baker and his wife were at home. Having checked that the street was deserted, he set off down the narrow alleyway between the two buildings. It smelt dank and his feet slithered several times on rotting rubbish. He could make out a side doorway, also boarded up, before the alley turned the corner behind Arontius' house. He could feel the rough timbers of a fence, over which he climbed into a tiny yard. The back door also had boards across it, but here the workmen had not been as thorough in sealing off the house. Victoricus was able to wrench two boards away and delivering a sharp kick at the door found himself inside.

The small square room into which Victoricus stepped had clearly been Arontius' workshop. That much was clear from the smell of wax and tanning. He let his eyes grow accustomed to the dark and then groped his way over to a wooden ladder in one corner and clambering up it emerged in a larger attic room under the eaves of the house. As far as Victoricus could make out it was bare except for some dry reeds in one corner. He supposed that these had been discarded from a mattress when the previous occupants had left. Not much caring, since he was desperately tired, he flung himself down on them and wrapping his clothes about him promptly fell asleep.

2

Victoricus was not sure whether it was the penetrating cold of the spring morning or the sound of the baker chopping firewood in the next yard which eventually woke him. Once awake, however, he was certainly aware of both cold and hunger. The long attic room spanned the full length of the building and once upright Victoricus was conscious of the roof timbers just above his head. He peeped out of a crack in the shutters overlooking the main street and saw one or two workmen in short tunics trudging up the hill. They reminded him that he now needed work if he was to survive in Isca.

Cautiously he descended the ladder into the room below. He could make out where the cobbler's workbench had stood against the wall. Brown staining splattered the wall from about waist height. Stones set into the earth floor near the alley wall were red from a hearth's heat. Passing between hurdles, which divided the room into two he glanced into the shop area next to the street. Not that there was much to see. The cobbler and his family had obviously removed what few belongings they had possessed. Grass was already sprouting through the floor and a lump of plaster had fallen from one of the walls.

Victoricus withdrew and peeped cautiously out of the back door. The yard was not overlooked, but he could hear the baker and his workmen busy next door. From the smells and sounds reaching him it was clear that the ovens were outside and baking was in full swing. The smell of baking bread reminded him that he was hungry, but it was not just lack of money which held him back. His gut-wrenching experience of the baker's wares on the previous day was still too vivid.

Crossing the yard he noted with some alarm a timber-lined well with only a slight kerb just off centre. Had he walked that way last night he might easily have pitched into it. He could make out water way below and hauled on a rope left attached to an iron hook driven into the kerb. A wooden bucket emerged with what appeared to be clean water and, unclipping it from the rope, he drank greedily. A lean-to shed on the fence in the far corner of the yard had served the family as a privy. It was just a hole in the ground and Victoricus made use of it, raising a second bucket from the well to flush it down.

Putting the planks back across the house door, he climbed cautiously over the fence and resolved to follow the alley round away from the main street to see where it led. Clearly from the undergrowth and rubbish the path was unused. It emerged onto a narrow street in which Victoricus was astonished to note hardly any of the houses were occupied. Wandering through he became aware that this quarter of the town, hidden behind the main street, was almost wholly deserted. Some of the buildings had been abandoned so long that they had tumbled down. Others had been ransacked. Shutters and doors had been removed. Timbers had been prised out of walls. Roof tiles were missing on some; others had been completely stripped and even roof timbers removed.

The first sign of life was the sound of a dog barking furiously inside one of the houses as Victoricus turned the corner. He had already noted that this house was not derelict. Its window shutters and door were painted. An elderly man with thinning red hair emerged holding back a huge dog on a chain.

'What is your business here young man?' he demanded.

'Just exploring,' was Victoricus' reply, which obviously did not satisfy his questioner.

'Thieving more likely,' came the quick response. 'One of Sorio's men looking for pickings. He's sending round boys now to look for materials. Be off, or I'll let the dog loose.'

Despite Victoricus' protest that he knew no one called Sorio and was not on the look out for anything to thieve, the old man still looked suspicious.

'What are you doing here then?' he asked. 'Even the council workmen don't come here any longer.

The only people I see are up to no good. You're certainly not one of Sorio's regulars. They usually arrive in teams with carts.'

Victoricus was cautious, not wanting to divulge the whole of his history, but he did explain that he had only arrived in the city yesterday and that he had been robbed. He was careful not to say where he had spent the night.

'I'm on my way to look for work,' he told the man.

A loud guffaw greeted this last remark.

'Not in this town, boy,' spluttered the old man, who appeared to be softening. 'Can't you see, the place is dying. Twenty years ago you might have got work. Then I could have told you the names of all the people in this street. Decent families with the men folk all in work. Our children played here. We all went along to the amphitheatre together occasionally. Now that's a rubbish dump. This house was a shop selling wooden bowls and cups. My wife was behind the counter, while I did the wood turning in the back. We did a good trade. Now she's dead and our eldest with her. The other two left, my daughter to marry a lead miner from east of here whom she met in town and my other son went overseas. All the folk are the same – they've gradually drifted away or died off. And now that thieving Sorio pulls their houses apart for his own gain and the rats play in the rubble. He wants me out so that he can clear the whole street, but I'll set the dog on him, first. I was born here and please the gods, I'll die here.'

The old man paused. It was some time since he'd spoken so long to anyone. He occasionally bandied words with the stall holders in the market, but he was always wary of being away from his house for too long. He'd taken to growing most of his food in his own and his former neighbour's garden behind the houses. He realised with a jolt how empty and lonely his life was now and felt sorry for himself. This young man standing before him looked honest enough. He even reminded him a little of his dead son.

'My advice to you is to get out of town. Look for work in the countryside. Labourers are often needed on some of the bigger farms, especially at this time of year. You'll do no good in Isca. I don't suppose you've eaten this morning. Look, I'll fill your belly and then be off with you out of this place.'

Victoricus smiled. Was this the same belligerent householder who'd confronted him only five minutes before? He'd soon changed his tune, he thought. He hesitated, but what had he to fear from an old man and a dog? He hastened to thank him and accept his food, but at the same time was determined to stay in the city at least for the time being.

With stomach full and his ears bombarded with more details of his host's family and friends, Victoricus emerged from the house. The man, whom he now knew as Rufus after swapping names, had been content to let him eat and had not tried to pry more deeply into his past life.

Fortunately Rufus had been content to ramble on happily.

'I shall try for work here in town,' Victoricus had said, in one of the rare pauses, and Rufus had not tried again to dissuade him.

His only comment was: 'I shall be interested to know how you get on.'

Striking uphill through the abandoned quarter, Victoricus came to a narrow alleyway which emerged between two houses into a paved street. Most of the buildings here were occupied with just an occasional one boarded up and as the forum basilica loomed ahead to the right, he realised he was near the centre of town again. He hurried along the main street and, retracing his steps from the previous night, eventually found his way through the gate into the quarry.

He was much more aware of the size of the quarry in full daylight. It had the appearance of an irregular bite out of the side of a cone shaped hill. The wooden shed, which he had dimly perceived the previous evening was to his left, but was empty. The only signs of life were two men working at the face.

As he approached them he could see that they were hammering wooden pegs into a section of the stone face which jutted out from the rest. The older man with the hammer looked up, wiping the sweat from his face.

'What brings you here then, youngster?' he asked, glad of a short break. Victoricus explained that he was looking for work but was half-prepared for their reaction as both men laughed out loud.

'I'm strong and not afraid of hard work,' he said, defiantly, 'and though I don't know this trade I'd learn it soon enough.'

'I don't doubt it, young fellow,' said the quarryman, looking him up and down, 'but there's still no work. We're to be paid off next week and the Council, which owns these works are closing them down. There's no call for stone from here any longer. Who can afford it? And anyway, look around town – there's plenty of stone just lying about in some parts for the taking.

'You'll be lucky to get work anywhere in this ghost town,' remarked the other man, speaking for the first time. 'My lads have all left and found work elsewhere. Two of them are in government service – now that's the sort of work to be in these days.'

'You could try the cattle station,' said the first man, 'between the forum and the north gate. They sometimes take on labour, but they pay a pittance and work you 'til you drop. As for me, the wife and I are off next week. My brother's got a farm near the coast and we're off to lend him a hand.'

3

Victoricus found the cattle station easily. Taking an alley, which ran between two houses opposite the forum, he was soon aware of the stench and sound of cattle. He found himself in an open area. A cobbled yard surrounded by a fence was full of cattle and on the far side stood a large house on its own. He walked round the fence observing the small black bullocks. They were fine animals, well fed and lively. Cattlemen were separating the herd out into pens, cursing at the animals and applying the sticks they carried liberally. There must be at least 100 head of cattle here thought Victoricus, marvelling at the size of the operation.

Reaching the house, he noted that one of the three wings around a small courtyard served as offices from which men emerged from time to time, some clutching wooden writing tablets. Entering the first room he encountered a clerk seated at a rough table furiously scratching out figures with a metal stylus. Ink stains littered the table and concentrated in a circle around the inkpot. The clerk muttered figures to himself and from time to time brushed the sweat from his forehead and wiped it on his tunic. He scarcely looked up as Victoricus asked about work, resenting the interruption.

'Try the third office along,' was the sole reply as the doorway was filled with the bulk of another visitor, apparently a driver, judging from the whip in his hand.

'Is that bill ready yet?' shouted the newcomer, as he advanced to the desk. 'The ship will miss the tide if it waits much longer and this last wagon load must be on it.'

'Two minutes,' replied the clerk 'will see it done, if I get no more interruptions.'

The driver eyed up Victoricus resentfully and he decided to beat a hasty retreat. In the second office Victoricus was confronted by a red faced, thick-necked barrel of a man, who was standing, hands grasping the window sill, bellowing out into the yard. This was a bullock in human form.

'What do you want?' was the blunt greeting as he turned from the window.

Victoricus came straight to the point: 'I'm look-ing for work. I was brought up on a farm, so I know animals and I'd be prepared to do anything.'

'I don't employ boys,' came the reply, 'this is men's work. Go back to your farm.'

Victoricus protested that he might be young, but he was strong and experienced and could start immediately.

'How come you're available then?' demanded the human bullock. 'Been caught thieving or have you chased one maiden too many? I'm not handing out jobs to every misfit country bumpkin that fetches up here with a hard-luck story. Get out and crawl back where you came from.'

Victoricus, normally slow to take offence, felt his anger rise, but realised there was little point in arguing. Nothing was going to change this man's mind. He left with as much dignity as he could. The cattleman, known as Castor, followed him out as if to see him off the premises. Pausing to let a cart rumble past, Victoricus crossed to the enclosure.

As he walked along the outer fence, the youth could see one of the workmen trying to entice a bullock out of one of the pens. He had a rope round its neck and was pulling at the animal and cursing it at the same time. He flayed at its flank with a long stick and must have caught it on a raw spot, as the creature suddenly dived forward, taking the man by surprise. He had foolishly wrapped the rope around his forearm and it now tangled, dragging the hapless victim along. He stumbled and fell and was dragged along the ground in the wake of the bellowing beast. Other cattlemen came running, but regarded the incident as a welcome diversion rather than offering any practical assistance.

Victoricus watched fascinated, but as the bullock turned towards the stretch of the fence where he stood he realised that its hooves were repeatedly treading the now inert body of the man. Without thinking, he mounted the fence and leaped into the path of the charging animal. Stepping to one side as it came near he grasped its horns and forced its head down. At the same time he pitted all his weight and strength against the forward motion of the animal. Of course, as he later realised, the bullock was by now tiring and his intervention just tipped the balance and slowed it to a halt.

'I thought I'd seen the last of you,' bellowed a familiar voice behind him. The overseer came up, kicked the prone figure on the ground and shouted to the others to get back to work. 'The show's over,' he yelled. 'Fetch a bucket of water over here, Petrus.'

While Petrus hastened to draw the water from the stone trough at one side of the enclosure, the overseer turned the body of his workman face up. Removing a knife from a leather pouch at his belt, he quickly cut the rope from the victim's arm. The bone of the forearm was sticking through the flesh – a bad break.

'No more work to be had out of him,' muttered his boss. He grasped the bucket and dashed the water into his face. The reaction was slow, but the wretched man did open his eyes. Pain registered almost immediately and he heaved and was sick out of the corner of his mouth.

'Get hold of one of your cronies and dump this useless carcass onto the straw in the barn,' spat the overseer to Petrus. 'When the vet comes to look at that sick bullock I might remember to get him to look at this creature here. The wages he's owed could just cover the cost of strapping up that arm, but his working days are over.'

Turning to Victoricus he said: 'You've got

yourself a job – temporary until I can find a proper replacement, but you've got work for today and tomorrow. You work 'til I say you finish and you turn up on site at sunrise. If you're late you don't get paid. Now get that bullock over to the slaughterhouse over there and then come back and see Petrus for the next job. Remember I'll be watching out for you.'

Castor had pointed to the end of the second wing of the house and Victoricus grasped the remains of the rope and persuaded the bullock to walk with him across the enclosure. He hardly needed directions. The stench met him part way over. Not that he was concerned – Victoricus was used to the slaughter of animals, though not on this scale. He persuaded the beast into the wide doorway. In one corner three men were sawing up a carcass, throwing the resulting joints into a series of tubs. As they were filled two men were carrying them through into a second room. They carried a long pole, which was slipped through the iron rings either side of each tub and then hoisted onto their shoulders.

The butcher, stripped to his waist, advanced, long handled axe in one hand, a hood of coarse wool in the other. He slipped the hood over the bullock's head, motioning for Victoricus to pull the animal to one side. With one swing at the animal's head he felled it. It went down without protest, falling onto its knees and then rolling onto its side. Taking his knife out of his pouch he slit its throat. The butcher's assistant began the task of skinning the animal without delay. Victoricus, marvelling at the efficiency of the operation, walked back, rope in hand, to find Petrus. Petrus was filling the water trough from buckets brought to him from a well. He paused as Victoricus approached.

'Have they killed that one?' he asked and when Victoricus nodded he went on. 'Keep them supplied, one beast at a time, all from that pen. When they want another they'll wave from the doorway. Keep a sharp look-out. In the meantime you can give a hand loading the carts. I'll take you over.'

Victoricus wound the rope around his middle and glanced at his companion. Petrus looked worn out. He was pale and thin and walked with a slight limp. His eyes were dull and fixed on the ground. Victoricus took the opportunity to find out more about his new employers asking first about pay.

'You'll get that, such as it is, after you've done eight days' work,' came the reply, 'but part of it comes in food, some of which you'll get about the middle of each day. Those are rations to be eaten here.'

'And where is all this meat going to? Where are the carts taking it?'

'Much of it's being shipped out down river from the town quay.'

'Yes, but where to?'

'You ask too many questions. Be thankful you've got a job. Just do the work.'

Is everybody here this irritable, thought Victoricus, as they came to the carts. Barrels were being rolled out from the back of the abattoir across a stone platform against which a cart had been backed up, with its tail end open. Two men were stacking them upright on the cart two deep. Victoricus recognised one of them as Cinhil, the driver from the quarry.

'I see you've got yourself a job, youngster,' he shouted.

'Help to roll those barrels out,' said Petrus 'and remember to keep a sharp look out for the butcher's call.'

Victoricus joined three others fetching the barrels out of a back room, rolling them up a ramp and across the platform. He soon found that it took some strength to get the barrels rolling, but once they were moving they were difficult to stop. Twice he only just managed to stop a barrel before it careered into the men loading the cart.

'Steady, youngster,' remarked Cinhil, 'you'll be breaking the cart and us too.'

Part way up the ramp with the next one his foot slipped and the weight of the barrel proved too much for him. He leaped out of the way as it rolled back gathering speed to crash against the back wall of the cellar. One of the loaders in the cellar stood back and gaped as the barrel split open, its wooden top coming off. Salted beef joints spilled out.

The silence was broken by Cinhil, standing at the top of the ramp.

'Fool of a boy,' he shouted, 'I told you to slow down. Look sharp and get an empty barrel from the store.'

As Victoricus moved, an ominous bellow came from outside. He recognised the unmistakable tones of Castor, the overseer. In the middle of a string of curses he heard the word butcher and realised that another beast was needed. Ignoring the chaos in the cellar, he mounted the ramp, jumped from the platform and ran. Butcher and overseer were standing outside the door of the slaughterhouse looking towards the bullock pens. As Victoricus came up, Castor turned and his face twisted.

'I should have guessed it would be you. Get the next beast over here quick and stay alert, if you want to be paid.'

Victoricus ran over with the next beast and the butcher went through the same ritual as previously. Castor stayed in the doorway until the beast was dead. As Victoricus wound the rope back round his waist, he stepped over. Before he'd had time to tie the rope, the overseer had struck him across the face with the flat of his hand and he found himself lying in the bullock's blood.

'Now, get back to work,' he spat out.

Angry as the blow had made him, Victoricus knew better than to show any reaction to this man's brutality; he had to accept whatever treatment was meted out to him if he wanted to keep his job. That was the way it was. He picked himself up and, carefully avoiding Castor, made for the door. Back in the cellar he realised that the broken barrel had been cleared away. Its contents had been transferred into a fresh barrel and the cart was almost loaded. He concluded that the workmen were probably not anxious to attract the overseer's attention, no matter who caused the problem. He resolved to take great care with the barrels and to keep a sharp look out for the butcher's signal.

The rest of the day passed without incident. He ate his bread and fat, brought round in a basket to the workers by an amiable old man in the middle of the day. By then the blood on his tunic had dried, but his face still stung to the touch. By the time the shout went up to finish Victoricus was so weary he could have fallen asleep in the cellar. But he dragged himself back to the cobbler's house, taking care not to be seen as he climbed over the fence and scrambled through the door.

He had no difficulty waking. He was used to getting up before dawn. He sluiced himself down with water from the well, noting with satisfaction the stubble growth on his chin, as he had decided to grow a beard in case any of Cynan's men came looking for him. Setting off in good time, he called on the old man and his dog in the back street to tell him of his good fortune. He guessed that Rufus would be up and about. Sure enough, as he approached the house the dog started barking and Rufus emerged. He invited Victoricus in, eager for news. Even the dog seemed pleased to see him.

The old man assumed that his visitor would eat some breakfast with him and Victoricus was too hungry to protest too much. He fell upon the beans, parsnips and chicken which Rufus put in front of him, explaining between mouthfuls about his job.

'At the cattle station across from the side of the forum. A big undertaking with lots going on but a pig of an overseer. I've been taking the bullocks for slaughter and helping load wagons.'

The old man confessed that he had not ventured that way.

'But I've seen cattle being driven into town and carts going out of the south gate.'

He had no idea who owned it or where the meat was being sent.

'How many days work have you got?'

Victoricus admitted that he had only been set on for a couple of days.

'I don't expect they'll keep working at this furious pace. There's bound to be slack days and no doubt I'll be stopped then. Still, it's work, if I can stand it.'

Rufus eyed his tunic with the dark streaks where the blood had dried. Victoricus did not admit to having been knocked to the ground, but passed it off as the result of slipping on the slaughterhouse floor. The old man fetched a clean tunic from a wooden chest in a corner of the room and urged him to put it on. The youth was reluctant, but Rufus thrust it at him, saying that it was only an old thing, which had belonged to his son.

'I'll wash yours while you're at work,' he said. 'It'll give me something to do.'

Victoricus gave in and changed quickly, his eye

on the light outside. The sun was beginning to come up.

'I'd better go – see you tomorrow and thanks for the food.'

The old man came to the door and reflected again as Victoricus hurried up the street, how the lad reminded him of his son. The same powerful build, broad shoulders and stocky legs. An open, trusting boy, he thought, with a steady gaze which missed nothing. Slow to rouse, but not one to cross.

Victoricus meanwhile caught up with Petrus part way down the alley on the way to the enclosure. Petrus was coughing so much he was red in the face. No chance of conversation with him. As they emerged they saw Castor leaning on the fence near the house.

'So you've turned up again,' was his greeting as they approached. 'Don't expect special treatment on your second day. We'll get some work out of you today. There's hides to be cleaned and bundled. That should improve your clean tunic.'

Turning to Petrus, he remarked 'Don't stand there coughing your guts up, go and sort out the rest of those bullocks. Make sure those from Lurio are done first.'

Victoricus was directed over to an area of the enclosure where several piles of hides were strewn about. Each one had to be spread on the ground and the fatty tissue adhering to it lifted off with the use of a flat metal blade. It could only be done from a kneeling position and he soon discovered that it was not only a messy job but also a back breaking one. The two men, who had loaded barrels with him the previous day, worked alongside him.

'You can drop one of these, young fellow, without putting us in fear of our lives,' joked one of them. 'When that barrel crashed back into the cellar yesterday, I thought the gods had deserted me.'

'Watch you don't make holes in that skin, Attius,' said the other, 'or Castor will be skinning you.'

'He doesn't scare me,' commented Attius, but he looked about him cautiously.

'How long have you two been working here, then?' asked Victoricus.

'Too long,' came the swift reply from the second man, called Silvius. 'But there's nothing else to do round here. I used to work on my uncle's farm, but when his own sons grew up I was no longer needed.'

The number of cleaned hides increased and Attius counted out five and trussed them up with a thin strip of hide.

'This lot will have to be ready for loading by mid-afternoon,' he commented.

'Where are they going?' asked Victoricus.

'I don't know,' answered Attius, 'but I guess they'll be shipped out of the Isc and westwards along the coast. We went with a load once all along the coast for a day and a night, finally ending up in a great bay with two large rivers flowing into it. We spent most of the voyage being sick over the side and were pleased to reach dry land. We unloaded barrels of beef and lots of hides near the mouth of one of the rivers and carts were there to pick them up. We brought great lumps of tin and copper back and landed those part way up another river not too far off on the voyage home. Strangely, we weren't sick on the return journey.'

Victoricus realised that this voyage must have taken his companions close to his home territory, but he made no remark about this. Glancing across to the house, he noticed that Castor had a visitor. The two of them were talking earnestly just outside the office. Victoricus thought there was something familiar about the newcomer and, straightening up and staring he realised with a start that it was Bruscius, his landlord's bailiff. He quickly bent back to his work, fearful that he might have been seen. What if Castor brought the bailiff over to where they were working? If he did then Victoricus was in trouble. He glanced about him to work out his best route for escape, resolved that if Bruscius sighted him he would make a run for it.

Just then, Attius decided that they should take some of the bundles of hides over to the store and bring more untreated ones out. The three of them set off with a handcart loaded with bundles, Victoricus making sure that he walked on the side away from Bruscius, steadying the load. They were soon out of his sight behind the second wing of the house and eventually beyond the barrel cellar of the previous day. Silvius pulled open a wooden door and they deposited their load with others against the far wall. Victoricus noted the pungent, familiar stench of animal flesh.

'Castor seems to have a visitor,' he remarked as nonchalantly as he could, 'I wonder who he is? Another seller as like as not.'

'Not him,' said Silvius, 'he only comes occasionally say once a month and I tell you this, Castor minds his manners with him. I don't know what he's called or where he comes from, though I don't reckon he's from Isca, but Castor takes orders from him.'

'Quick, finish loading that cart,' called Attius, 'there's someone coming.' Victoricus braced himself, sure that Bruscius was approaching and he was cornered. All three were hastily loading up the cart when Petrus appeared in the doorway.

'You're to come with me,' he said, looking at Victoricus. 'There's a new herd of cattle due in and we're to fetch them from the north gate.'

Victoricus glanced around as they walked across the yard, but Castor was now talking to one of the drivers and Bruscius appeared to have gone. They drove some twenty weary looking beasts from the north gate into the enclosure. They made eagerly for the drinking trough on arrival. One of the drovers told Victoricus that they'd come some seven miles down the Isc valley that morning from a farmstead close to the river and that he and his companion were planning to set off back straightaway.

4

Castor appeared to have forgotten that he had only employed Victoricus for a day or so at most. On the eighth day Victoricus duly lined up with the other men outside Castor's office to receive his pay – a handful of small bronze coins, four joints of salted beef and a bag of wheat flour – all duly noted down against his name by a clerk at a table. He was asked to make a mark in the right hand column to show that he had received his due, but astonished both the clerk and his workmates by writing out his name.

'You write better than you roll barrels,' laughed Attius, next in line.

Victoricus took the meat and flour back to Rufus on his way home. The old man was grateful. 'I don't have meat much these days, except when I kill one of my own chickens and I'll bake us some loaves with the flour.'

The old man and the youth were getting on well together. Rufus enjoyed having someone to talk to and to fuss over and Victoricus was pleased to have someone outside work to whom he could talk freely. By now he had confessed his whole story to Rufus and kept no secrets from him. Here he could talk freely of his family and their farm and they could share reminiscences from their pasts. But always he returned to the cobbler's shop late at night to bed down in the attic. Sometimes the old man suggested that he stay with him, but Victoricus seemed to want this degree of independence and Rufus never pushed him to stay.

By now the attic was more comfortable. Under cover of darkness he had smuggled in some straw and a blanket supplied by Rufus and he had a stool and drinking mug from the same source. With his own money he had purchased a few personal items such as scissors to trim his fast growing beard, a pumice stone to help remove grime from his hands and feet and spare boots. He'd even enjoyed the luxury of a scrub down in the public baths between the forum and the south gate on one of his rare days off. He had visited the baths only once with his father and had been frightened by the noise, the heat and the steam. Now only one of the hot rooms was still open and that was at best luke warm and there was only the barest trickle of a water supply into the cold room. The great open plunge bath, which he remembered full to the brim with clear water was now dry and empty, its mortar lining crumbling. The attendant told him the baths would close soon as the building needed repairs and there was no money for them. In any case, he added, there were not enough clients to keep it open.

One night he was awoken by voices on the

pavement outside the front of the shop. He crept to the shutters to listen. He could hear the pie man and his wife from next door. They appeared to be arguing with two men.

'No one's tampered with this lock,' he heard one of them saying. 'You must have dreamt it.'

'But we've heard noises from the building,' insisted the pie man 'and the other morning I thought I heard water splashing in the yard.'

'You should put more water in your wine,' came the reply, 'you've called out the watch for nothing.'

'Now we're here we may as well just check it out,' said the first man. 'Get the lock open and let's have a look.'

Victoricus didn't wait to hear more. Wriggling into his breeches and tunic and snatching up what belongings he could he pelted down the ladder and out through the back door. Pausing only to put on his boots, he quickly scaled the fence, realising only when he reached the top that the darker shadow in the alleyway was a third man. At the same time his outline against the night sky became clear to the watcher, who hollered that someone was escaping from the back.

Victoricus hesitated, debating whether to drop back into the yard or into the alley. He'd almost certainly be trapped if he stayed in the yard, he reasoned. Better to take his chance against the one pursuer in the alley, rather than be faced with at least three if he delayed.

As he dropped from the fence he was immediately aware that his opponent was coming full tilt

at him and from the sound of boots in the passageway someone was already running to join him. He
flattened himself against the fence and stuck out his
boot just as the first man drew alongside him. He
fell heavily and Victoricus darted away, running as
hard as he could for the back streets. Remembering
the shell of the roofless house he'd passed many
times on his way to Rufus', he turned in and
crouched in a corner, trying to get his breath back.
Three men emerged from the alley, two of them
carrying lanterns. Peeping out of a window opening Victoricus could see the flames of the oil lamps
flickering as they were carried. They had spread
out across the street and were walking cautiously
forward, looking to right and left.

'We'll never find him here,' said the first man,
'there are too many places to hide.'

Away from the main street they appeared wary
and ill at ease.

'Come on, we've scared him off,' said another.
'He won't be back. Let's report to the pie man and
have a search of the cobbler's old place.'

Victoricus stayed in hiding long after his pursuers had gone. He was thinking over his situation.
Over the weeks he'd felt secure in the cobbler's
shop and he realised he'd become careless, taking
it for granted that the pie man and his wife would
not hear him or perhaps would not care if they did.
On reflection he realised he had been foolish,
staying on at the cobbler's for sentimental rather
than practical reasons. After all there were lots of
empty properties away from the main street, where

he could have made himself a home and been secure.

As the sky lightened he crept out of his hiding place. He felt more miserable now than he had done at any time since he came to Isca. Memories of his family and their home came back to him. Maybe he should have stayed and gone to work for Cynan. Isca seemed less and less attractive.

Wearily, he made his way to Rufus' house, where over a large breakfast of cold salt beef and his host's fresh vegetables, his spirits revived. Just recounting the events of the night to a sympathetic listener was a tonic. He was even able to laugh at himself crouching in the ruins, while the watchmen discussed him in the street outside.

'You can move in here,' said Rufus. 'There's plenty of room and to tell you the truth I'd be glad of your company. Sorio's demolition gang have been active round here again this week. They were clearing a street just down the hill near the town wall a couple of days ago. I could do with a strong lad around the place.'

'But why are they pulling houses down?' asked Victoricus, puzzled, 'and why take the debris away? I must go and see what they're up to.'

'My advice is leave them alone,' said his companion. 'Don't interfere and maybe they'll leave us in peace.'

Rufus didn't seem at all sure that he would be left alone and Victoricus agreed to stay with him, at least for the time being. Fortunately he'd been leaving most of his meagre pay with Rufus, who kept the coins with a few of his own treasured possessions in a cavity in the kitchen wall. Last night he would have been hard put to rescue his money as well as himself. One day he might be able to rent a place of his own.

Victoricus went off to work feeling more cheerful. Even the first few drops of rain falling on him as he made his way uphill failed to dent his natural buoyancy. By mid morning, when a third heavy shower threatened to drop out of a leaden sky, he was soaked and cold. His breeches stuck to his legs and his boots were full of water. Plastered all over with mud and manure, he was trying to separate off some lively bullocks, newly arrived, into their pens.

Petrus was supposed to be helping, but his cough had worsened over the weeks and he was no longer capable of doing the work. The others covered up for him, whenever Castor was about, but he would not be able to go on much longer. Victoricus had first realised that Petrus was seriously ill when he had seen him coughing up blood. He had then tried talking to Petrus trying to find out who was at home caring for him. But all attempts at enquiry had been firmly rejected.

Castor, barely recognisable in a long woollen cloak and hood, splashed over to the fence. ' Look lively now and finish off, we need you two in the salting room this morning giving a hand.'

Castor had lost some of his fire, recently, Victoricus thought. He was still coarse and lost his

49

temper with the men. He even lashed out at them occasionally, but he seemed preoccupied. He spent much more time in his office, venturing out only occasionally and then only to give orders. When Victoricus had started at the cattle station Castor was everywhere, darting about poking his nose into everything, checking on the men. Now they saw him less and less.

Victoricus and Petrus made their way over to the salting room. Rain was still coming down, flung into their faces by violent swirls of wind.

'Stroke of luck getting some inside work on a morning like this,' commented Victoricus without getting any response from his companion.

The salting room was next to the slaughterhouse. Tubs of meat joints, still bloody from freshly killed beasts, were lined up at one side. Attius worked stripped to the waist, his torso glistening with sweat. He was delighted to see help arrive.

'Silvius didn't turn up for work this morning, so I'm on my own. The butchers dump the tubs through the doorway, but they're short handed as well and can't help with the packing. This lot's supposed to be done by the lunch break, but we'll never be finished in time.'

Breaking an oblong cake of grey brown salt with a wooden shovel in a side stall, he turned to finish off layering the meat in a barrel with shovelfuls of salt.

'Fetch me a lid,' he called to Victoricus, ignoring Petrus, who was shivering violently just inside the door. Together they hammered down the wooden lid, forcing it onto the seating with mallets, before securing it with iron nails.

'Another one out of the way,' said Attius. 'You roll it through while I fetch another tub and no fancy tricks this morning.' He glanced at Victoricus and then upturned a barrel in the far corner. 'You sit on that Petrus and get warm. You can do your stint later.'

Petrus made to protest, but he was so weak that he allowed himself to be ushered out of the way into the corner.

'He'll not keep going much longer, by the look of him,' whispered Victoricus on his return. 'He's lucky that Castor has not been doing his usual checks, otherwise he'd have been thrown out weeks ago.'

'He should be in bed,' said Atticus, 'but he struggles in every morning, never late. He has a widowed mother and sister, who rely on his wages, but I think their income's about to dry up.'

The two of them now worked in harmony together to get the barrels of salt beef ready for loading. Petrus came over a couple of times, but it was all he could do to stand upright let alone work alongside them and they urged him to get out of their way. He retreated back to the corner.

They were down to the last two tubs, when Attius noticed that Petrus was slumped on the floor. He shouted to Victoricus and the two of them went across to check.

'He's fainted,' said Attius. 'Fetch some water and we'll revive him.'

'He's not breathing,' whispered Victoricus in shocked tones, as he bent over Petrus. 'I think he's . . .'

Attius gasped. 'It can't be true, not Petrus. We were talking to him only a few minutes ago. I know he was ill, but I hoped he would recover with a bit of time.'

'I'm sorry,' said Victoricus, 'but I think he has died. One of us had better fetch Castor.'

Attius arrived back with Castor within a few minutes. Castor was clearly not pleased with this latest interruption. 'I could have done without this,' was his opening remark as he entered the workroom. 'Why did the silly fool choose today to die? Bring him over to the yard on that board.' He pointed to the remains of a table propped against one of the walls.

They carried Petrus over to the yard. Castor directed them into what appeared to be a spare room in the same wing of the house where his own office was. Attius was detailed to go across to Petrus' house, which Castor explained was close to the south gate.

'Find out what they want us to do with the body,' he urged.

'In the meantime, you finish off the salting,' he said to Victoricus. 'The wagoner will be back soon and we must get loaded up.'

Victoricus resumed work on his own. He was shocked by the suddenness of Petrus' death, but he tried to put it out of his mind and concentrated on packing the meat. He was only half-way through the first barrel, when he heard the wagon drawing up. Cinhil was driving the team and was impatient to be on his way. He began loading on his own, as he had no mate with him and was completely indifferent to the news of Petrus.

Victoricus emptied the last tub and brought the barrel through to the loading bay. He and Cinhil worked in silence, rolling the barrels up the ramp and onto the cart. They were interrupted only by the return of Attius.

'Did you contact the family?' asked Victoricus, wiping the sweat from his forehead.

'They were in alright,' replied Attius, 'but I'd sooner manage a herd of wild boars anytime than go through that again. The old lady set up such a wailing when I told them and her daughter fainted away onto the floor. Several neighbours came in and they started weeping too, until the house was full and I didn't know where to turn. Fortunately the daughter recovered and begged me to fetch the priest from the church close to the forum and I was glad to get away.'

'Which church is that, then?' enquired Victoricus. On one of his rambles he'd noticed a small church in a cemetery beyond the south gate, but he knew of no church near the forum.

'It's really the priest's own house,' said Attius, 'but there's a chapel on the first floor, where he holds services occasionally. He's gone round to comfort the family and he's making arrangements to pick up the body, so Castor's pleased.'

'That's enough gossip,' interrupted Cinhil, 'let's

get this loading finished and then one of you had better come with me to the quay.'

Castor arrived as they were finishing off. He looked pleased. The priest had already sent men for Petrus' body, so it was no longer the overseer's responsibility. He ordered Victoricus to travel with the wagon to the quay and to return with the docket from the ship's captain.

Victoricus was eager to see the ship and the quay. The rain had almost stopped, though gusts of wind still swept across the enclosure. Perched on the seat next to Cinhil they started off, all eight oxen straining to shift the load. Their passage out through the south gate was easy, but as Cinhil turned his team downhill into the quay road he warned Victoricus to put plenty of pressure on the wooden lever between them so as to slow the wagon down. Oxen and wagon wheels were slipping on the wet cobbles and they had a tough time keeping control of the load. Eventually the road levelled out and they came safely out onto the quayside.

5

One ship lay at the quay, its sails furled, creaking and heaving in the choppy water. Stacked on the quay close by were roof tiles, timbers and dressed stone, which Victoricus realised with a jolt must have been removed from buildings inside Isca. Here were the results of the work of Sorio's demolition gangs neatly arranged ready for loading.

The captain appeared out of a small cabin built onto the aft deck of the ship. He stared for a moment at the wagon and then, wrapping his cloak about him, he walked down the plank onto the quay. Pushing back his hood, he revealed a head of dark curly hair with a pair of sharp blue eyes in a well-tanned face.

'It's no use unloading this lot,' was his opening comment. 'I reckon this wind is going to get worse and we may be stuck here for some time. By then I'll be late for taking the rest of my cargo along the coast to Durnovaria and won't be able to ship your barrels into the Taen.'

Cinhil swore in a great tumult of oaths born of tiredness and frustration. 'What am I to do with this lot then?' he asked finally, jerking his thumb in the direction of the load behind him. 'I can't take it back to Castor.'

'You'll have to,' came the swift response, 'and then it can wait for one of your own ships to pick it up in a week or so. You know I was only fitting in this extra voyage as a favour and the weather's against it. I'm sorry, but there's no more I can do.' As if to emphasise the point, he turned his back on them, flicked his hood up and walked back to his ship.

'What do we do now? ' asked Victoricus.

'You heard,' snarled the driver, 'we go back. You get down and help pull the team round. Take it slowly. We don't want to end up in the river.'

Castor was not pleased to see the wagon back in the yard once more. 'These seamen always use the weather as an excuse for ducking out of work. You can leave the cart loaded up 'til the morning and then the two of you will have to drive across with the load yourselves.'

'What, all the way to Duriarno?' asked Cinhil.

'There's a good road most of the way. Get an early start, stay overnight and you'll be back in two days. Better than hanging around for the next ship.'

Castor's mind was made up and the driver accepted it. Perhaps he saw it as a break from the local routine. Victoricus was probably the more disturbed. He recognised the name and knew it was in Cynan's territory, close to his own family's former lands. It was with mixed emotions that he viewed the journey. He was keen to see the area again after all these months in Isca, but would he be recognised? His beard was now full-grown, but would that be enough to save him from discovery?

After he'd helped unharness the oxen and stable them for the night, he sped back to Rufus with all his news. After a normal day's routine there was not usually much to tell, but tonight he had the details of Petrus' death, his visit to the quay with the building materials stacked up there and above all his trip over the next two days.

But Rufus was bursting with news too.

'I went over to the market this morning and the forum was all locked up. There were just a few stalls on the pavement outside, but no one was being allowed in. Apparently the magistrate has gone. His house in town is all shuttered up and I was told he'd left for his estates east of the city and is not coming back. The last few councillors have given up, not that they do much now anyway. Even the clerks were locked out. They were outside hollering that they hadn't been paid for weeks and the watchmen with them.'

'So, how will the town manage, then?' asked Victoricus. 'Who will clean the streets, do repairs, keep the water supply going?'

'It's been running down for years, as you know,' Rufus reminded him. 'Look what's happened just while you've been here. People don't want to live in Isca any longer and no one wants the job of running it. The governor hasn't travelled here from Corinium for at least five years. Even he's abandoned the place. He used to come regularly when I had my shop. Isca was full of people on the days of his visit. Once I went to listen to the governor acting as a judge in a case in the basilica. I remember he was very impatient to get the case finished.'

'Someone will take over, surely,' said Victoricus. 'Isca can't just fade away.'

'I'm afraid it'll be men like Sorio and his gang who'll become the law in this place now,' said Rufus, 'so we'd all better watch out.'

After dinner, while there was still an hour or so of light, Victoricus offered to walk out with the dog. Rufus was busy in his garden and Victoricus wanted to take advantage of his early homecoming. It was unusual for Castor to let the men go early. He set out downhill, but instead of entering the alley behind the cobbler's shop, he cut across in the opposite direction into the south-west quarter of the town. The buildings here were obviously unoccupied and many were dilapidated. Some had fallen into decay, but others had been robbed of materials, leaving them prey to the weather.

After passing across two streets the buildings thinned out dramatically. Victoricus emerged into an area pitted with trenches, from which foundations had been removed. He was struck by the thoroughness of the demolition workers. They had even stripped out stones lining drains and pulled out the posts which had formed the frames of the houses. The resultant trenches and pits had been left open with piles of soil between.

Picking his way across he was astonished to discover that beyond this recently worked area lay a large expanse of levelled ground beyond which the town walls were clearly visible. His amazement increased once he realised that this earth had been ploughed and sown. Someone was trying to grow crops inside the walls of the city. Perhaps Rufus was right after all: the city was dying. Was its fate to become just one more great estate owned by someone like Cynan?

As he stood staring and trying to take in the meaning of all these changes Lupus began to bark and at the same time Victoricus became conscious of movement behind him. Someone was coming out of the abandoned buildings which he had just passed. Victoricus patted the dog and encouraged him to stay at his side. A man was striding rapidly over the ground towards them. Victoricus thought he looked familiar and as he drew nearer he realised that it was Silvius from the cattle station.

They each asked simultaneously ' What are you doing here?'

Silvius explained that he had taken the job of caretaker.

'I was set on yesterday – that's why I wasn't at the cattle station. Work there was coming to an end anyway. I just have to check that no-one trespasses onto this land, so I've set up head-quarters in that house over there and I act as watchman during the night.'

'Who are you working for?' asked Victoricus.

'A man called Sorio. One of our neighbours put

me onto him. He lives in the upper part of town and appears to run a lot of enterprises in Isca.'

'Why is he growing crops here inside the city?' persisted Victoricus.

'This is only my first night working for him,' laughed Silvius, 'you'll need to give me longer to find out all about him. In any case he doesn't exactly invite questions. Now I'm supposed to run you off his land, which he acquired from the Council. Suppose you tell me how you come to be here.'

Victoricus explained that he was lodging nearby, was out for a stroll with the dog and that his wanderings had brought him in that direction.

'When I saw the ploughed land I was curious,' he said.

The two of them walked back together as dusk was creeping in and Victoricus was anxious to get back to Rufus.

'I'll look you up again,' remarked Victoricus 'and see how you're getting on. It will be a lonely vigil out here. I shouldn't think you'll be much disturbed.'

At first light the next day as Victoricus arrived at the cattle station, he found Cinhil already there and impatient to be off. He had harnessed the oxen and within a few minutes they were descending the hill past Arontius' shop, out through the west gate and over the river bridge. The rain seemed to have passed over, but the wind promised by the sea captain was driving into their faces, bringing white clouds out of the south-west. Victoricus was retracing the route which had brought him as a fugitive to Isca. He was fearful of returning to his home area, but at the same time excited at the prospect of seeing familiar country again.

Cinhil, who seemed quite cheerful once they were on their way, took the oxen at a slow pace.

'We've a long way to travel – perhaps 20 miles – and we mustn't tire the beasts.' Cinhil was about twice his companion's age, tall and thin. He managed the oxen well, thought Victoricus, applying the whip sparingly, just enough to remind the beasts that someone was in charge.

Near the foot of the great hill, on the top of which Victoricus had paused all those months ago, Cinhil told him to get down and walk with the leading oxen.

'Keep encouraging them,' said he, 'until we reach the top. This is a stiff climb for them, but if the leaders keep going we'll manage it alright.'

The surface was rutted, where the rain of the previous day had poured down the hill and the track surface was soft, but at a steady pace they reached the top without mishap. Here they paused to rest the beasts before following the track along the broken ridge which lay beyond. The wind caught at them on this high ground, tugging at their cloaks and causing the lead oxen to falter. Cinhil was forced to make greater use of the whip. Victoricus glimpsed familiar stone topped hills in the distance. These had been a constant backcloth throughout his childhood, whenever he was out of doors.

Soon the grey streak of a great river estuary became visible ahead of them and far away to the left the horizon opened out to the sea.

'You see how easy it would have been,' said Cinhil, 'to ship these barrels round from the Isc to the Taen. Instead we're flogging our way over these hills and nearly getting blown away in the process.'

'No ship would venture out in this wind,' offered Victoricus, 'He'd be blown ashore.'

'Well, perhaps you're right.'

Some time later they were following the straight track off the hills towards the river crossing. They'd halted twice near streams to allow the oxen to rest, water and feed, but Cinhil was keen to arrive at the bridge over the Taen with time to spare for a lengthy stop, before moving on to arrive before dusk. Once at the bridge they released the oxen to wade in the water and graze the bank. Keeping an eye on the beasts, they settled down next to the wagon, away from the wind. Victoricus, suddenly conscious of hunger, was pleased that he'd remembered to pack food and drink. He was curious to know about their destination. Cinhil had referred to it as Duriarno and he did recall a prominent hill of that name in the area. He remembered tales about it too. It had once been the stronghold of a king, who had ordered huge ditches and earth banks to be dug around the hilltop. But the stronghold had been neglected for a long time and it had become overgrown.

'You'll notice a difference,' said Cinhil, 'the ditches have been cleaned out and deepened and the ramparts built up. Wooden gates have been hung across the entrance and there are buildings inside.'

'Who would want to do all that?' asked Victoricus, realising in the same instance that he already knew the answer. There could only be one man around here powerful enough to command such work to be done. This would explain Bruscius' presence at the cattle station. Cynan was building himself a fort and stocking it with food and materials. But the Roman government wouldn't allow that. Once they knew what was going on, they'd be sure to put a stop to it.

Sure enough, Cinhil confirmed Victoricus' suspicions:

'The landowner, Cynan has ordered this work to be done. He says he's going to build a house inside the ramparts and live there.'

'He'll be chased out soon enough, when the governor hears about it,' said Victoricus, without too much conviction.

'Not him,' remarked his companion. 'It's a long while since the governor bothered with these parts. Cynan can do pretty much what he likes and there'll be others like him. We might be glad of them, too. These men will protect us, feed us and give us jobs.'

'Yes, but at what cost?' queried Victoricus. 'We'll be tied to them worse than those oxen to the cart. I don't want to be ordered about for the rest of my life.'

Cinhil laughed out loud. 'What do you think

Castor has been doing then for the last few months? You've jumped to do his bidding quickly enough.'

'I take Castor's orders alright,' said Victoricus, 'but I take his money too. Anytime I've had enough I can leave.'

'You'll think differently when you've got yourself a wife and family to keep. You'll be glad of regular work and food then. And if shiploads of pirates come up our rivers again, as they did in my grandfather's time, you'll be glad to put yourself under Cynan's protection or somebody like him. Anyway, time to round up the oxen and push on. We want to see this load safely installed at Duriarno before nightfall and find some dry place to get some sleep.'

6

Crossing the wooden bridge, the ox cart breasted the next rise with ease. The oxen seemed fresher after their long stop or perhaps they sensed the end of the journey coming.

'There's Duriarno,' shouted Cinhil as they reached the top and Victoricus looked ahead to a prominent hill on a ridge rising sharply out of the surrounding countryside. Even at that distance he could make out activity around the fort. His sense of unease increased. He was bound to meet some-one he knew and since his beard was his only disguise he felt sure they would recognise him.

As they drew nearer the earthworks around the hill stood out. A great earth rampart encircled the top of the hill and it was clear that a wooden palisade fence had been erected on top of it. Further down the slope a second earthwork was visible running some way below the highest defences. They began to meet travellers on the same track. An assortment of carts, men on foot and men on horse back passed them in both directions. Duriarno was a hub of activity. Victoricus drew his cloak around himself and pulled his hood well over his face. Fortunately it seemed the right action to take in the teeth of the gale now blowing. Recognised or not, he would be pleased to arrive.

Close to the foot of the hill they were hailed by an old man leaning on a stick, his left hand trying to keep his hood over his long grey hair. 'What's your load?' he demanded, looking at the wagon.

'Salt beef from the cattle station at Isca,' was Cinhil's equally terse reply.

'Take it round by the track and report to the man there. He'll direct you up to the gates.'

'It's a stiff haul up to the first gate,' they were warned, when they met the next guide. 'We'll hitch up an extra ox team to get you up there, but don't be in a rush.'

'You'd best get down,' instructed Cinhil 'and help lead the teams. This will take some skill.'

Victoricus found himself slithering up the churned up track, his hand on the harness of the leading ox, while another youth held onto the other leading beast. It was difficult for him to gain a foothold, but the oxen by contrast seemed sure-footed and hauled the load relentlessly up the slope.

Passing through the outer gateway, the timber gates of which were set back, flanked by ramparts on either side forming a passageway, they found themselves in a large triangular-shaped area. Here they were instructed to pull in to the left of the gate.

Victoricus, looking round, noticed with horror Bruscius walking towards the cart. Fortunately his companion was trying to separate the two teams of oxen and Victoricus was able to busy himself helping. The youth went off down the hill with the fresh team and Victoricus was in time to hear Bruscius' instructions as he lingered at the side of the wagon.

'Take your team over to the shelter.' Bruscius pointed to the far side of the enclosure. 'There's fodder and water there. Then I'll get some men to help you unload. The cart can stay here for tonight. We've got a part load for you to take back to Isca and you can collect that on your way out in the morning. I've fixed up quarters for you inside the fort. I'll detail one of the men to show you where to go. You'll be able to eat and drink just as soon as the cart's unloaded.' His instructions over, Bruscius made to turn away and Victoricus breathed a sigh of relief, but too soon, as the bailiff turned and looked straight at him.

'How was the journey?' he asked in friendly tones, encouraging the newcomer.

'Not bad, cold enough,' grunted Victoricus, drawing his cloak and hood about him as if to emphasise his point.

'You get used to the wind up here,' remarked Bruscius, still staring.

I'm done for this time, thought Victoricus, he's sure to recognise me. But to his intense relief the bailiff went on his way.

Having unloaded the barrels and stacked them

on a wooden platform erected just behind the rampart, Victoricus went with Cinhil to check on the oxen. The animals appeared content so the two of them went in search of food themselves. As they approached the gateway of the inner enclosure, one of Bruscius' men met them to show them the way. Both were impressed with the layout inside the fort. A long timber hall stood close to the centre of the enclosure. In size it was the equal of the houses in Isca and Victoricus was impressed.

'That's the Lord Cynan's house,' remarked their companion seeing Victoricus' stare. 'It's nearly eighty feet long and has massive posts inside holding up the roof. We can have a look inside later if you want. He's at his estate at the moment, so it's not in use.'

Victoricus noted the low stone walls, with timber uprights set in them and the painted plaster work in between. He had seen similar buildings in Isca and a few on farming estates between the Isc and the Taen. The roof had the characteristic red tiles. Cynan clearly aimed to live well in his new fort.

'Is he often here, then?' asked Victoricus, pleased that Cynan was absent that night.

'Every two or three days,' came the reply. 'He divides his time between his estate and here, but he's gradually spending more time at Duriarno. I believe he'll abandon his farmhouse soon and live here permanently.'

Victoricus sniffed the air. He could smell food cooking. A pig was being roasted over a fire in the tail of the rampart. He and Cinhil were invited to take a wooden platter from a pile, while the cook sliced off layers of the meat. This was then coated in a thick sauce, studded with caraway seeds. It smelt good.

Having collected their food, the three of them made for a timber building nearby in which several men were seated at tables eating. Knives were available in a container and jugs of beer and wooden beakers were on the tables. The travellers soon fell to eating and conversation failed.

Victoricus leaned back on his stool, as he cleared his plate and drained his beaker. As he did so he caught the eye of a man on his way out of the hut.

'Why, it's Tadius' lad, isn't it? What are you doing here?' The man, swaying slightly on his feet, had stopped and was addressing Victoricus. The latter realised with horror that it was Clemens, one of their old neighbours from home

He tried to explain that he was making a delivery and would be gone in the morning. Victoricus became desperate for the man to leave, as he was beginning to draw attention to them, but Clemens was clearly full of beer and was not to be brushed off so easily.

'Where are you living now?' was the next question and then 'how did you manage to get out of Cynan's service?' The man was well meaning and genuinely interested. He had no idea of the problems he was causing Victoricus.

Everyone in the hut was now listening and

watching, as Victoricus tried to give brief explanations without being rude. But as luck would have it, Bruscius chose exactly that moment to enter the hut searching for one of the workmen.

He paused, sensing some undercurrent in the atmosphere. He saw Victoricus on his feet and Clemens facing him. 'What's going on?' he asked.

Before Victoricus could stop him Clemens blurted out: 'here's Tadius' son returned, Bruscius. I never thought to see him again'.

So saying, he clung onto Victoricus, partly for support and partly out of friendliness. Victoricus struggled to loosen the man's grip but at the same time Bruscius moved forward, gesturing to two men to follow him. He looked closely at Victoricus, drawing in his breath.

'You're right it is Victoricus returned to us. You'd better come along with me, lad and explain yourself.'

His two companions dived forward, shouldering Clemens to one side, and took firm hold of Victoricus, one on each arm.

'What's going on?' asked Cinhil, bewildered.

'You've been sheltering a runaway. That's what,' replied the bailiff. 'I shall have to supply you with a new mate for the return journey.'

Bruscius strode out of the building, motioning to the men to follow him with their captive. Victoricus was helpless in their grip and with sinking heart allowed them to lead him away.

In the twilight they crossed to another building, which appeared to serve Bruscius as an office. It was sparsely furnished with a table and two chairs. Notes in ink on wooden tablets were piled to one side of the table. The bailiff motioned Victoricus to sit and asked the other two to wait outside.

7

'I thought we'd lost you forever,' was Bruscius' opening remark. 'After you fled from your father's house, we did search for you for a few days, but we had better things to do than spend time looking for a runaway youth. Now you're back Lord Cynan will expect obedience this time. I'll speak up for you. We understand the difficulties you faced when your family died. I don't think you'll find Cynan too harsh on you, but you will now have to settle down to work. Where have you been hiding yourself all these months?'

Victoricus had decided on the short journey in the arms of Bruscius' men, that his best option was to seem to accept his fate, offer no resistance and give himself precious time to think. He sidestepped any explanation of his recent whereabouts and asked what was happening in Cynan's territory.

'Why has he rebuilt this old fort and stocked it with foodstuffs? Produce arriving by wagon and by sea – all this activity. What is he planning?'

'There are changes coming,' replied the bailiff, 'and they're coming quickly. Lord Cynan saw some while ago that the Roman government wasn't interested in this area any longer. The governor and his officials stopped visiting. The town councillors in Isca gradually gave up. Cynan himself stopped bothering to go to Isca six years ago. He still makes use of the old town and its quay, but not for much longer. Lord Cynan saw that in the future the people round here would need him.'

'Need him for what though,' asked Victoricus, puzzled, 'surely they can just get on with their lives?'

'And think of the squabbles there'd be if people were left alone to sort themselves out,' interrupted Bruscius, becoming passionate in his argument. 'They'd soon start fighting over food, land, womenfolk. And what if we were attacked – from the sea perhaps or even by people better organised than us from further west. Think, lad, you've had a bit of education, we must prepare ourselves and someone must lead us. We can't rely on the Roman government any longer. We must look after ourselves. Lord Cynan has rebuilt Duriarno. He'll come and live here soon. He has plans to rebuild a couple of other forts too. He'll make sure food and other supplies are stocked up so that any of his people in need can be helped. In return he'll expect his people to work the land and bring him gifts from time to time and obey him – for their own good.'

'This means collecting an army together,' mused Victoricus, more to himself than to Bruscius.

'Of course', came the reply, 'men are being

trained at the moment. Lord Cynan can't offer his people protection without a band of warriors.'

Yes and with warriors at his back Cynan can force people to do what he wants, thought Victoricus. He's doing just what my father said – he's creating a kingdom, just like his ancestors had and to think my father thought it was a joke.

The bailiff broke into his thoughts: 'Lord Cynan will be here tomorrow and I'll speak up for you. Remember you're his man and show respect. One way or another Cynan will get work out of you now. If you show willing, he'll use your talents in a good position. But he also has work gangs where life is hard and you wouldn't want to end up in one of those. In the meantime I shall have to lock you up. I still don't know if I can trust you and you're not slipping through my fingers again.'

Victoricus was taken over to another hut, which was empty, apart from some straw on the floor. It smelt as if chickens had been in it recently. There was just the one door, no window openings and in any case Bruscius was clearly taking no chances as two men were ordered to remain outside the locked door for the rest of the night. Since he had no other option, Victoricus, exhausted, lay on the straw and promptly fell asleep.

He was awoken the following morning by someone pulling back the bar securing the door. He blinked as the early morning sun penetrated into the hut and sat up. Someone was bringing him breakfast. He became conscious too of sounds around the hut – sounds of people and animals starting work and realised with a start that Cinhil would be off without him today.

Victoricus glanced at the intruder and then looked harder with growing astonishment. Surely this was Arontius the Isca cobbler, whose house he had been occupying for so long.

'What on earth are you doing here?' he asked.

Arontius motioned him to lower his voice. 'I thought it was you,' he said. 'I noticed you last night crossing the fort with Bruscius and thought I recognised Tadius' son. I'm working here now – preparing hides for the Lord Cynan and doing leatherwork occasionally. I had to close my business in Isca.'

Victoricus explained that he knew Arontius had left Isca and went on to tell him about his own occupation of the old shop. Arontius was astonished.

'My wife and I were in despair. No work coming in and my two daughters growing up. Then Bruscius called one day and offered me work in this place. I had no choice. It's not ideal. They work me all day and I just get food supplies for the family and occasional extra gifts of honey and such like. We live in a draughty hut in one corner of the outer enclosure between the two gateways and my wife hates the place. It's not the right place to bring up our daughters. The men eye them up and make obscene comments and the bailiff has even hinted that the Lord Cynan might want a hand in deciding who they marry. But enough of my troubles, what about you? Why did you come back?'

Victoricus explained what had happened and told Arontius of his conversation with Bruscius the previous night.

'Well, my advice is to escape and get well away from here as soon as you can,' said Arontius. 'Don't let them set you on. You'll regret it. Cynan will have power of life and death over us all soon and many of us will be little more than slaves.'

'What's this about slaves?' interrupted the familiar voice of Bruscius, as he stepped through the doorway. 'Don't go filling the lad's head with all your moans, Arontius. Get about your business and leave him to me.'

'There's a bucket of water here,' he said to Victoricus. 'Get yourself cleaned up. The Lord Cynan will be here soon and he'll want to see you. Remember what I said last night. I'll be back soon.'

When Bruscius returned it was to conduct Victoricus over to the great hall in the centre of the fort. 'I've spoken to Lord Cynan and he's ready to look favourably on your misconduct. Watch what you say and show respect.'

The great door in the end wall of the hall was open, but guarded by two men carrying spears. This was a new experience for Victoricus, who had only ever seen men with weapons out hunting. He walked forward down the central aisle of the building between the pairs of timber posts. Wooden tables were stacked away neatly in the side aisles and the earth floor had fresh rushes strewn on it.

Cynan was talking with others at the far end of the hall. Here was a raised platform with a centrally-placed ornate chair. Victoricus noted its leather padded seat and carved legs, ending in animals' feet. Close by was a high, three-legged table with a bowl of fruit and a beaker of drink set upon it.

He noticed Cynan, standing with the group of men to one side and dominating them. He was certainly an imposing figure thought Victoricus. Tall, thin and erect with bushy eyebrows turning grey, like the hair on his head. He dismissed the men with a nod and turned to Bruscius and Victoricus. Settling himself into his chair, he looked at Victoricus, who was immediately aware of piercing ice blue eyes fixed on him. Victoricus recognised he was in the presence of a formidable personality, perhaps born to rule, as Cynan himself obviously believed.

He returned the stare coolly. He was not going to be intimidated. He could not think of Cynan as a king.

'You have returned to our territory, Victoricus, but not freely. You came in disguise and with no intention of remaining.' Cynan spoke slowly, enunciating every word clearly and precisely. 'However, Bruscius tells me you are now willing to work for us and I will forget your escapade if you will settle down and support us.'

'Sir, when my family died eighteen months ago,' replied Victoricus with equal clarity, 'I hoped I would be allowed to continue working the family's farm. You chose not to allow this. I decided then that there was no future for me in this territory and it is only chance which brought me back. I would still prefer to go my own way and seek employment where I will. You are holding me a prisoner, even though I believe I have done no wrong.'

Cynan's face darkened at these words, but it was Bruscius who interposed, stepping forward, his face set and angry: 'What answer is this to give the Lord Cynan? Fool boy, do you want to end up in the labour gangs? You're being offered the chance to work honestly for a leader who will protect you.'

'He's stubborn and disobedient,' said Cynan, 'I'll trouble myself with him no more. See that he's suitably employed, Bruscius.'

With that dismissal, Victoricus was ushered out of the hall. The bailiff was still fuming at what he took to be a personal insult. He'd done his best for this youth, who'd made him look foolish in front of Cynan. For the sake of Victoricus' father he'd tried to help the youth. Now he could take what was coming to him.

Shouting to two of his men, Bruscius gave instructions to take Victoricus over to the smith in the outer enclosure. There he was forced to submit to the fitting of wrist irons linked by a heavy chain. He was then dragged across to a post close to the gate and to which he was chained. Three other men were already similarly attached, seated uncomfortably on the ground. It was not possible to stand or to lie back, as Victoricus soon found out. He was forced to sit upright and his back and legs were soon aching.

The other three were not inclined to talk. They

looked downcast and dazed by their predicament. However, from the little conversation Victoricus had with them it emerged that all three had run away from one of Cynan's farms, but they had been caught after two days and brought to the fort. They believed their lives were threatened and feared for the future.

Few passers-by took any notice of the prisoners. Victoricus thought he might get a glimpse of Cinhil leaving, but perhaps he was already gone. The wind was still strong, but it was not cold and the occasional showers were refreshing. If he leaned back letting the chain become taut he could get some comfort until the pull on his wrists became unbearable and he had to lean forward again. He tried closing his eyes and dozing, but the discomfort always woke him in the end.

In one of his dozes he was jerked awake by a touch on his shoulder. Arontius had come over and squatted beside him.

'How did you get in this mess?' he asked, clearly troubled.

'By not speaking politely enough to Cynan, I suppose,' said Victoricus. 'I just told him the truth and he wasn't keen to hear that.'

'Just like your father,' remarked Arontius, 'speak your mind and damn the consequences. Well, you've landed yourself in trouble this time. I wish I could help, but I can't see how. I wonder how long they'll keep you here?'

'Keep away from the prisoners,' shouted a guard, who'd approached from the gateway. 'Get back to your cobbling and look to your daughters, Arontius. Your family will suffer if you end up in chains.'

The day passed slowly. No one approached the prisoners except a guard bringing water and bread near the middle of the day. Victoricus ached all over his body. No position was comfortable any longer and one of his fellow prisoners had set up a continuous moaning sound, which was really irritating.

Victoricus found that there was a faint movement on the staple through which his chain was threaded. He tightened his chain regularly to put pressure on the staple to see if he could loosen it. By mid-afternoon he was sure there was more play on it, though it still held fast. He was sure by now that being exposed to the weather chained to this post was part of the punishment and speculated how long they would be kept there before being taken to the labour gang which Cynan had mentioned. The water brought at midday seemed a long while ago and the roof of his mouth was dry and his tongue swollen.

8

During the night all four were restless, constantly moving and groaning. At one point in response to their cries, a guard came over to them and they begged for water, but received only kicks and curses instructing them to keep quiet.

Before dawn it began raining, the wind dashing the spots into their faces but despite the cold wind, which set them shivering, they welcomed the rain with open mouths and tongues out. All except one, whom Victoricus noticed lay still, his head towards the post, paying no heed to the rain. He must be unconscious, thought Victoricus, one way to get relief.

Victoricus was so intent on trapping the rain which was now streaming down his face, that he was only aware of Arontius at his side at the last moment. The cobbler was on his belly and motioned to Victoricus to keep quiet.

'I'll try to free you,' whispered Arontius, 'but keep still.'

He removed a pair of pincers from his tunic. 'The chain's too thick to cut out here; it would take too long, but I might be able to free it from the post.'

Victoricus, now fully alert and excited at the prospect of action, explained to Arontius in a low voice about the staple. It proved difficult to turn, with the chain through it and Victoricus suffered agonies of pain from wrists and arms before Arontius finally freed him. They were about to crawl away, when one of the other prisoners, who had noted the escape hissed: ' You'll free me, or I'll holler for the guards as soon as you move away.'

'There's no time,' whispered Arontius in alarm, 'we'll all be caught.'

'We're caught already,' said the man. 'Just free me. I know a place where I can hide and I won't trouble you afterwards.'

Arontius had no choice. He worked as quickly as he could with Victoricus helping as far as possible, but his whole body was so stiff and he was so impeded by his own chain that his help was minimal. Eventually the staple gave way.

'Now free my mate,' ordered the prisoner and Arontius, resigned, did as he was told.

They failed to arouse the fourth prisoner and had to abandon him, fortunately as the intense blackness of night was beginning to lighten, even in the rain. It was agreed that Arontius and Victoricus would crawl away first and that after a short interval the others would make good their escape.

Arontius led the way. Victoricus found it difficult to crawl. His knees were numb and his legs refused to obey him. He had rubbed his arms and legs before setting out, but every foot of the way was agony to him. He was just thinking that he wouldn't be able to crawl any further when Arontius stood up and pushed open the door of his hut. His wife, Anicilla, was waiting anxiously just inside.

'Come in quickly,' she said, helping Victoricus as he stumbled through the door. The room was in darkness, so that no light showed outside. Arontius barred the door and drew a leather curtain across it. Only then did his wife light a small oil lamp which threw a circle of light into the centre of the room.

Victoricus was rocking slightly on the balls of his feet. He was coated with mud all over and water continued to run from his hair down his neck onto his soaking tunic. Anicilla pushed him gently towards the hearth on the back wall and at the same time Arontius removed a metal screen, which had been placed before the fire. The embers threw out a welcome heat and added to the light.

Anicilla brought a piece of sacking. ' Rub yourself down with this while we decide what to do. It'll be light enough soon for the guards to realise they've lost their prisoners and then there'll be a huge outcry.'

As Victoricus' eyes grew accustomed to the light, he realised that their hut was simply one large room. At either end of the room space was screened off with hurdles and he surmised that these were the sleeping areas. In the centre was a rough wooden table on which was the lamp. If he had to hide he could see no obvious place where he wouldn't be found in less than a minute.

'I'm only going to cause you trouble,' he said to Arontius, 'now I'm warm I'd better go and take my chance. If I can get over to the rampart without being seen I might be able to lie low and slip through the gate once it's open. If the guards find me here you'll all suffer.'

'No, if you leave here now,' said Anicilla, busy at the fire, 'you'll be caught. We've got some ideas about getting you away. Eat this – you'll need your strength.' She thrust a bowl at him and he spooned soup into himself, feeling its warmth spreading in his body.

A movement behind one of the hurdles caught his attention and he was instantly on the alert. A pair of eyes was looking out at him from between the slats and the hurdle moved slightly. Anicilla followed his glance.

'I suppose it was too much to expect Viventia to sleep through all this. She knew something was afoot earlier. I sensed her excitement. Come on out, we know you're awake and don't disturb your sister.'

Viventia slipped between the hurdles and stepped into the room. Victoricus was struck first by the resemblance to Anicilla. Viventia was a younger, slimmer, version with the same features. He imagined that Anicilla had looked like this some twenty years ago. He saw black hair drawn tightly into a bun at the back and an erect young woman, about his age, not afraid to look him straight in the eye. Despite a long thin cloak which covered her from neck to toe, Victoricus realised he was in the presence of a confident and beautiful girl, mature and lively. He was suddenly conscious of his own wretched position and of his appearance. He coloured and quickly closed his mouth, which had been gaping.

'Don't worry about Viventia', said her mother, 'she'll have that effect on men once too often and some good it'll do her.'

9

'It'll be light soon,' remarked Arontius, who had been busy in one corner of the room. 'As soon as the gate guards realise the prisoners have gone a search will be started. They'll realise quickly enough that their quarry must be within the fort, so they'll poke about into every corner. Our only hope is to get you out at the beginning, as soon as the gates are opened for the day.'

'Assuming they do open the gates today, how am I going to get through?' asked Victoricus, his gaze slipping frequently from the father to linger on the daughter.

'And what of the other two prisoners? If they're caught they'll give us away and then your whole family will be in danger. I should not have let you help me. Now you are all at risk!' he continued.

'If we act quickly, we could still save our skins,' said Anicilla ignoring his protests. 'It could be some time before the men find the other prisoners. But let's get on,' she urged, anxious to get the escape organised.

'Often at first light,' explained Arontius, 'as soon

as the gates are opened my wife takes one or both of the girls out to pick herbs or mushrooms. They don't go far away from the fort and they're only gone a short time. Occasionally I go out at about the same time to check on the hides in the stream bed. I have been known to take one of my daughters with me. We might be able to smuggle you out with us.'

'But they're bound to notice a bearded youth with you,' said Victoricus in some despair. 'Let me take my chance outside now. You can always deny helping us to escape and Bruscius may believe you.'

'No, we've gone too far,' said Anicilla, patiently. 'This is what we're going to do. We'll shave off your beard and put you in one of my long linen dresses. Then, wrapped in Viventia's cloak, you might just pass as my daughter. We'll rouse Armea soon and she can accompany us.'

Viventia giggled. 'You'll make a fine girl,' she said, looking him up and down. 'I hope the guards don't try any tricks with you.'

'Be serious, daughter,' said Arontius sharply, 'You've forgotten that if we're caught you could end up dead or someone's slave. You won't be giggling then.'

Victoricus was deep in thought.

'If I take Viventia's place,' he said to Arontius, 'how are you and she to get away and what will you all do? You'll never be able to come back here.'

'That is the difficulty,' agreed Arontius. 'Viventia and I will leave a short while after you and hope that the guards are not alert enough to notice the increase in my family. It's a risk, but in the confusion of the search we might get away with it. As to leaving the fort, as I've said, we'll be happy to get away from here and start a new life elsewhere.'

'We must get on,' urged Anicilla. 'Its the only plan we have. Hope for the best and trust in God to see us through.'

Victoricus reluctantly agreed. He was anxious because he had put this family in danger, but he realised that they now had to act to save themselves. He understood why Arontius had brought a cloth, a bowl of water and his bronze razor to the table. He submitted to Arontius clipping his beard with small shears and finally shaved himself as closely as he could.

In the meantime Anicilla was busy. Armea was awoken and instructed. She'd obviously dressed hurriedly and was still sleepy. Victoricus felt sorry for the young girl, no more than eleven or twelve years old he judged and her life about to change so drastically. Viventia was sent to fetch her mother's gown and her own thick cloak.

Shaved, the ample gown fastened around him and the cloak and hood hiding his face and figure, Victoricus looked so unlike the slim and graceful Viventia, that the family despaired.

'He'll never pass through the gate without the guards challenging him,' sighed Arontius.

'In the half-light we might get away with it,' said his wife. 'You must keep back, Victoricus and let me do the talking. If Armea and I show our faces we may just convince the guards.'

Just then shouts were heard in the distance. Arontius peeped out of the door. It was now light enough to see across the enclosure. A knot of men stood around the prisoners' post and orders were being given. The gates remained closed. He withdrew, closing the door quietly.

'They've discovered their loss and the search has begun. Pray now that someone opens the gates.'

The next few minutes all were silent, the risks they were about to take starkly vivid. Then they heard the rumble of a wagon and Arontius went to the door again to announce that the gates had been opened to let it in.

Three hooded figures passed through the doorway and out into a cold, damp morning. There was a light drizzle, which Victoricus noted might be of help to them. He could see men searching the enclosure and its buildings. They'd left the cobbler's house at the right moment. It would be searched soon.

Later on he would remember how well Anicilla had acted at the gateway. She had made no attempt to slip past the two guards, but strode straight up to them.

'What's all the fuss and shouting this morning?' she demanded. 'You woke us all up.'

'Just some prisoners loose in the fort,' came back the reply. 'Don't you worry, we'll soon catch them again. Where are you off to so early?'

'I've noticed some mushrooms near the spring. They should be ready today and since my girls were awake I thought I'd bring them along. We might be able to fill the baskets.' She pushed her basket forward to emphasise the point.

'How's Viventia this morning?' asked the other man, smiling. 'Come and guard the gate with me. You don't want to go mushrooming.'

Now we're caught thought Victoricus, bitterly regretting involving Arontius and his family.

'You wouldn't want her this morning,' laughed Anicilla, 'she's got the sulks.' She moved forward at the same time beckoning the girls to follow and to Victoricus' intense relief the guards made no further attempt to hinder them. He could only admire the woman's coolness, when his own mouth was dry as sand and his heart was thumping.

Armea quickened her pace and made as if to run.

'Slow down,' hissed her mother 'and walk normally. We're in no danger now. If we meet anyone we must act naturally.'

Near the bottom of the hill they turned off towards the spring, but hid in a clump of trees at the edge of a ploughed field, a spot pre-arranged between them. Now they faced an agonising wait, anxiously peering out from the trees for the other two. Anicilla sank to her knees and prayed aloud to God to save them and Armea joined her.

Victoricus, baptised a Christian and a regular church attender when his mother was alive, sensed in himself a curious reluctance to take part. He had felt no urge to go along to a church during his months in Isca. In fact he'd divorced himself from all religious practices. He realised with a jolt that this was the first time since leaving home that he'd been forced to think about religion. His parents had attended the tiny church which served their rural community and had been friendly enough with the priest to invite him to the house occasionally. He and the twins had been baptised and it was natural that the whole family should go along and worship together. Yet he knew that not all their neighbours were Christian. Some still looked to ancient gods to protect themselves and to make their lands fertile. Roman gods like Jupiter were still worshipped as well as local mother goddesses and some still sought the protection of Cernunnos, the horned god. The death of his family had left him numb and in a curious way resentful against all gods and less ready to seek solace in religious ritual.

Arontius and Viventia came into his thoughts. Was it possible that they too could get away? Viventia stayed in his mind's eye. He had met girls only rarely in the past and his thoughts had seldom dwelt on them, so he was worried at the impact Viventia had had on his sense of well-being. He was disturbed without fully understanding why. Such a brief meeting to lead to such turmoil in his thoughts. He found it difficult to contemplate what he would do if Viventia and her father failed to escape.

10

Arontius had witnessed the scene at the gateway through the slightly opened door. Once he was assured that the three of them were safe for the time being, he relaxed a little. At least it was no longer possible for the guards to find Victoricus in his house. He watched the men searching the enclosure and turned to make sure there was nothing left in the house which would betray the presence of Victoricus. Viventia had hung Victoricus' cloak with her own clothes, having brushed it thoroughly. The hair from his beard had been burned on the fire. The shaving materials were put away. Arontius was satisfied that all was well.

Within a few minutes the searchers arrived at his door. Bruscius was in charge.

'We need to search your house, Arontius, for these fellows who escaped during the night. Did you see or hear anything last night?'

'Nothing,' replied Arontius. 'You won't find them here, there's just me and my daughter.'

'This man was talking to one of the prisoners last

night,' said a guard pointing to Arontius. 'I had to shoo him away from them.' The cobbler knew this stout, loud-mouthed ruffian, who constantly tried to intimidate himself and his family. He'd approached Arontius a few weeks before to demand Viventia's hand in marriage. The cobbler judged that the guard was driven more by lust than any desire to provide a home for his daughter, but he had judged it better not to antagonise the man, saying that Viventia was too young to marry anyone.

The bailiff stared at Arontius closely. 'Is this right?'

'I knew his father some while ago,' said Arontius evenly, 'and I just asked him how he came to be in such a plight. No harm in that.'

'So long as that's all you did,' said Bruscius, still staring suspiciously.

'Where's your mother?' he shot at Viventia, suddenly.

'Gone out to pick mushrooms – she'll be back soon,' came the reply.

The search was thorough, fuelled by the searchers' suspicions. A simple wooden chest was emptied of its contents, beds were shifted, screens moved, but it was quickly obvious in the sparsely furnished cottage that there was nowhere for a person to hide.

Viventia stayed in the background, but the stout guard sought her out deliberately and under pretext of examining the fireplace behind Viventia, grabbed hold of her.

'What are you hiding?' he asked, his arm round her waist and his face close to hers. Viventia scraped her wooden soled sandal hard down the man's shin and he recoiled in pain.

'You little slut,' he spat at her and raised his hand as if to strike Viventia across the mouth. 'You'll pay for that.'

Arontius leaped forward and grabbed the man's arm. 'Leave my daughter alone.'

Bruscius intervened. 'You keep your hands to yourself, Briginus. We're supposed to be searching for prisoners. There's nothing here, let's move on.'

Arontius felt it would not be long before the other prisoners were caught. It was essential that he and Viventia were away by then. He collected tools together in a leather bag and told Viventia to pack some food and drink, but his chief worry were the guards at the gate. They would be sure to remember that his two daughters had already passed through the gate that morning. Once they were ready, he dared not delay any longer and, wrapped in their cloaks, he and Viventia left the house.

In one way their luck held, for the night guards had been changed, but Arontius' sense of unease increased, when he saw that Briginus was one of the replacements.

'Where do you two think you're going?' was his initial greeting.

'I'm just off to tend to the hides in the stream,' replied Arontius, 'they need regular attention as you know.'

'She's seeing to them as well, is she?' said Briginus, indicating Viventia.

'Viventia helps from time to time,' Arontius pointed out.

'Well, the two of you are not going anywhere this morning,' crowed Briginus. 'The bailiff's orders – no-one is to pass through the gate without his permission.'

Despite the churning in his insides, Arontius tried to appear as calm as possible. 'I'm sure Bruscius won't want my work interrupted,' he said, 'we'll go and have a word with him.'

The bailiff was supervising the search of the inner enclosure and did not welcome the interruption. However, he strode over with them to the gate and gave orders to allow them out. But then the blow fell. Briginus was told to accompany them. Arontius protested that there was no need for this precaution, but Bruscius was adamant.

'Just keep an eye on them, Briginus, and none of your nonsense. I'll send a replacement to the gate.'

As he turned to go, there were loud shouts from inside the fort and Bruscius hurried away. They've found the prisoners, thought Arontius, we must get away and grabbing his daughter's arm he urged her down the track.

'Here, what's the hurry?' shouted Briginus following on. 'Slow down.'

They had no alternative but to make for the stream and Arontius began work unpegging the hides from the stream bed and turning them.

Nevertheless he was troubled and kept an eye on the track from the fort. Any minute Bruscius might send men for him and all would be lost. He knew the others would be anxiously waiting in the copse and was desperate to join up with them. They must get well away from Duriarno as soon as possible.

Viventia worked with him for a while. Briginus stood and watched them, but soon retreated up the bank to sit and watch from a distance. Viventia's skirts were getting wet and heavy in the swollen waters, so Arontius told her to rest. She was sitting with her back against a tree, when Briginus sidled up. Giving her a leering look, he thrust his hand over her mouth and at the same time used the weight of his body to force her down to the ground. Arontius was busy, bent over with his hands deep in the stream and noticed nothing. Viventia struggled and tried to bite her attacker's hand; she could feel his other hand exploring inside her dress. She twisted and arched her back but his weight and strength were too much for her and the pungent smell of his body made her faint.

Suddenly Briginus relaxed and fell across her, only to be heaved away. Viventia lay unable to catch her breath, still terrified. It was only when Victoricus called to her father that she realised he had saved her. Briginus lay sprawled out to one side.

'I clouted him over the head with this,' said Victoricus, pointing to a stone. He knelt beside

Viventia to re-assure her. She tried to stammer out her thanks but he shook his head, unable to meet her eyes. Putting an arm about her waist he helped her to her feet. She clung to him overcome with weakness and relief but recovered herself quickly when she saw Arontius approaching.

'We saw three people come out of the fort gate and guessed that they had sent a guard with you. Anicilla and Armea stayed in the trees, while I scouted about towards the river, in the hope of causing a diversion to lure this brute away. I am pleased I arrived when I did, but we must go quickly now,' urged Victoricus. 'Follow me.' He set off downstream and Arontius, plucking up his bag, plunged after the two of them.

They were soon all together among the trees, where Viventia threw herself into her mother's arms but there was time only for a hurried account of events, before plans had to be made. They were certain to be pursued. Even now, Bruscius must be hearing of Arontius' part in the prisoners' escape. They would hardly remain silent, when their own lives were threatened.

Victoricus urged that they make for Isca. No-where would be wholly safe, but he felt there were places in the city where they could hide, whereas a family arriving on any estate in the area would be suspicious. Arontius was reluctant to return to Isca, but after Anicilla added her voice to Victoricus he eventually agreed that in the short term it was perhaps the best solution.

Victoricus suggested striking across to the Isca

track, which he and Cinhil had travelled only two days before. 'We'll be safe perhaps for a mile or two, but we must keep a sharp look-out. At the first sign of pursuit we'll have to cut across country.'

11

Victoricus led the way, with Arontius bringing up the rear. Glancing fearfully around them they emerged from the trees to walk along the edge of a newly ploughed field, sheltered on one side by a thick hedge. From time to time they had glimpses of the fort in the distance, the gateway clearly visible. There appeared to be no activity. Indeed as far as Victoricus could make out the gates remained closed. Within a few minutes they came to the track, which was empty and walking in a group to one side they started towards Isca, the fort gradually receding into the distance behind them.

Victoricus was conscious of their slow pace, aware that mounted men would quickly overtake them, but at least they were making steady progress on the track. Across country they would be much slower. All were immediately alert to the sound of a cart coming towards them.

'We mustn't be seen,' said Arontius, 'let's get off the road.'

'But, there's nowhere to hide,' called Viventia,

'and no-one coming from that direction will bother about a few early travellers.'

'No, your father's right, Viventia,' said Anicilla, 'if we're seen the report may go back to the fort. We must hide in the ditch until the cart passes.'

They stumbled across the wide verge and into the deep drainage ditch at the side of the track. It was overgrown and hid them easily, but it was also wet and muddy. Armea slipped down the bank and ended up coated with mud and in tears. The vehicle passed slowly, the driver completely unaware of their presence.

In the next hour they had to scurry back into the ditch three more times to escape the notice of travellers. Despite the urgency, Armea had difficulty keeping up even a moderate pace and gradually she lagged behind, a parent on either side urging her on. Victoricus strode on with Viventia, both constantly looking back over their shoulders to check the road and the progress of the rest of the family

They had walked a short way, when Viventia broke the silence: 'You came to my rescue just in time,' she said. 'Briginus has chased after me ever since we came to the fort. He even asked father for a marriage contract a few weeks ago. Just think marriage to that pig! Fortunately father refused him, but in any case I wouldn't have had him – I'd have run away first. I shall choose someone myself. Someone I can truly love.'

This said, Viventia glanced flirtatiously at

Victoricus, who tried to cover his embarrassment by pretending to study some trees on the horizon. Nevertheless she noted with pleasure that he blushed at her words, the redness spreading from his neck upwards and over his cheeks.

Viventia next persuaded Victoricus to give an account of his life in Isca and she in turn told him about their flight from that city.

'I loved living in Isca,' she said. 'The baker and his wife were good neighbours in their way and when I was young there were several children around to play with. I'd go to the forum market regularly with my mother. There was always something to do. Then father began to lose business. Families moved away. The day the bailiffs came from the Council was awful. Mother was weeping and father was practically out of his mind. A friendly carrier offered to take us and our few belongings to an estate he knew near the Taen. The owner wasn't at all keen to take us on but he allowed us to put up in his barn as long as we all four worked in his fields.'

'So how did you finish up at Duriarno?' asked her companion.

'Bruscius came visiting and discovered that father had worked with hides. Father was taken away to work at the fort straightaway. We followed along later.'

Viventia was going to carry on, but Victoricus suddenly gripped her arm and swung round. At the same time, some way back down the road the rest of the family had also turned. The unmistakeable sound of horses, ridden fast, had come to their ears.

Victoricus seized Viventia and urged her to the side of the road. As luck would have it the ditch here was tidy and afforded little shelter. The youth jumped the ditch and urged Viventia to follow. Clambering over a fence, they ran for the safety of a small clump of trees. Panting, they reached it just as three horsemen came into view. They flattened themselves against the trees and peered out.

'What's happened to the others?' called Viventia. 'I didn't see where they went.'

'I think that they headed for the ditch on the other side,' said Victoricus. 'Let's hope they've found a safe place.'

The riders were clearly visible. Victoricus recognised Bruscius in the lead with two of the guards behind him. He heard one of the men shout and the horses slowed on the stretch of road below the watchers.

'They're looking our way,' gasped Viventia, shrinking back into the trees. 'They're ignoring the ditches.'

'That guard at the back is pointing over here,' said Victoricus, watching intently. 'Perhaps he caught a glimpse of movement as we fled into the trees. Get ready to move on.'

'I can't abandon my family,' wailed Viventia.

'We'll meet up with them later, but we mustn't get caught. I wouldn't like to be at Cynan's mercy.'

'They're going on,' said Viventia, as the bailiff's horse trotted on.

'No,' said Victoricus, 'they mean to trap us – look Bruscius is going on alone, but the others are dismounting. I bet he's aiming to get behind us and cut us off. They're climbing the fence – it's time to go. Follow me and run for your life.'

For a short time the trees afforded them shelter, but they soon faced open ground, with little cover except field hedges, the land sloping uphill. Victoricus paused, not anxious to leave the trees, but as Viventia caught up with him he plunged on running bent double along the edge of a small field. Climbing over a fence, Victoricus halted to assist his companion, but Viventia urged him on, ignoring his outstretched hand. Near the top of the adjacent pasture, Victoricus looked back and saw the two guards appear at the edge of the trees. They would have no doubts now that they had sighted their quarry.

'If we can get to the top of the ridge,' panted Victoricus 'we might be able to find a hiding place before the men come up, but keep an eye out for Bruscius. He'll know this country well.'

Viventia nodded and went on.

At the top they paused, studying the landscape ahead. Ploughed fields and pasture lands stretched away down to the Taen in the middle distance and the hills on the horizon. Victoricus noted with alarm the lack of cover. He was looking upon a treeless countryside with a spattering of farmsteads, several built within enclosing banks and ditches. There was no sign of Bruscius. After rapid consultation they decided to make for one of the farmsteads, which lay some two miles off.

Victoricus made a mental note of the route and plunged down the slope, Viventia keeping pace with him. He looked back periodically to check when their pursuers reached the skyline and noted with satisfaction that they were obscured by a high hedge as the guards appeared. Clutching hold of Viventia, he flung her down flat on the ground, none too gently, her eyes widening with fear.

'Why did you do that?' she protested.

'They've just reached the ridge and I don't think they've spotted us. If we lie low for a bit they might go the wrong way.' So saying, he cautiously lifted his head to peer through the hedgerow. Sure enough, he could see the men hesitating on the top of the ridge, scanning the countryside.

'Let's see what they do,' said Victoricus.

'It's no good,' replied the girl, 'we'll be spotted as soon as we start off again. We should keep going.'

'Hold on,' said Victoricus, 'I think they're walking along the ridge away from us, probably aiming to keep on the high ground until we break cover. Give them a few minutes to increase the gap between us.'

Viventia lay on her back, still panting with her exertions. The hems of her cloak and dress were coated with mud and her hair, normally drawn back neatly into a bun, was beginning to escape from its pins and straggle over her face. Despite their peril, Victoricus stole a glance at his companion, noting the high colour in her face and the curves of her body. She was beautiful and he realised that he wanted nothing more than to be with her and to hold her. Viventia caught him staring at her and their eyes met. Her smile of flirtatious amusement faded away as she responded to the intensity of his look and she in her turn lowered her eyes, confused by the emotions stirred in her.

Suddenly alerted to the danger of their situation, Victoricus raised himself up and stared through the hedge, failing to spot their pursuers on the ridge. Hard as he looked, they were nowhere to be seen. Viventia joined him, kneeling. 'They must have started down off the hill,' she said, 'and be out of our sight.'

'Yes, but which way did they go?' rejoined Victoricus, cursing himself for being distracted at this crucial moment. 'Come on, we must move.' Crouching down, they began to run down the hedgerow and into the next field.

12

Some time later, they were approaching the farmstead by way of a sunken track, which Victoricus noted had been used by cattle in the past, but not recently. Banks rose above head height on either side of them. They had seen nothing of their pursuers and both felt uneasy and vulnerable in the lane. Victoricus scrambled up one bank to peep cautiously over the top but nothing out of the ordinary was visible.

The track eventually widened as both banks turned away from them to surround a level area, where the grass was exceptionally lush. Across it they could see another low bank with a simple gap in it. Both looked anxiously round, but seeing no movement they went on. The ditch outside the inner bank was overgrown – clumps of nettles had started up in the bottom and along its sides. Piles of rubbish littered the area. Weeds, encouraged by the recent rain, were rapidly greening over the remains of kitchen waste including, Viventia noticed, large numbers of oyster shells and animal bones.

Viventia was puzzled. 'This place looks abandoned,' she remarked. 'The fields are ploughed and there are sheep and cattle grazing, but no-one has walked this way for a while.'

'You're right,' answered Victoricus, 'it appears to be deserted. The land is obviously being worked from elsewhere. This could be another tenant farm that Cynan's taken back for himself. Let's have a look at the buildings, but go carefully. We still don't know where Bruscius and his men are.'

Within the enclosure were timber buildings, becoming dilapidated, but as Victoricus judged, not long abandoned. Grass and moss were beginning to sprout in the thatch of a small round house at one side and one plank built shelter in the lee of the bank was leaning at a crazy angle. Animal pens of upright posts and hurdles lined another length of bank.

Viventia froze, a sharp cry escaping from her involuntarily. Victoricus swung round, but it was only a hare breaking cover out of long grass near them, disturbed by their approach. Both laughed after the release of sudden tension. Victoricus was convinced that no-one had been in the enclosure for some time: no-one was waiting to pounce on them.

They explored the round house. Its earth floor still had small pieces of pottery, charcoal and bones trodden into it and the hearth at the centre contained the remains of the last fire, a kerb of stones holding them in place. Weeds had begun to grow through the floor and birds were nesting in the thatch above their heads. But it remained a sound structure, thought Victoricus, as he looked around appreciatively. The timbers of its walls were still upright, with the infilling between the posts intact and the roof struts though blackened with smoke still formed a perfect cone above their heads.

'Sit here and rest,' said Victoricus 'and I'll go and take a look.'

Viventia sank down gratefully onto one of the kerb stones, but not before she had warned her companion to take great care.

Victoricus mounted the inner bank and lying flat out on his stomach peered cautiously over the top. He could see no movement between the farmstead and the ridge and was about to turn away, when something caught his eye. There, just one field away he glimpsed the brown tunic of one of the guards moving against the hedge and as he watched, concentrating hard on the spot, he saw that both men were there. He slid down the bank out of sight, but as he did so a shout came from the other side of the enclosure. He jerked his head round to see the head and shoulders of Bruscius, clearly on horseback approaching rapidly. They were trapped.

Viventia had heard the shout and came running out of the house. Victoricus joined her. What were they to do?

'Bruscius will have to use the entrance, unless he abandons his horse,' said Viventia. 'He'll never get that animal over the ditch and bank. Come on, we still have a chance.'

So saying, she was off out of the inner enclosure,

running as hard as she could and Victoricus obliged to follow. She veered left at the entrance into the open ground between the two banks and continuing on reached the side furthest away from the gateway. Here, the roof of the house was visible above the inner bank.

'If all three make for the entrance we might survive,' she panted. Victoricus was not so sure. He felt trapped between these banks and thought that if they tried to climb out they would be exposed.

The horse was the first thing they heard, as they waited at the foot of the outer bank. The jangling of harness, more than the sound of its hooves, muffled by the long grass. Victoricus was on his feet immediately.

'He's riding round here,' he said, listening intently. 'What do we do?'

'Up the bank, quick,' replied Viventia and without waiting she started up. They were over the top and down the other side before the horseman rounded the corner. Pausing in the weed-filled ditch, they looked at each other, wondering what to do next. The decision was made for them. Bruscius loomed momentarily above them at the top of the bank, his horse abandoned, before hurtling down straight towards them.

Victoricus rose to fend him off.

'Escape while you can,' he flung back at Viventia as the bailiff jumped the last few feet into the ditch. Viventia stifled the scream forced from her as she realised Bruscius was holding a sword. But her mouth gaped as the bailiff in turn screamed and fell over, his ankle twisted and broken as he landed awkwardly.

Victoricus, mesmerised, just stared at the fallen figure, writhing in pain. His instinct was to help, but Viventia urged him away, reminding him of the two guards, who must be nearby.

'They'll look after Bruscius,' she said 'let's get away, while we can.' They left him hollering for his men and moaning in between at the pain and set off down the field at a run.

Before they reached the end of the field, Victoricus glanced back to see two men hurrying, not in pursuit of them, but towards the ditch where the bailiff was lying.

'We're safe for the moment,' he said. 'They'll not come after us any more.'

Nevertheless, as they re-joined the track they took care to keep a sharp look out. There might be other search parties out for them, though Victoricus doubted it. Viventia was anxious about her family and was hoping to encounter them somewhere along the way. They decided not to hide from the few travellers who passed them going west. A group of five was conspicuous, but two cloaked and hooded figures were hardly worth a second glance.

The thick cloud of the early morning had thinned out and shafts of light from a fitful sun appeared occasionally above the sea far to their right as they trudged on. The wind continued to swirl about them, rippling pools of rainwater in the road and flinging the broken cloud over the hills ahead of them. Both were weary and hungry, drained by the events of the morning, but anxious to keep going.

They approached the bridge over the Taen river with caution, but the only living things visible were oxen lazily wading in the shallows on the far side. Coming closer they noticed a wagon drawn up close to some trees on the further bank.

'There must be someone around, but I don't see them,' said Victoricus. 'Let me go ahead and check.'

'We'll both go,' came the reply. 'I don't want to separate again. We'll face it together.'

Victoricus was content and they passed over the bridge without incident. The driver appeared to be asleep under the wagon. They looked down on it from the end of the bridge and Viventia became aware that Victoricus was gripping the rail and staring intently.

'What is it?' she asked.

'I think I recognise that wagon,' said Victoricus slowly, 'and if I'm right then the man asleep below it is Cinhil and we're in luck. Let's go down and find out.'

Sure enough, it was Cinhil, who emerged, smiling broadly from beneath the wagon. He was almost as pleased to see Victoricus as the latter was to see him, gripping him by the arm and only reluctantly letting go.

'When Bruscius dragged you off from the meal that night I was so amazed I didn't know what to say. Then I pieced together your story from that drunken neighbour of yours and from the snippets which came back to me while I was waiting for the return load. They kept me kicking my heels all the following day and try as I might to see you I was always refused. Then, just as I was getting ready to leave all this hullabaloo about your escape. That delayed me further. And then to cap it all, when I did get away your substitute mate, whom Bruscius thoughtfully provided, proved to be dead drunk and useless.'

'Where is he now?' asked Victoricus.

'I kicked him off miles back down the road – I was better off without him. I've lost a mate and you look as if you've found one, young Victoricus,' remarked Cinhil, eyeing Viventia.

'It's a long story,' said Victoricus, 'but this is Viventia, who's also fled from the fort.'

'Well, you can tell it to me on the way to Isca,' said Cinhil, 'I assume that's where you're heading.'

'And you need a mate,' grinned Victoricus. 'How were you going to get this load over the hills to Isca on your own?'

'That was puzzling me, too, but now its solved,' came the reply. 'Let's get those oxen hitched up.'

'Just a moment,' called Viventia, coming forward. 'Did you see a young girl with her parents on the track from Duriarno? We got separated on the way.'

'Ah,' said Cinhil suddenly enlightened, 'that would be Arontius the cobbler and his wife – your parents and your sister – am I right?' Viventia

112

nodded and he continued: 'no, I can't say I saw them on the road and I think I would have recognised them. Sorry. But don't worry they'll turn up. Now, let's get moving if we want to be in Isca before dark.'

13

The journey back to Isca was uneventful. The three of them sat together on the front of the wagon as the oxen slowly plodded home. Viventia was silent most of the way, wrapping her cloak closely about her and thinking of her family and of the future. Victoricus gave Cinhil a detailed account of the last two days.

'I'm not sure how safe you will be in Isca,' remarked Cinhil when he had finished. 'There's fewer people and fewer places to hide these days. You'll have to take care. You've made Cynan look foolish and he won't forget that in a hurry. His control over the city is strong, even though he has no residence there now. You might be better going east, getting away from Cynan's lands. If he ever lays hands on any of you again you'll be sorry.'

'We agreed to join up with Viventia's family at Isca,' said Victoricus, 'so we'll decide what to do then.'

'You'll stick together, will you?' asked Cinhil, looking pointedly from one to the other.

Viventia in her turn stared fixedly at Victoricus.

'I've no family of my own left,' said Victoricus, choosing his words carefully 'and I probably owe my life to Arontius and his family. They've lost their home and become fugitives by helping me, so yes, I'll certainly stick by them now.'

'Powerful reasons,' remarked Cinhil, grinning widely, 'excellent reasons. What other could there be?' But he got no answer as Viventia was studying something on the horizon and Victoricus was watching the oxen closely.

They rolled over the bridge into Isca just as the light was beginning to fade. As the wagon mounted the main street, Viventia looked out eagerly for her old home and shed a few tears as they passed the boarded up shop. Victoricus agreed to go along to the cattle station with Cinhil to help stable the oxen.

'But we won't unload tonight. I'll park the wagon next to the house and see to it in the morning,' said Cinhil.

The cattle station seemed silent, deserted as they turned in. There were a few bullocks in the pens, but Castor was nowhere to be seen. They halted the wagon and Victoricus began to unhitch the oxen and walk them over to the water troughs.

'So you're back then, I was expecting you two yesterday,' said a voice, putting Victoricus instantly on the alert. He swung round to see Attius close to him.

'Who's this handsome clean shaven youth? You seem to have lost your beard crossing the Taen. What's been happening?' His glance took in Cinhil,

115

but then rested on Viventia, standing to one side. 'Lost your beard, but acquired a beauty. What have you two been up to? You've missed out on all the fun here, but had some of your own, by the look of it.'

Victoricus ignored the taunts and asked 'Where's Castor? And what fun's this you're talking about?' By now Cinhil had joined them and Viventia came over and was introduced.

'When I came into work yesterday there were two carts drawn up outside Castor's rooms and a couple of men were loading up his belongings. He took me on one side and was quite friendly, for Castor. Said he was getting out – going east with his family. The cattle station was running down and there'd be work only for a few more weeks. Sure enough, an hour after daybreak he was gone and he left me in charge until someone else was sent. So you take your orders from me now,' Attius concluded with a laugh.

Victoricus gave only a brief explanation of the events at Duriarno as he and Viventia were weary and anxious to be off. He was sure that Rufus would welcome Viventia and take her in and he was keen to see the old man again.

They slipped away as soon as possible, after Victoricus had agreed to report to the station in the morning. He guided Viventia through the streets holding onto her arm.

Cinhil had been able to pass on some food to them, but both were hungry and Viventia was so tired she leaned heavily on him. Passing slowly through the familiar alleyway from the north gate street, Victoricus anticipated their welcome from Rufus. Soon they'd be near the fire and eating some of Rufus' home grown produce. The sense of unease crept upon him gradually. There was something wrong. The buildings outlined against the setting sun were thinning out. It dawned on Victoricus that Rufus' street had gone. His house, his garden, the street itself had all been swept away. In their place were pits, heaps of rubble and timbers and stone lying about. They were standing on the edge of an empty landscape – a vast quarter of the town without buildings or streets.

'What is it?' whispered Viventia sensing the profound shock which Victoricus was experiencing.

'It's Rufus' house – my home – all gone. There was a street of houses here when I left Isca. And where's Rufus and Lupus? I must find out what's happened to them. This is Sorio's work. His men have been clearing this area for some time and they've finally driven the old man out.'

'Who is this Sorio and where can we find him?' asked Viventia.

'He has a house close to the forum – but wait, Silvius his night-watchman should be somewhere around. He may know what's happened to Rufus.'

They picked their way around the edge of the area with Victoricus making as much noise as he could, throwing stones and tossing timbers around to try and flush Silvius out. It worked. After a few minutes Silvius stepped out from the remains of a building.

'Oh, it's you, Victoricus – if you're out for an evening stroll with your girl you're making plenty of noise about it.'

'The noise was to attract your attention, Silvius. What's happened round here – the whole area's been demolished since I was here last.'

'Sorio came in with a large gang two days ago at sunrise,' explained Silvius. 'He was determined to demolish the whole area in one go and he pretty well succeeded.'

'What happened to the old man Rufus with the dog?' asked Victoricus in some trepidation.

'He resisted, but it was no good. Sorio was sympathetic but absolutely firm. When he released the dog one of the men thumped it with a post and after that the old man gave in. Sorio brought up a cart and loaded all his belongings onto it. He's found him an empty house near the east gate and all his stuff was taken there, the old man riding on the cart. He was in a state, threatening Sorio with all manner of things, but Sorio just laughed. Within an hour his house was roofless and by the end of the morning it was gone.'

Victoricus turned away from them, wiping away tears. He had been through so much in the last few days and then to return to this: his old friend, who'd treated him so well, driven from the house and garden he loved so much, his dog dead for all he knew. It was almost too much to bear. Shock soon gave way to a burning anger that Rufus should have been treated so in the short time that he had been away.

Viventia, despite her own troubles, sensed Victoricus' loss of well-being. The world which he had built up around him here in Isca was breaking apart. She hugged him, but added to his embarrassment at displaying his emotion.

'Can't we go and find this Rufus?' she asked. 'Then we could see for ourselves how he is.'

Silvius offered to take them over to the house quickly, though he dared not be absent from his job for very long.

The house lay far into the opposite corner of the city, with the town wall rising sharply above it. The rooms lay around two sides of a yard, which was full of rubbish and shutters hung at crazy angles from the window openings. The rooms had once had corridor access by a paved way, its roof supported by small columns set on a wall, but this had collapsed and was strewn about the yard. Great patches of plaster had fallen from the walls revealing the timber frame beneath.

Silvius left them staring about and scurried back to his watchman's job. Victoricus thumped on the one door, which seemed to be on its hinges. There was no response. He knocked again, but no reply was forthcoming.

'Wait here, under the shadow of the wall,' he said to Viventia. 'I'll go in and take a look.'

He found Rufus in a small room at the end of a hallway. He was huddled in one corner, staring straight ahead, his belongings scattered around him.

'Rufus, it's me, Victoricus.'

The old man's eyes swivelled, but otherwise there was no response.

'I know what's happened, Rufus and I'm as sorry as you, but let's try and make the best of it, eh? You and I together could make this place into something, couldn't we? There's even room for a garden outside. Come on, it's not like you to give up. I've a friend outside who's desperately tired and hungry. She's lost her parents and sister – doesn't know where they are – can't we give her a welcome?'

Victoricus went out to fetch Viventia and when they reappeared the old man was on his feet. Viventia's plight had struck a chord with him and his sense of chivalry and his protective instincts now came into play. He welcomed them both, embraced Victoricus and all three ended up shedding tears.

'Now, where are your lamps?' asked Victoricus, peering into the gloom. 'Let's get some light in here.'

The scene which met their eyes, when the lamps were lit was chaotic. Rufus' belongings had been dumped by his carriers in the next room. Furniture, clothing, cooking pans and tools all in a heap. The hall was blackened with smoke from a fire, which someone had lit recently in the middle of the floor. The plaster of the walls and ceiling had a grey coating, beneath which were just visible painted panels stretching up from a strip painted wine red at floor level. Rubbish was piled in another room and included the remains of a meal eaten some while ago. It smelt foul, even to Victoricus, who could endure most odours.

'Why don't we clear up enough to get a night's rest and then explore further in the morning?' suggested Viventia, clearly tired out.

Rufus by now was his old self again. He had rescued some of his foodstuffs and utensils and was busy putting a meal together. 'It'll only be cold stuff tonight, but it'll have to do. We'll sort ourselves out tomorrow. You two clear a space and try and find some bedding. There should be some mattresses somewhere among my belongings.'

Victoricus was astonished at how quickly they sorted themselves out. The day had begun with him chained to a post in Cynan's stronghold. Since then he'd met Arontius, escaped, nearly been recaptured and returned to Isca on the same wagon on which he'd left. Now here he was reunited with Rufus in this strange house and with Arontius' daughter sitting on the mattress opposite him. He felt secure, although he admitted to himself that they must still be in danger. What of Arontius and Anicilla, who had put their own lives in danger by rescuing him? Where were they now?

Many of the same thoughts were obviously going through Viventia's mind. She had worked with him cheerfully getting the room ready, but now she was silent and pre-occupied. They had finished their cold meat and green beans – sadly the last from Rufus' garden – and a tear ran down her cheek, hastily brushed aside. Victoricus moved to comfort her, putting his arm around her shoulder.

'I know you're worried about your family,' he said. 'I won't deceive you – I'm worried too – but they knew we were making for Isca and I feel sure they'll turn up in the next few days. Then we'll make plans for the future. In the meantime Rufus and I will look after you. You'll come to no harm while we're here.'

'I feel sure they've been taken,' whispered Viventia, 'and that I'll never see them again. We can't go back. It wouldn't be safe, but I must have news of them somehow.'

'We've a few friends in Isca,' said Victoricus. 'We'll ask about for news from the west. We're sure to find out something in the next few days. In the meantime we must prepare for their arrival. This house looks big enough for us to have a room each. That should please Armea.'

'Let's get some rest,' put in Rufus, 'things will look brighter in the morning.'

The three settled down on their mattresses, keeping to the one room as all agreed it would be safer, until they had explored the building more thoroughly. Victoricus had just fallen into a deep sleep, when he was aroused by Viventia shaking him violently. He was not fully awake for some moments and then his drowsiness was replaced with astonishment. ' What is it Viventia?' he whispered, puzzled and then alarmed at finding her kneeling at his side, her warmth and smell so close.

'Shh, and listen,' came the reply, 'there's someone in the house.'

Now fully alert, he froze and concentrated. He

thought he heard a sound within the house. There it was again, like a low moan or whine. What was it? Just a window shutter or a door moving in the wind? He turned to re-assure her. 'It's just something moving in the wind, I think.'

'No, it's not regular enough for that and the noise has changed. I've been listening for some while. I'm convinced we're not alone here.'

By now Rufus too was awake and they decided to investigate. Victoricus struck a spark from the flint and lit one of the oil lamps. Shielding the flame with his hand he stepped into the corridor. Here the noise was louder. It was coming from the end room close to the outside door. Motioning the other to stay he crept forward, pushing the door ajar. Cautiously he peeped into the room. The sounds were coming from one corner. He lifted the lamp high and moved across the room.

'It's Lupus,' he called. 'Bring another lamp.'

Rufus came with a rush. 'I thought he was dead,' he said, a grin lighting up his face. 'When they bundled me onto the cart and brought all my stuff out of the house, piling it onto the back, I was sure they'd left Lupus behind, dead. He's tough, of course. It would take more than a clout on the head to finish him off.'

'Let's have a look at him,' said Victoricus, pleased to see old friends reunited, but anxious in case the dog was permanently injured. 'Here, hold the light, Rufus. Why don't you get back to sleep, Viventia? We can manage here.'

Victoricus ran his hand over the dog's back and

legs. 'No problems there,' he said. 'He's got a nasty wound on the side of his head, see, where the blood has run but there doesn't seem to be any great injury. If we bathe it in the morning, he'll soon be well again. Meantime leave him to sleep. That's the best thing for him. Have you got a blanket we can put over him to keep him warm?'

Turning his head, he realised that Rufus had already disappeared, but by the time Victoricus had straightened up, he was back, blanket in hand, having anticipated the need. He wrapped up his companion gently causing Lupus to whimper and snuffle. Then the two resumed their broken sleep, Rufus happier than at any time since their return.

In the morning Victoricus was determined to go along to the cattle station. Viventia and the old man urged him to be cautious.

'Cynan may already have men searching for us in Isca,' she said. 'Don't take any risks.'

Victoricus assured them that he would be careful, but he was anxious to keep contact with Cinhil and Attius.

'They may have news from Duriarno. Attius is bound to hear something soon.'

Viventia relented, her anxiety for her family persuading her the risk was worth taking. She and Rufus would explore the house and clear out some of the rooms, while Victoricus was gone, but she begged him not to be long.

14

The city seemed quieter than ever as Victoricus made his way to the cattle station. Few people were about and those figures, hooded and cloaked, whom he did encounter, passed him by without a glance, seemingly preoccupied with their own cares. Cinhil was unloading the wagon as he approached and seemed pleased to see him.

'Come to give me a hand, have you boy? Where have you left that girl of yours?' he asked in rapid succession. Then seeing Victoricus glancing anxiously round, he assured him that he and Attius were the only people on site.

Victoricus relaxed a little. He did not like to point out that Viventia was not his girl but at the same time he was rather pleased that Cinhil should think so. He told the wagoner about Rufus and the events of the previous night, at the same time grabbing one of the empty barrels and rolling it into the storeroom.

Attius joined them as they finished unloading.

'I'm still in charge,' he grinned. 'No-one's arrived to relieve me. Castor's desertion has not been noticed yet or perhaps they've got other things to do. There's no work, no money and no food and unless I get orders soon I'll be off myself.'

'Petrus is being buried in the south gate cemetery this afternoon,' added Attius. 'There's to be a service in the cemetery chapel beforehand. His mother and sister won't have many friends there. You should come along with us Victoricus.'

All thoughts of Petrus had gone from Victoricus' mind with the events of the previous days, but the picture of a thin body shaken by coughing came abruptly into his mind. Overworked and under-nourished Petrus, struggling to provide for his family and finally toppling over so silently off the barrel. Images of everything which had happened since flickered before him. Was it really only four days since Petrus had died?

No pursuit appeared to have reached Isca yet. Perhaps he could risk attending the funeral. He might learn something there. He made arrange-ments with the two men to meet near the south gate and they would go along to Petrus' funeral together.

Viventia was uneasy at the mention of Petrus' funeral, on his return to the house.

'Funerals attract people and the cemetery is such a public place. You might be noticed by one of Cynan's spies.'

'I'll be careful,' Victoricus assured her, 'but apart from paying my respects I might pick up news from Duriarno.'

A discussion ensued into which Rufus was drawn

and finally it was agreed, with some reluctance on Victoricus' part, that all three would attend the funeral.

Rufus and Viventia had spent the morning tidying the house and exploring. In daylight it was clear that sets of rooms one storey high were arranged around two sides of a yard. The stone-built house backed onto the street behind the city wall, with pathways leading off the street either side. Across the yard was another house, which appeared to be occupied. It had probably not been long deserted before Rufus was dumped in it, although some roof tiles were broken and window shutters were either missing or hung loosely. Within, the two of them had cleaned out some of the rooms and set out furniture. Painted wall plaster in two of the rooms had been washed down with water drawn from a well in the yard. Rufus had found charcoal somewhere and the stove was working.

'It's not home, he remarked, 'but it'll do for the moment. We'll just need the rooms on this side of the house, so I've nailed up the doorway between.'

Rufus was cheerful again. Lupus had met him on his return and Victoricus was sure that the animal's recovery had helped revive the old man's spirits.

The three met up with Attius at the south gate and together they walked along the road leading downhill away from the city. Passing the road to the river quay, they soon came to the family burial plots, with their stone walls and monuments, lining both sides of the route and stretching back from it for some distance. Many were uncared for, over-grown, with tombstones lying at odd angles and the simple brick and stone built tombs crumbling and shattered. A few more cloaked and hooded individuals were moving in the same direction.

Viventia drew closer to Victoricus.

'I hate these old tombs,' she said. 'When we lived in Isca I always tried to avoid this road. I feel our ancestors watching and waiting, ready to pounce when we least expect with all the old gods in their wake.'

Rufus tried to re-assure her.

'Its the monuments themselves, rearing up on either side, which seem to threaten you,' he said, 'but don't believe that the dead are evil. Your ancestors live on in you and would not want to harm you, rather they'd want to protect you.'

Eventually they came to the small chapel perched on a knoll above the river, surrounded by tomb-stones and wooden grave markers. They entered through the west door, crossed the tiny vestibule and, pushing aside the curtain, joined the con-gregation. Victoricus surveyed the twenty or so people standing in the body of the church. A board on trestles set up before the altar bore the body of Petrus, wrapped in a white shroud. Attius nudged him and pointed out Petrus' mother and sister to one side. Their weeping was the only sound break-ing the silence.

The priest appeared out of the chancel behind the altar and immediately began to intone the service. Prayers were said, the priest standing before the altar and extending his arms and hands palms outwards. Victoricus could follow some of the Latin if he concentrated hard, but he was already out of practice. The Celtic tongue he used to talk to his friends and workmates was much more familiar to him. Attius, he sensed, was not following the service at all, while Viventia and Rufus did appear to be concentrating. In a short time it was over and the priest led out the small procession, with first the body of Petrus carried out on the board by four men, followed by the family and the rest of the congregation. They assembled around a freshly dug grave close to the chapel.

After a few more words from the priest, Petrus was lowered into the grave. Small sweet biscuits in the shape of leaves were handed round to the mourners by two women, who also poured out a thin wine into wooden cups for them. The grave was then filled in by a waiting labourer.

This brief ceremony at the graveside gave Victoricus and his friends a chance to study the faces of the mourners. Victoricus recognised only one person – Silvius, whom he'd half expected to see. As the mourners began to move away he joined them. At the same time Rufus was drawn away into conversation with an elderly woman, standing close to one of the gravestones.

Silvius was agitated and could hardly contain himself. Sorio himself had visited him in the night.

'He doesn't usually visit while I'm keeping watch. Occasionally one of his men might check on me in the evening or just before I go off duty, but last night he arrived with about twenty men. He wanted to know if I'd had any trouble or seen anything unusual. I told him it was as quiet as ever. 'Keep a sharp look out,' he said. 'From now on I'm putting three more men on night watch. They're to patrol the area between the two gates and report in to you regularly.' When I asked him what trouble he was expecting he would only say that he had enemies, who were jealous of his position in the city and might be planning an attack on his lands.

Later one of his men said that Sorio had followers keeping watch on the Isc bridge and at the quay at night as if he expected a threat from the river or out of the south-west.'

'Cynan!' whispered Viventia. 'He'll be behind this. He's not content with his base at Duriarno. He's trying to extend his power.'

Victoricus agreed with her. 'Bruscius said Cynan was looking to take over other forts. I'd not thought of him trying to take Isca, but it makes sense. A great walled town like this, even if it is run down, would be a rich prize for Cynan.'

Attius cut in excitedly that he'd had a visitor at the cattle station just after Victoricus left that morning.

'It was one of Sorio's men. 'From now on', he said 'you're working for Sorio. We'll have a gang in tomorrow to pull down that house of Castor's and remove it. You can live above the barn and you'll take your orders from Sorio. He'll see that you're fed regularly and from now on any cattle sent in will be processed for him.'

'What will you do?' asked Silvius.

'I've had no contact with Cynan and Sorio's here on the spot so from now on you and I are working for the same boss,' grinned Attius.

Rufus, having finished his conversation, returned to the group.

'An old friend,' he explained. 'I used to meet up with her regularly in the shops, but haven't seen her for some time. She's leaving Isca soon to live with her son near Lindinis.'

They walked back together into town. Attius and Silvius turned down an invitation to return with them to the house, so the three made their way through the narrow streets near the dilapidated bath-house towards home. Victoricus told Rufus what they had heard of Sorio and Cynan.

'So those two are rivals to take over our world are they?' retorted Rufus. 'What a state we're in when a man can't live decently in his own house and is threatened from all quarters. We'll be stuck in the middle of this trial of strength.'

'Listen!' called Viventia urgently.

'What is it?' said Victoricus as they stopped.

Then they could all hear it. Furious barking from ahead.

'That's Lupus,' shouted Rufus and plunged ahead.

'Wait,' yelled Victoricus grabbing his cloak. 'We must go carefully. Let me investigate.'

They were approaching by the street at the back of the house. Victoricus entered the narrow path at the side of the house, moving cautiously. A glance round the corner of the house revealed two men sat in the yard, obviously waiting for their return. Lupus continued to bark at intervals. Victoricus returned to the street.

'Two of Cynan's men by the look of them,' he reported. 'We can't go in.'

'What are we to do?' pondered Viventia in despair. 'We'll never be free of them.'

'Attius will give us shelter for the moment and then we must leave Isca,' said Victoricus. 'It's not safe here any longer.'

'I must find my family,' wept Viventia. 'I must know that they're safe.'

Victoricus offered what comfort he could. Placing his arm around her shoulders he drew her to him.

'First thing in the morning we'll go west towards the Taen. We won't take the road – it would be too dangerous. We'll travel by paths until we get news of your family. Someone's bound to have heard of them.'

Still holding on to the girl, he turned to Rufus.

'They don't want you – you'll be safe in a few days, when the search dies down. You could stay on in Isca.'

'And have another home demolished around my ears? No, I'm coming with you, but first I'm going to rescue Lupus.' With that he walked on down the street.

'Go after him,' said Viventia, wiping away tears. 'He'll get us all captured.'

Victoricus caught up with the old man, who was determined to retrieve his dog.

'I'll climb in through one of the back windows,' he said.

'They're too high up and in any case those men will hear you.'

'I might do it standing on your shoulders,' put in Viventia, coming up behind them.

Victoricus would not hear of it, but, after a hurried argument, was finally persuaded. When action was needed Viventia was confident and resourceful, quite unlike the tearful girl of a few moments previously. She squeezed into the window opening easily. Then there were tense moments while the two below listened intently. Would the waiting men investigate once Lupus ceased barking? Viventia appeared at the window once more. Leaning out, she dropped the silent dog into Victoricus' waiting arms, before heaving herself out onto his shoulders. By now Rufus was caressing his dog and they prepared to move off as quickly as they could. Victoricus looked round frequently as they retreated but there was no pursuit.

15

They made their way cautiously towards the cattle station. All were fearful of encountering more of Cynan's men in the streets. Emerging from the alleyway they skirted the pens and approached the barn. Attius was nowhere to be seen.

'I expect he's busy in one of the sheds,' said Victoricus. 'We'll go into the barn first then I'll go and find him.'

Lupus began growling as soon as they were through the door.

'What is it, boy?' called Rufus.

A slight forewarning, but not enough. Before they turned, four men were on them, pinning their arms and flattening them against the wall. Victoricus tried to resist but it was useless. Lupus bared his fangs at the man holding Rufus, but the attack never came.

'Control your dog old man or I'll lay out your precious Victoricus with this,' yelled a familiar voice. 'It will save the Lord Cynan the job of executing him.'

So saying, Briginus emerged from the shadows

brandishing a length of lead pipe. He held it beneath Victoricus' nose.

'We meet again and this time you won't escape. You've crippled Bruscius and annoyed Lord Cynan, but I'm taking you back and claiming my reward.'

He eyed Viventia hungrily and Victoricus felt sick with despair. Why had he delayed in Isca? They could easily be 30 miles further east now away from the clutches of men like Briginus and Cynan. He knew now that he loved Viventia. It had grown out of their easy companionship and her bravery. Admiration had grown into love, as yet unexpressed. He should have protected her, even if it meant abandoning her family for the time being. Now they were all doomed – he to death and Viventia to a living death with this oaf Briginus.

Briginus, boor that he was, sensed the emotions the youth was experiencing. He moved towards Viventia, flicked back her hood with the pipe and thrust his face into hers.

'Like it or not, you'll be mine, when we get back to Duriarno and we won't wait for your precious father's consent, even though he'll be taken soon enough. Arontius and your mother helped a prisoner escape. They deserve death, but I might ask for their lives from the Lord Cynan once we're related. Then they can end their days as Cynan's slaves together with that sister of yours.'

The clout across his cheek caught Briginus entirely unawares. He flinched, as his companions guffawed, but was only momentarily off balance.

Seizing Viventia by the hair, he twisted her head until she cried out.

'Spirited eh? I shall enjoy breaking you in – and I might not wait for Duriarno.'

Victoricus raged against his captors, flinging himself sideways, but to no avail.

'Put them in with the other and muzzle that dog,' yelled Briginus. 'Make sure they're well secured. We'll move off at dusk.'

Slumped against a wall, with legs and arms firmly tied, Victoricus recognised the cellar where the meat barrels had been stored. As his eyes grew accustomed to the dim light he could make out the outlines of his companions, all similarly trussed up and propped against the wall. Even Lupus was tethered and had rope tied around his muzzle. Victoricus moved painfully towards Viventia.

'I'm sorry to have involved you in this mess. Your family have paid dearly for helping me to escape. I wish I'd never agreed to go to Duriarno, back into Cynan's territory.'

'Next thing you'll be saying you regret meeting up with me,' cut in Viventia, unable to see the colour rising in her companion's face. 'It's no good wanting to change the past. We have to make plans. Didn't you hear what that pig Briginus was saying? They haven't caught my family yet, which means they must still be hiding out in Cynan's lands. We've got to get away from these men before they drag us back to Duriarno.'

'The girl's right,' called Rufus. 'No good giving in now.'

'There's five of them to the three of us,' remarked Victoricus, in despondent mood.

'Four,' said a voice on the other side of the room, making them all stiffen.

Attius, tied up like the rest of them, was pushed up against a barrel. He was still dazed from a blow on the head, received when he resisted Cynan's men, but he was able to relate what had happened to him. They had been waiting for him on his return from the funeral. Cynan must have heard of Sorio's growing power and they'd been sent to recover their lord's property. Attius was convinced that a trial of strength between the two lords was imminent and that it might result in their rescue.

'Cynan's men can't wander freely about Isca any more. They're very wary within the walls of the city.'

'That's right,' said Viventia, remembering. 'Briginus did say they wouldn't move off with us before dusk and he was quick to lock us up out of sight.'

They continued to discuss their plight and ways to escape, but in the end were forced to agree to await opportunities on the road.

Some hours later the door to the cellar was flung open and Briginus appeared with his men. They were brought out one at a time to be fitted with shackles and chains, which eventually linked them in one line. To Rufus' dismay Lupus was left tethered in the cellar. His protests were met with threats to kill the dog there and then, which promptly silenced him. They were escorted out into the main street, Briginus leading the way. There were very few people about so late and the few passers-by wrapped their cloaks tightly around themselves and hurried on ignoring the little procession. The chains set up strange echoing clinking sounds in the stillness.

As they approached the gate they were confronted by a small knot of men, who eyed them closely. One held an iron tipped spear and others wooden staffs.

'We're about to close the gates,' said one. 'What's your business here?'

'Our business is for Lord Cynan,' said Briginus, 'returning some of his property to him. We're just setting off back to his headquarters.'

'So late in the evening,' rejoined the other 'with a dark night coming on. I'm not sure I should let you pass. The Lord Sorio should hear of this. Who are these prisoners and what's been your business in Isca?'

Briginus had stiffened on hearing Sorio's name and title.

'Since when has Sorio been styled Lord here?' he said. 'The Lord Cynan controls all in these parts. Dare you interfere in his business?'

Victoricus began to hope that salvation was at hand. The two sides looked as if they might come to blows, or at least their departure might be delayed.

'This youth,' said Briginus pointing to Victoricus 'and the girl are runaways from the Lord Cynan's service and these two have harboured and assisted them. I am taking them all back to Duriarno and I advise you not to hinder me.'

Victoricus was surprised to hear a more conciliatory tone from Briginus. He must be anxious to get away. The guards conferred and to the dismay of the prisoners, the party was allowed to leave. Their only hope now lay in escape during the journey. They could expect little mercy once at Duriarno.

Victoricus was aware first of bright stars in a blue black sky. Then quickly the stiffness in his limbs and the sore places on his ankles and wrists intruded. He listened as Briginus called a halt and all sank gratefully onto the grass at the side of the track. Rufus had struggled to keep up the pace over the last few miles, dragging the chains which linked him to Attius and Victoricus and causing them increased discomfort. He was still breathing hard and would have difficulty in going further. Viventia had fared better. She was determined not to show weakness and had managed a smile in answer to Victoricus' query about her well-being.

One of their guards carried water in a leather bag and passed it to each in turn to drink. Briginus chided him in a half-hearted manner for spoiling them. He too appeared weary and ill at ease. Anxious to be back at Duriarno and hand over responsibility, thought Victoricus.

Back on the road the pace was slower. No amount of urging or cursing could make Rufus go faster. Even Briginus came to accept that the old man had been pushed to the limit. His solution was to take Rufus out of line and release him from his leg shackles, leaving him handcuffed only. One guard was attached solely to Rufus to assist him onwards. Victoricus was puzzled that Briginus was taking so much care. Was he regretting bringing Rufus along, fearful perhaps of Cynan's reaction?

The sky to the east, over the sea, was just beginning to lighten as they topped the hill towards the Taen bridge. Attius and one of the guards shouted almost simultaneously, drawing everyone's attention to fires burning down near the estuary to their left. The whole party stopped. Briginus studied the flickering lights, conferring with his men and reaching no conclusion. It was a clear night, with a strong breeze blowing off the sea. The flames were bright points piercing the blackness. One fire might be accidental but two in the same area must be deliberate. Meanwhile the prisoners had sunk to the ground, glad of a further rest. It was brief, as Briginus appeared satisfied with a suggestion from one of his men that the Lord Cynan's men were punishing miscreants. Nevertheless Briginus was wary and ordered his men to keep careful watch as they descended the hill towards the bridge. Two of them were sent ahead. His unease was plain when Rufus slipped and stumbled sending stones clattering across the surface of the track for he whipped round snarling:

'Go quietly old man or I'll shut you up permanently.'

They were close to the bridge an hour later. Nothing had happened and Victoricus, who saw any diversion as an opportunity for escape, was bitterly disappointed. Once over the bridge and deeper into Cynan's territory their chances of escape would be minimal. Not for the first time, total despair overwhelmed him.

Briginus went ahead to join his scouts, leaving the prisoners in the charge of his remaining men.

'Sit the prisoners down at the side of the road,' he ordered, 'and don't take your eyes off them. I'll be back shortly.'

Victoricus and his companions sat in a circle. Rufus looked utterly drained. Sweat poured down his grey face and his mouth drooped open as he took great wheezing breaths. Victoricus placed his hand over his and the old man looked up, shaking his head but incapable of speech.

Attius was keen to take action, to seize the opportunity.

'With Briginus and two of the guards gone, we might manage to get away,' he whispered. 'It's our best chance.'

'Shackled together, we wouldn't get far,' returned Viventia. 'We'd need to delay or divert the guards so that we could hide up for a while.'

Their hurried discussion was interrupted by screams and shouts ahead close to the bridge. Sounds of fighting reached them. All looked up, peering in that direction. Their guards stood in the middle of the road, anxious and bewildered, not knowing what to do.

'Now's our chance,' muttered Victoricus, 'let's move down the bank slowly and see if they notice.'

Sliding backwards on their stomachs, trying desperately not to make too much noise, they reached the bottom of the ditch. They were just in time to hear one of Briginus' men return.

'Briginus is wounded. Flee for your lives,' he shouted. 'We walked right into some Scottic raiders near the bridge. They've pulled their ships onto the sand and are fanning out in this direction. There must be two dozen of them, at least, well armed.'

16

Their prisoners forgotten, Cynan's men fled back up the road they had come, their terror tangible to the listeners in the ditch.

'We are in more danger than them,' said Viventia as soon as the guards were out of earshot. 'I've heard of these raiders from Ireland attacking coastal areas further west. They're on the look-out for slaves and chained as we are we'd be a perfect catch.'

'Straight from one danger into another,' said Attius. 'If these raiders really are moving this way we need to take cover quickly. I'd feel safer with these shackles off.'

'Let's move away from the road,' ventured Victoricus, 'and try to find somewhere to hide. They'll not move far away from their ships and I suspect they'll sail off when its light. Cynan will have been alerted and is sure to send men to investigate.'

They made their way through a belt of bushes and trees. Progress was slow and painful as they tripped over roots and jerked their limbs against their chains. Eventually the vegetation thinned out and small ditched fields were visible in the half light. Pausing, they surveyed the landscape. A slight mist hung about the river to their right and the higher ground ahead was a solid grey mass.

'Someone must farm this land,' ventured Attius after gazing for some time. 'They might have tools, which would free our shackles.'

'But what if it's one of Cynan's supporters? We'll be handed over immediately.' This from Viventia.

'We can't stay here,' said Rufus. 'It'll be light soon. We must get rid of these chains.'

Victoricus agreed. 'Why don't we try to keep to the edge of the fields, using the hedges and fences as much as possible and keeping a sharp look out? We might find a friendly farmer out early, who'll help us. Failing that, we must find a safe hiding place before daylight.'

Several square fields lay behind them and they were about to start on another, when Victoricus stopped so abruptly that they all collided.

'Into the ditch quick as you can,' he hissed with such urgency that they fell rather than scrambled down its side and landed in a heap.

Rufus' groans ceased abruptly as he too now heard on the still early morning air the sound of people on the move, which had alerted Victoricus. They were close to a narrow drove-way, which snaked downhill between the fields in the direction of the river. Two men paused not far from where they lay. They looked back up the track and as they did so Victoricus saw the outline of round shields on their left arms and spears in their right hands. They spoke hurriedly in what Victoricus soon recognised was a language at once different yet similar to his own. He gathered that they were anxious to get on more quickly and it became apparent what was holding them up. The watchers in the ditch heard rather than saw a large group of farmers and their families being jostled along by warriors behind and beside them. Whips were being used to drive them along and every so often a thong found its mark and a sharp cry ensued. The Scottic raiders had rounded up their prey and were driving them towards the river and their ships.

As the throng passed Viventia stiffened and cried out. Victoricus threw himself upon her as far as his chains allowed, wrenching Attius' arms painfully as he did so. Rufus, gingerly peeping out between the nettles noticed that one of the rearward guards had stopped and was peering in their direction. Viventia struggled, while Victoricus tried to calm her.

'Quiet,' he hissed between his teeth, 'you'll get us all captured.'

'But, you don't understand,' returned Viventia desperately, 'that was my mother crying out there – they've taken my mother captive. I must help her.'

Victoricus, devastated as he was by this news, nevertheless kept his head.

'We won't help her by getting captured ourselves,' he stressed, trying to lift his hand enough to touch Viventia and comfort her.

By now the sounds of the slave party had died away and the guard had hurried on to catch them up. Viventia was sobbing uncontrollably now and nothing any of them could say or do brought ease. Separated from her family, threatened by Briginus, being bound in chains, hunted as a fugitive and now witnessing her mother being dragged away was too much for Viventia, resilient as she normally was. The others watched helplessly, sympathetic but at a loss what to do. Victoricus tried whispering words of comfort, resting his arm on her shoulder, as she lay on the bank.

'I'll take care of you Viventia,' he said. 'I love you so much. We'll survive this and then find all your family together. We'll rescue your mother. Let's make plans.' Viventia, unable to reply, could only answer his declaration of love by burying her face in his chest. It was enough. Victoricus knew his feelings were returned and he experienced a rush of contentment and protective love. This was quickly followed by a surge of anger as he railed against his fate, against Cynan and against the world in general. Why couldn't he have been left in peace in Isca, with Viventia at his side and her family re-united with them? As quickly as it came, the mood passed and a more sombre consideration of their situation took its place. He sat up, his chains pulling against Viventia on one side and Attius on the other.

'We must decide what to do,' he said. 'Our first priority must be to get these shackles removed. We

146

can't help ourselves or your mother, Viventia, until we're free. Let's walk up that track and see what the Scots were raiding.'

A few minutes later they were trudging in a line up the track hemmed in on either side with earth banks topped with hedges. The half-light of approaching day had been replaced by a gloomy morning with gusts of wind beginning to ruffle the trees and a pall of grey cloud masking the sun. Caution gone, both Victoricus and Attius were eager to push on and force a change in their circumstances. Rufus sensed a new determination and throwing off his weariness took pleasure in the prospect of action. Even Viventia, red-eyed and downcast, was caught up in the new spirit. In her heart she knew Victoricus was right. Had they dashed out to rescue her mother all would have been easily taken by the Scots. It was much more sensible to get their chains removed and then take stock of the situation. But it was painfully hard for her to walk in the opposite direction, away from her mother.

They soon came to buildings which had clearly been visited by the raiders. The remnants of the wooden door of a neat circular house still swung on iron hinges. It had been shattered with great force. Someone had tried to set alight the thatched roof, its timbers resting on rough stone walls, but it had failed to do more than smoulder, before going out leaving a large black patch just above the doorway. But it was not this which drew everyone's eyes. A man's body lay across the

147

threshold, a pool of his blood beneath him. They approached cautiously.

'There's nothing we can do for this poor wretch,' said Victoricus bending over him. 'He's been stabbed several times. He must have fought to defend his family.'

Two timber buildings lay either side of the yard. One was clearly a barn, with open doors wide enough to back a cart in. Attius was keen to explore it.

'There may be tools in there which we could use.'

All were reluctant to step over the body into the house and welcomed this diversion eagerly. The building appeared almost empty. One wooden stall held the remains of a heap of grain. Great circular scoops in an otherwise orderly pile together with driblets of grain across the barn floor betrayed the activities of the marauders taking what they could carry away. They turned their attention to the other end of the building, which was dark, but proved more promising. On a shelf at the back Rufus located a hammer, with a great square iron head and a short haft and a couple of iron chisels.

'Let's move into the light in the doorway and see if we can put these to work,' he said, grinning.

It was not easy. Attius suggested that they knelt in a circle and reaching backwards, half turning, he was just about able to clasp the hammer between his two hands. Rufus held a chisel, trying to direct it onto the head of the pin which held his handcuffs together. Several times Attius missed the chisel and hit his companion's wrist. At other times the chisel flew off and had to be recovered. Eventually Rufus' hands were released. Once freed, he made short work of releasing the others. Rubbing arms and legs, stretching their backs and walking slowly round the barn, they took pleasure from their new freedom.

Victoricus had noticed iron shod spades in one corner of the barn and he and Attius proceeded to bury the body they'd discovered at the house. The fine night had been replaced with an overcast morning. Rain was falling and the wind, stronger now, caught at their cloaks as they bent to their work. They buried the dead man at the edge of the nearest field.

In the meantime Rufus and Viventia looked for food. The raiders had been less than thorough in their search of the house and they found salted pork, vegetables and goat's cheese in the kitchen. Rekindling the fire they soon had a meal ready.

'We can find no trace of anyone else around the farm buildings or in the nearest fields,' remarked Victoricus, when he and Attius returned from their melancholy task. 'The raiders must have taken away everyone else.'

'Did you recognise the dead man?' asked Viventia.

'Never seen him before,' they confirmed.

'They must have captured my mother somewhere in this area,' suggested Viventia, 'But what's happened to father and Armea? Were they in the slave party or are they still around here or might they be dead?' So saying her lips quivered and her eyes filled again with tears.

Much the same thoughts had already gone through Victoricus' mind and glancing around the kitchen he guessed that similar ideas had occurred to his other companions.

'Let's not fear the worst, Viventia,' he said putting his arm around her. 'As soon as we've eaten I'll go down the track to the river and see what's happening.'

'I'll come with you,' said Attius.

'No, Cynan has no quarrel with you and Rufus,' offered Victoricus. 'You two were taken only because you were with me and Viventia. You can make your way back to Isca and be safe.'

Protests greeted this. Rufus and Attius were determined that they were staying around and Victoricus, secretly pleased, ceased to try and persuade them. Finally it was agreed that Victoricus and Attius would go swiftly down to the river and seek out news. Rufus was in need of rest and Viventia, although she would never have admitted it, was also close to exhaustion. They would therefore stay behind in the house and lie low. Victoricus was loathe to separate and Viventia constantly urged caution on them both, but each could see that the arrangement was necessary.

17

An hour's walk brought Victoricus and Attius within close sight of the river. They judged that the tide was going out as sand banks were already beginning to appear. There was no sign of any ships in the stretch of the estuary which they could see.

'No wonder the Scots were in a hurry with their prisoners,' remarked Attius. 'They needed to catch the tide'.

'But how far will they have got,' pondered Victoricus, half aloud, 'with this wind blowing and squally showers they'll surely not have ventured out to sea?'

The drove-way brought them right to the sandy shore. There were signs that cattle had been driven along it recently and other scuffles in the sand marked the passage of human cargo. They stood at the water's edge, straining to look out. There was no sound and nothing moved.

'Let's walk along the shore towards the river mouth for a while,' suggested Attius. 'You never know we might be lucky and pick up some news.'

'We must go carefully,' replied Victoricus, 'we're exposed on this shore.'

'The rain will cover us and we'll get on quicker on this hard sand than crossing fields and ditches. Just keep a sharp look out. There'll be few people about because of the raiding party and any of Cynan's men will be travelling in large groups – easily heard and seen.'

'With any luck,' said Victoricus, 'Cynan won't yet have heard about our capture and escape, so his men won't be out looking for us especially. In any case they'll have had their hands full with the Scots.'

The water seemed to be ebbing out of the estuary swiftly, the flow of the river settling into the one main channel at some distance from them. Both were weary after an eventful night and spoke little as they walked on, occasionally having to jump the small streams draining from the hills above them. But they were careful to look around them at all times and it was Attius who noticed a small boat half-hidden in some bushes close to one of the streams. It was upside down and they noted its simple wooden frame with leather stretched tightly over it. Its length was less than the height of a man and they judged it could carry only one or two people.

They were turning to go when at the same time they both heard sounds in the bushes nearby and they were instantly on the alert. Four men sprang out at them, sticks in hand.

Victoricus, taken at first by surprise, saw

straightaway that these were local men. The oldest, a short, swarthy individual with bent back and bow legs, demanded to know their business. There was some relief on his face too, thought Victoricus, presumably he was half-expecting raiders, but he remained wary.

'We've lost friends to the raiders,' said Victoricus, 'and thought we'd check the river to see if they'd gone. It's a forlorn hope, but we couldn't imagine the Scots setting sail out of the estuary in this weather.'

'And what was your interest in our boat, then?' asked one of the youths. Now they were close Attius was struck by the resemblance each to the other – the unruly shock of black hair above dark skinned faces, which were round with deep set eyes. All were of medium height with broad frames and barrel chests and even the youngest, whom he judged could hardly be into his teens yet, had slightly bowed legs. They must be a father and three sons he concluded.

'We just noticed it drawn into the bushes here and were curious.'

'You wouldn't be thinking of stealing it by any chance?' the father asked.

'Not us,' replied Attius, smiling a little to ease the tension. 'We couldn't handle a boat. Horses and dogs are about our limit.'

'You're not from these parts though. I know everyone between the hills and the river and you're both strangers to me.' The father had relaxed a little, but he still watched them closely.

'You farm Cynan's land then,' remarked Victoricus, skirting the questions until he knew more of the family before him.

'Some good it did us last night,' rejoined the eldest son, bitterly. 'Where was Cynan when the Scots rampaged through our lands, burning good farms and taking away our neighbours? Where was his so-called protection then?'

'You and your mouth,' hissed his father savagely, glancing with some apprehension at the two men before him. 'We've not done badly out of the Lord Cynan. He can't have men out patrolling every farm and the raiders did descend on us without warning.'

Victoricus felt that some explanations could be given to allay the family's suspicions and perhaps gain information. He told them their story briefly, admitting that they were four travellers, not prisoners, and omitting to explain the whereabouts of the other two except to say they were hidden. He admitted that a party of raiders had passed close to them in the early morning and that they had recognised a friend among the prisoners. They had followed them after an interval down a track leading to the river.

'Have you lost anyone to the Scots,' he asked 'or suffered damage to your farm?' He seemed to the strangers to show genuine concern and they visibly softened.

'They came close by,' admitted the old man, giving his name, Natalinus, 'and we hid. Our farm is not too obvious – it lies in a fold above here.' He gestured with his arm. 'They passed the end of the valley without noticing us thank the gods, but our neighbours were not so lucky. They were all dragged off and their buildings burnt. I have heard that the raiders anchored in the pool just before the Taen mouth. As you say, the weather's against them and they'll be there a few days.'

'The Lord Cynan might raise forces against them,' suggested Attius, 'and rescue your neighbours.'

'I doubt it,' put in one of the sons. 'He has men and horses right enough but he doesn't have many ships. There's nothing he can do except keep an eye on them and hope they'll go away. He'll have men either side the river mouth by the end of the day, I expect, but you can say goodbye to your friends. Like our neighbours they'll end up slaves to some household in Ireland.'

Victoricus decided that now was the time to mention Viventia's family. He admitted that they had heard only one of their friends among the prisoners.

'The mother of a girl travelling with us,' he explained, 'and we're anxious to know if the Scots took away her father and sister too. We came into the area to try and locate them after the family were separated.'

The father looked keenly at Victoricus, his eyes glinting below his prominent eyebrows. Victoricus guessed the man was going over the story in his mind and filling in some of the gaps. He was shrewd and would not be deceived easily. But could he be trusted? Victoricus imagined buying cattle from him. He'd drive a hard bargain, making sure he came out of it well. But would the man betray him and inform Cynan at the first opportunity? It was a risk he had to take.

'What are their names, this lost family?' asked the man.

Victoricus took the plunge.

'The father is Arontius, married to Anicilla and their daughter is Armea.'

There was no reaction from any of the men standing before them. Clearly the names meant nothing to them.

'What do they look like?' asked one of the youths.

'Arontius has grey hair and is well built. Anicilla is tall for a woman and holds herself well. Their daughter is about 12, thin and ungainly, with blonde hair. If she takes after her mother and sister she'll be a beauty in a few years.'

This jolted no memories either and the family appeared to be losing interest.

'Father, Aeternus has some visitors, doesn't he?' blurted out one of the sons. 'There was talk of it. Cousins, they were reckoned, but no-one's had sight of them. He keeps them hidden away on the farm.'

The old man scratched his head.

'There has been talk, sure enough in the last few days, but Aeternus always has kept himself aloof. His farm's so out of the way I doubt if even Cynan's men look him up very often.'

'Is it near here?' asked Victoricus, keen to follow up the first lead they'd had.

'It's at the end of a deep combe over the brow of the hill, difficult to reach from this side, easier from the beach near the red cliffs up the coast. Aeternus' not too sweet tempered at the best of times. He and his wife keep themselves to themselves. They've no children, but he loves his animals. He's been raising cattle and sheep on the sides of the combe for years now and he has a name for every one of them. I've seen him at market on occasion, but he has more time for his animals than for any human being, except his wife and he's always glad to get back to them. It's unlikely he'd take anyone in, cousins, friends or strangers. That's why I discounted those silly stories. Folk round here have nothing better to do than gossip.'

This seemed to set off a chain of thought in the old man and he turned rather abruptly, as if conversation was at an end and he was anxious to be off. His sons obviously thought so too as they prepared to leave.

'You've not given us your names I notice,' he flung over his shoulder, 'nor said where you're staying.'

'These are desperate times,' said Attius. 'Men need to take care and besides,' he added, smiling, 'this was hardly a social call. But I'm Attius and my friend is Victoricus.'

The last word clearly struck a chord as all four swung round again.

'You're a hunted man,' said the eldest son,

looking straight at Victoricus. 'Cynan's men were round yesterday asking after you. There's danger for you in these parts.'

Attius cursed himself for letting the name drop. It would have been easy enough to have invented a name for his friend.

Victoricus however, looked relieved, rather than angry. Perhaps he felt it was better to be honest with these farmers. It might be the way to gain their trust.

'I've done nothing wrong,' said Victoricus. 'Cynan tried to force me to work for him after my family died and I lost the farm. All I've done is escape from his clutches.'

'We all owe service to him, now,' remarked the old man. 'We keep our farm going, but the Lord Cynan takes much of our surplus and there's precious little of that these days. My sons will have to work the lord's land, when I go. They already have to do several days a year for him. Marcus here,' he indicated his eldest son by a jerk of the head, 'will soon be leaving to marry a girl Lord Cynan's arranged for him and he'll work on the lord's land near Duriarno. If you can get out, then good luck to you, but I can't risk any suspicion falling on me or my family from helping you.'

'The last thing I want is to get you into trouble,' said Victoricus, 'but at least allow one of your son's to show us the way to Aeternus' holding. After that we'll shift for ourselves.'

The old man was reluctant to be parted from any of his sons, but his curiosity to know what if anything had happened to Aeternus made him waver. When Marcus said he'd show them the way and then return home, his father relented. They walked together up the narrow path by the stream. The surface was well worn, so the path was in regular use. Eventually it forked and the old man led his sons off to the left, leaving Marcus and his new companions to go straight on.

18

The path rose steeply away from the river and the three were panting by the time they reached the top. The rain had stopped, but gusts of wind were sweeping across from the sea, so that they had to hang onto their cloaks. Marcus had difficulty making himself heard, but he tried to point out certain features to them. He pointed towards the mouth of the river behind them.

'You can see the course of the river from here all the way to the sea. Its channel swings to this side just before it turns sharply in two great curves to flow out into the sea under those red cliffs. The raiders' ships are anchored in the river under the high land out of our sight. With the tide out they might be feeling a bit threatened.'

'And where is Aeternus' farm?' asked Victoricus.

'We need to walk on a bit for that,' said Marcus, 'so if you're ready we'll get on.'

Walking through trees, Victoricus and Attius were astonished to find that they'd scaled a narrow ridge. Within a few minutes they'd crossed it and were looking down into a steeply sided narrow valley.

'There's the sea again,' pointed Marcus, indicating a grey streak to their right 'and below us to the left is Aeternus' farm.'

They could make out nothing but fields and clumps of trees overshadowed by high ground on the extreme left.

'We'll walk along the ridge a little, 'said Marcus and then take an easy route down into the valley.'

They found themselves walking in a semi-circle round the head of the valley. The narrow ridge broadened out onto an open hill with coarse grasses, and occasional trees and bushes. Their feet disturbed lumps of grey flint and they had to tread carefully despite their thick hobnailed boots.

'You wouldn't scratch much of a living out of this land,' remarked Attius.

'It's no use for ploughing, that's for sure,' said Marcus, but we do graze the cattle up here in the summer. The best soils are on the sides of these valleys – rich red earth, which turns easily and grows all the crops you want. My grandfather's buried over there – another use for this high land.'

He pointed to mounds of flint and earth sharply outlined against the sky on the top of the hill.

'He died a pagan and my grandmother insisted that he had to be buried in that old mound over there with his drinking cup, a few coins and his knife. He was over eighty when he died and he kept to the old religion all his life. Even sacrificed a chicken after the seed was planted each spring and let its blood drip into the earth. He reckoned he'd seen Cernunnos, the horned god, dancing around those graves on autumn evenings after the harvest, but mother always said it was only after he'd had too much of the local beer. I tell you, though, I wouldn't come up here after dark and nor would any of my friends.'

'What's that ahead of us?' asked Victoricus, pointing towards a bank of earth surrounding a small circular area. 'It looks too big to be a farmstead and in any case its in the wrong place.'

'Oh, that's the old fort,' said Marcus. 'They say our ancient leaders used to live there. We call it Hendinas. Grandfather had tales about that place too. This is where we turn into the valley. A path leads down to Aeternus' farm.'

So saying, he plunged off to the right between two bushes and began to descend a steep, narrow path. Attius and Victoricus followed picking their way gingerly down the side of the valley.

Within a short time Aeternus' farmstead was visible. It was tucked away in a slight fold in the valley side, the buildings invisible until you suddenly came upon them. All seemed peaceful, but they approached the round timber and thatched house quietly. Victoricus noted a lean-to shed built into the side of the hill on a natural flat platform with sheep pens nearby. Close by was a timber barn and some way away what looked like a cattle shed. All looked neat and intact, with no signs of destruction. Judging by the buildings,

Aeternus was a successful and well-organised husbandman. Victoricus approved.

They approached the house through the yard. There appeared to be no-one about, so they were taken by surprise when a man suddenly appeared before them, wooden staff in hand, demanding to know their business.

'Don't you recognise me?' asked Marcus.

'I know you right enough, lad, but who are your companions and what are you doing here?'

'I showed them the way here, Aeternus,' said Marcus. 'They're looking for a lost family – father, mother and daughter. We wondered if you had seen them.'

Victoricus noticed that Aeternus' face tightened and became a blank as Marcus was speaking. This man knows something, he thought, but is it news of Arontius and his family?

'Where are you from then and why are you on the look-out for this family?' Aeternus directed his question directly at Victoricus, having sensed his special interest in the matter.

'It's a long story,' explained Victoricus, 'but I was with the family of Arontius the cobbler, when we were separated. His daughter Viventia came with me and is now close-by, but her parents and young sister were lost to us. We have been searching for them in this area after a clue that they were hereabouts. My friend Attius has been helping me search.'

Aeternus appeared stony-faced throughout Victoricus' explanation.

They'll get nothing out of this old fool, thought Marcus. He knows nothing. Aloud he made his excuses.

'You can make your own way back, now,' he said, 'I'd best be getting back home.'

He hardly waited for thanks before departing back up the path.

Aeternus seemed to relax a little after Marcus' departure, but he continued to question the youths.

'I notice you say nothing of how you became separated, young man and why your search has brought you all to me.'

'I'll be frank with you,' said Victoricus, having reached a decision. 'we were running away from the Lord Cynan. Arontius and his family felt threatened and I had incurred his wrath because I refused to serve him. I wanted a free life in Isca after my own family had died. His men were chasing us when we became separated. We know that the rest of Viventia's family were not taken captive, so they must have been hiding out somewhere. We were re-taken in Isca along with two friends and were being returned to Duriarno, when we escaped. In the early hours of this morning we saw a band of Scottic raiders dragging away prisoners to their ships. Viventia was sure she heard her mother among them.'

Aeternus seemed satisfied. He threw down his staff and invited them into the house. His wife looked up from tending to a figure on a makeshift bed made out of straw and heather. She looked scared at first until she made out her husband in the gloom. He motioned for Victoricus to step forward to the bed. As his eyes grew accustomed to the light, Victoricus was shocked to see a white-faced Arontius laid out on the bed. Beads of sweat stood out on his forehead and his hair was plastered to his skull. Blood had soaked into the right hand side of his linen shirt, which was ripped from neck to hem.

'Arontius!' he wailed, 'What's happened to you?'

'He can't hear you,' said the woman, 'he's in a deep sleep. He's been stabbed in the side, but the wound is clean and I've put a poultice on it. He's lost a lot of blood, but I think he'll live, given rest and quiet.'

Victoricus turned to Aeternus.

'This man saved my life a few days ago. Now he's fighting for his own life. How has this come about?'

'Those same robbers came up our valley yesterday afternoon. They'd landed on the sands at the stream mouth, close in under the red cliffs and they moved through the countryside like rats picking up everyone they met and eventually they carted off their pickings over the ridge to their ships in the river. Those who resisted were killed. Fortunately we are so well hidden that they failed to see our farm, but as luck would have it Arontius' wife and daughter were down at the spring near the bottom of the valley and they were caught. Arontius was on his way to join them and must have stumbled on the pirates, because I found him later like this. He'd been left for dead.'

'So the Scots made off with Armea as well as Anicilla? That's an awful blow,' said Victoricus, thinking desperately of how this news was to be broken to Viventia. Misfortune was piling on misfortune and he was despondent, not knowing which way to turn.

Attius had great sympathy for his friend's predicament. He tried to think what practical steps could now be taken. The situation seemed hopeless.

'We must get back to the others, ' he suggested to Victoricus. 'We've abandoned them now for a long time. They'll be anxious for us and might be tempted to stray away from the farmhouse.'

'Have something to eat and drink before you go,' put in Aeternus' wife reaching for a flask on a shelf.

'Look,' said Aeternus, 'Arontius can't be moved at the moment and he'll need several days of rest. You must be in danger in this area. Once Cynan has driven off these Scots he'll have men out looking for all of you again. He's very determined. Why not bring Viventia here? She'll be safe and she can help to nurse her father. It will give her something to do. Return here with her and your friend Rufus. We can't put you all up in the house, but you three could stay in the barn until you decide what to do.'

Having rested and fed Victoricus and Attius decided this was the best course of action and they started back to pick up their companions. Descending the same track the Scots had used to drive their captives from the ridge to the estuary, they came directly to the abandoned farmhouse. All was quiet and they found Rufus and Viventia having rested now anxiously looking out for them.

Victoricus explained quietly to Viventia what had happened to her family. Attius took Rufus outside to give him a complete account separately, leaving the other two alone. Viventia wept, but seemed more resolute and determined through her tears. Naturally she was anxious to see her father, but she still hoped that her mother and sister could be rescued. She hoped for action. She relied on Victoricus' steadiness and ingenuity. He was gentle and resourceful and clearly adored her. As she had rested in the cottage, she thought over his words to her when they'd lain in the ditch, with her mother and, as she now knew, her sister, being dragged past. He really loved her and wanted to live with her. She'd prayed to God before falling asleep for her family to be re-united and for Victoricus and herself to be settled somewhere together.

Attius and Victoricus were exhausted and needed to rest. It was agreed that they should sleep while Rufus and Viventia kept watch. The wind was still blowing strongly off the sea and Attius was sure that the pirate vessels would not be able to make it out of the estuary.

'They're stuck for the time being,' he said.

Some hours later, as evening drew on, Victoricus awoke to the smell of cooking. Viventia and Rufus had kindled a fire in the kitchen range, using charcoal from a lean-to shed at the back of the house. Rufus had explored and found two chickens, which he'd killed and plucked. They were now boiling in a large saucepan, while Viventia prepared a sauce with honey, thyme and fennel found in the kitchen. She'd also prepared some honey cakes and baked some bread.

In a different world, she reflected, she could be cooking her husband's evening meal in a kitchen just like this after he'd finished his day's work in the fields. Would they ever escape to enjoy such peace?

Having eaten, there was time before dark to walk over to Aeternus' house and for Viventia to see her father for herself. He was still in a deep sleep and she was shocked by his appearance, but at least she was re-united with him. Nursing him back to health would occupy her and leave her less time to brood. Aeternus and his wife, Tullia, made her very welcome.

'You can stay here as long as you like,' said Tullia 'and together we can look after Arontius.'

One question was uppermost in Viventia's mind.

'Why did my family come to seek shelter with you?' she asked Tullia.

'My husband sold hides to Arontius when he was in Isca,' she replied 'and once he even came out here himself to look at some cattle, so he knew where to find us when they were on the run from Cynan's men. After you became separated he made his way here. He'd resolved to stay a few days and then to travel to Isca alone to see if he could find you. Apparently he trusted that young man of yours – Victoricus – and was convinced that he would protect you and treat you honourably. He seems to have judged him well.'

Here, Tullia stared hard at Viventia, who, much to her own annoyance, was unable to stop herself blushing.

'Victoricus and his friends have certainly looked after me and kept me safe,' she said.

Tullia's kindly face registered that she fully understood. This short, rotund woman, with weather beaten face and soft brown eyes was a close observer of character. She knew within a few minutes of meeting any newcomer whether she approved of and trusted them. In a lifetime of over fifty years she had rarely been wrong in her assessment. Arontius had secured her approval on his first visit and she was well prepared, beforehand therefore to accept Anicilla, which she had wholeheartedly. Now here was their graceful, strong-minded daughter, strikingly beautiful and self-assured, despite the hard knocks she'd received in the last few days. Tullia was sure that the girl was a credit to Arontius and Anicilla, just as certain as she was that there was a clear understanding between Viventia and this solid young man Victoricus, who accompanied her. In her heart she wished them both well.

Aeternus showed the men the barn. It was well stocked, with plenty of straw at one end.

'It's the best we can do,' he said, 'but I think you'll be comfortable bedded down here.'

'We've slept in a lot worse places,' remarked

Attius, thinking back to their night on the road with Cynan's men.

'Attius and I are going to slip over the ridge to look at the Scots' ships before we turn in,' explained Victoricus.

'I'll come with you,' said Rufus. 'I'm fully rested now.'

Victoricus was sure that Rufus would slow them down but he did not want to hurt the old man's feelings. He suggested to him that someone should stay behind to keep watch at the farmhouse. It wasn't fair to leave the responsibility for the women and for Arontius solely to Aeternus. Rufus accepted the importance of this and agreed to stay behind.

'We'll keep an eye on things here, but you two take care. Don't go tackling those boat loads of Scots on your own.'

19

Victoricus and Attius set off with no clear intention except to take a close look at the raiders' ships. The wind which had blown now for more than 24 hours was still fierce and Attius seemed confident that the ships would still be in the river. It was getting dark as they reached the ridge and Victoricus suggested that they walk along it to the end nearest the sea, so that they would be directly above the river mouth. Then they could descend to where the ships lay. The ridge was so narrow that they could easily make their way along it in the dark. It was more difficult to judge their position, however, when they began their descent. It was only when they managed to identify a path going in their direction that they became more confident.

The path linked two farmsteads. As they reached each in turn, on the lower slopes of the ridge, the pungent smell of recent burning reached their nostrils. At each they stood briefly on the earthen bank surrounding the burnt out buildings. There was no sign of life, human or animal.

'It's just as Aeternus described,' reflected

Victoricus aloud to his friend. 'One party of raiders must have swept up his valley aiming to rejoin the ships at the Taen mouth over the ridge. In the meantime the ships anchored and another group poured out to terrorise the folk here.'

'And it was these farms, which we saw burning from the top of the hills the other night,' put in Attius. 'I wonder how many ships they have?'

'We should be able to see when we get nearer the river,' Victoricus rejoined, 'the moon is coming up and should provide enough light on the water to give us some idea.'

They continued their slow descent of the path until the land began to level out close to the river.

'The tide should be going out by now,' said Attius. 'I suggest we make for the shore. If we stay away from the water's edge we'll be well hidden from view.'

The wind off the sea continuously assaulted their ears and, masking other sounds, it almost proved their undoing. Attius grabbed his friend's arm and motioned him back.

'What is it?' hissed Victoricus.

'Can't you hear?' whispered Attius. 'Over there men and horses coming this way.'

They moved back a few paces and sank to the ground just in time as a black shape materialising as a man on horseback passed within a few feet of them. He was followed by others. Eventually a group of men on foot appeared and all kept pace with each other. The muffled sounds of their progress was carried back to the two watchers on the wind, for some time after they passed out of sight. Attius and Victoricus retained their position.

'Who were they?' Attius pondered, 'and where are they going? They didn't look like Scots.'

'No, they were Cynan's men I'm sure,' said Victoricus, 'and they're so close to the raiders' ships it must be connected with them. Perhaps they're going to patrol the shores and keep an eye on the raiders. Cynan's authority and pride will have suffered by these raids and he'll want to know all about the movements of the Scots.'

'It's a bit late to send patrols out,' suggested Attius. 'Surely he'd have had men out on watch by now. Anyway, we'd better go cautiously now and keep a sharp look-out. Let's make for the shore.'

They reached the sands, still wet from the waters of the retreating river. Having checked that no-one was about, they walked on in silence towards the river mouth. They'd walked only a short distance when Victoricus dropped to his knees and said in a low voice: 'Look, the sand is disturbed here – horses have been ridden past and there are foot-prints all over.'

Both stared into the blackness ahead. Moving off again, each was struck simultaneously with the notion of numbers of men and animals halted just ahead of them. They could even detect the faint odour of horses. Without saying one word they flattened themselves onto the sand. Victoricus motioned with his hand to move into the bushes on the bank. Attius followed him. Having reached the shelter of the vegetation, they took stock of the situation.

'It looks as if Cynan or one of his captains is assembling a force secretly on the shore here,' remarked Victoricus. 'Why would he do that?'

'It's too big for a patrol,' said Attius 'more like an attacking force, but what can he possibly attack? Unless his horses can ride on water he can hardly lead an assault on the ships. They're anchored safely in the middle of the river.'

'We can only keep watch and see what happens,' said Victoricus.

The thinning clouds gradually cleared and light from a half-moon began slowly to reveal more of the scene. Attius was right, a large force of men was drawn up on the beach on the far side of a rocky point, which separated them from the natural pool in the river, where the ships were anchored. The moonlight reflected from the narrow ribbon of water, which was the river channel. Attius thought he could detect movement on the far side of the river too and said so.

'Do you think those are Cynan's men too?' asked Attius.

'They could be,' replied Victoricus, 'though I can't make any sense of it.'

'Isn't there a large flat muddy area in the estuary, when the tide's out?' asked Attius. 'Is Cynan trying to get men across that nearer to the ships?'

'Something's certainly happening,' said Victoricus. 'Why don't we work our way round this point and try to get nearer any action. If Cynan is going to try and rescue the prisoners we need to be nearby.'

They were successful in reaching a high point above the river and were then able to see the outlines of three ships each with a single mast anchored in the river. The ships were swinging from side to side as the wind and currents caught them. The only sounds were made by wind and waves. The two youths watched and waited, peering into the gloom.

'Victoricus,' said his companion, 'one of those ships is moving towards our side of the river.'

'It's just the wind pulling it against the anchor,' returned Victoricus, but both watched intently.

Then they heard cries from the ships and they could make out figures moving on the deck. All three ships were being pushed inexorably by the wind towards the beach below them. Flames lit the scene as beacons were set alight on the beach and on the mud flats on the far side of the river. These revealed men drawn up waiting for the ships to ground. Cynan had prepared well for this assault. If it was successful his reputation would be greatly enhanced.

'We must get down there,' shouted Victoricus. 'We'll stand no chance of rescuing Anicilla and Armea as far away as this.'

The beach was now a writhing mass of fighting men some on horseback, struggling to reach the water's edge and to board the vessels. Two were already beached when the friends arrived, having seized branches as makeshift weapons. They were easily absorbed into the throng, but tried to keep together. Victoricus judged that they would be safe unless someone recognised them, which was unlikely so long as they kept well away from the fires. They endeavoured to get closer to the ships, which were all now beached. Two were upright, but one lay almost on its side, its mast pointing at a low angle towards the cliffs on the other side of the estuary. Fierce hand-to-hand fighting was in progress close to and on the ships. The Scots knew they were fighting for their lives and were well armed, most with thrusting spears, but several with swords. Cynan's men could match neither their weaponry nor their skill, but they had the advantage of superior numbers.

No prisoners had appeared yet and Victoricus imagined that they were probably secured below the decks. They could only watch and wait.

'Over there,' yelled a voice behind them. They swivelled round to see a horse rider directing them to join a group close to one of the ships. He gestured with his arm to the right.

'Don't stand idle: join that company.'

Victoricus and Attius recognised the voice simultaneously.

'Briginus,' hissed Attius out of the corner of his mouth. 'He can't have been hurt that badly.'

They turned in the direction indicated, having no choice but to obey. The wet sand soon turned to mud which slowed their progress, sucking at their boots and threatening to remove them. The rider followed at a slower pace, as if he wanted to check on them, but fortunately the thick mud deterred him and the horse stopped.

'Do you think he recognised us?' said Attius.

'Not him,' replied his companion, 'he would have said something for sure. It's just our luck to encounter Briginus again. We must be wary.'

They approached the first ship. Some seven or eight Scots were successfully defending it. They stood in a line along the deck rail and were beating off all attacks. Some of Cynan's men lay in the mud below the ship. The cries of the wounded could be heard and some were being dragged away by their comrades. The ship sat on the edge of the river channel still partly in the water.

'If the tide goes out further,' remarked Attius 'the Scots will be in trouble. They'll be attacked from all sides then.'

Another assault began with men clambering up the side of the ship only to be repulsed savagely by the raiders. One was pierced by a sword thrust and fell back screaming into the mud. The attack wavered and broke. The surge forward towards the ship, with Victoricus and Attius on its outer edge, slowed and stopped. Victoricus collided with one of the assailants and nearly fell, remaining upright only by clasping onto the man's shoulder. He turned and Victoricus recognised Marcus.

'What brings you two here?' asked Marcus looking from one to the other. 'We all came down in answer to Cynan's call. We'd have come anyway. Most people in this area have got relatives or friends trapped on these ships, but this is not your fight.'

'Viventia's mother and sister are on one of these ships and we're here to rescue them,' said Victoricus. 'It is our fight.'

'Well,' returned the other, 'we can certainly do with the help.'

'How did Cynan get the ships to move?' asked Attius.

'That was clever,' said Marcus. 'He sent men out into the river once the tide lowered to swim over and cut the anchor ropes. He knew the wind would do the rest. Once they were beached he knew he could get his men over to them.'

The shouting grew louder and the men surged forward once more.

'What's happening?' shouted Attius as they kept pace with the rest.

Men were swarming over the ship's sides in larger numbers than before. This time surely the Scots would be overwhelmed. Victoricus got a toe-hold on one of the planks and a firm shove from someone behind gave him the reach to haul himself onto the deck. His branch had slid from his grasp, leaving him unarmed but he could see no sign of the Scots. Marcus appeared beside him and they stepped warily across the planking. A man lay spread-eagled over the deck, dead. The shield still strapped to his arm identified him as a raider. Cheering broke out ahead of them and they came up to see prisoners being released from below.

Marcus was astonished at the swift end to the

fight. Recognising an old neighbour, he enquired how it had happened.

'Some of the prisoners got free and attacked the pirates from behind,' said the man. 'They were taken by surprise and our boys coming onto the ship at the same time overwhelmed them completely. One of the prisoners died and two are badly wounded, but at least its finished.'

As the prisoners were brought out and lowered down the ship's side Victoricus checked them carefully. Many were weeping and laughing by turns, thankful their ordeal was over. As the last of them came out and the ship was searched Victoricus realised with dismay that neither of the women he sought were among them. It was too much to expect success at the first try. Attius was nowhere to be seen. Marcus was busy helping one of his friends. Victoricus moved to the ship's side and looked down into the throng just below him. Groups of people were beginning to make their way back across the mud to the beach. He saw reunited families clinging on to each other, prisoners being helped along and horsemen shepherding men towards the other ships. Among them he thought he recognised the outline of Briginus' bulk, his back towards him. There were fires dotted all over the beach, their flames illuminating first one and then another knot of people on the move.

One fire was out of place. It seemed to be above the river itself. Victoricus' attention became fixed on it. Suddenly he realised its significance. One of the ships was on fire and as he watched the fire began to spread. Leaping down from the side of the ship he landed ankle deep in the dark mud. He decided to cut across the beach as fast as he could, but progress in the thick mud was slow. He was some time reaching the burning vessel and as he reached it he could see that it was well alight. The area of the deck around the mast was blazing furiously, the flames being fanned across the deck surface by the wind. There was a terrible wailing sound from within the ship.

'What's happening here?' he called to an on-looker, whose right arm hung loosely by his side, blood streaming from a gash. His left hand rested on a long handled axe.

'I don't rightly know,' came the reply. 'The Scots fought off all our attacks. They've killed a number of our men. Then in the middle of it all a fire started and our men backed off at first. I think they were puzzled by the fire. Next we heard men jumping into the water on the far side of the ship and realised the Scots were trying to escape. I guess they'll be picked up or drowned. Our men on the ship are trying to get the prisoners out, if they have time. Others are trying to put the fire out.'

Victoricus darted forward to help. He pulled himself up by a rope he found dangling over the side of the ship. A few paces across the deck brought him close to the fire, its heat scorching his legs. He worked his way round to the windward side. Here men were beating at the flames with sticks and spears, but it was no use. Near the stern of the ship others were trying to lift a trapdoor, the cries of frightened prisoners beneath it spurring them on. Victoricus recognised one of them as Attius.

'It's stuck or locked,' Attius remarked as soon as he saw Victoricus.

The latter remembered the wounded man on the mud had an axe. Swiftly he returned to persuade the man to give it up. He was reluctant to allow it out of his sight, but was hardly in a position to argue.

'I'll bring it back,' Victoricus flung over his shoulder, as he leaped again for the rope.

Legs apart, he flexed his shoulders and brought the axe down on the edge of the trapdoor. It shuddered, but gave hardly at all. Blow after blow he rained down on the timber, a circle of men gathering to encourage him. Eventually the timbers splintered and Victoricus was able to open up the crack with skilful blows of the axe. All the time the fire was spreading across the deck.

'Wait,' said one man, advancing and putting his hand into the crack. He felt an iron bolt and tried to move it.

Victoricus glanced at the crowd below, his hood thrown off, and chest heaving with his exertions, but noticed to his horror, Briginus on the edge of the crowd. He had abandoned his horse and was watching the drama. Has he recognised me, he wondered, hastily pulling his hood around his head, as if to shield his face from the heat?

'Direct some blows there,' shouted the man

having despaired of sliding the lock and pointing at the spot.

After further blows the door collapsed inward with a crash and men rushed onto the steps below. The flames of the fire flickered through a swirling grey smoke onto upturned faces. The prisoners were tied to iron rings secured into the frames of the ship. Their coughing and choking could be heard by all.

Attius was one of the first into the hold. He immediately had problems getting his breath, but, dropping to his knees he crawled from one to the other cutting with his small knife the rope which secured each to the ship. Others hustled them away, half -dragging half-carrying them up the steps and out of the door. On the deck willing hands carried them to the ship's side and dropped them into the mud for others to remove from the blazing ship.

Victoricus, on deck and increasingly threatened by the heat of the fire, tried to look out for Anicilla and Armea, but failed to see them. In the hold, with all the prisoners free, Attius himself had to be dragged out choking from the smoke. Victoricus lifted him to the side and together they plunged into the mud. Attius was still retching and coughing as his friend urged him away from the ship. Briginus was nowhere to be seen. Flames were licking up the mast and smoke was pouring out of the seams in the forward part of the vessel. Even as Attius was led away the prow of the ship erupted, with huge tongues of flame shooting out on all sides. Soon after the ship was totally engulfed in flames.

Downstream a little, fighting was still going on around the third ship. Don't they know when they're beaten, thought Victoricus, wearily contemplating joining a third assault. Attius was trying to breathe, taking in great gulps of air. They approached a huddle of figures covered in mud around one of the fires. Some had been identified by relatives or friends, who, by hugging and kissing their loved ones had become encrusted with mud themselves. Victoricus looked eagerly about him, but recognised no-one, except Marcus and his father, Natalinus. They were standing in a small group, which apparently included their rescued neighbours. Victoricus wondered if they might be the family who owned the abandoned farm, where they'd sought shelter. He stayed on the outer edge of the crowd, not wishing to be recognised himself. Attius seemed to be breathing normally, but was still unable to speak. One of the men nearby offered him a drink of water from a leather bottle and he drank greedily.

As the man turned, Victoricus saw two figures huddled together. They had been hidden from view by the large number of people of which he was part. Victoricus studied them, his hopes rising. They looked like two women shrouded in one cloak. They swayed gently together, holding onto each other tightly.

'Attius,' he whispered, 'I may have found them. We need to work our way round the edge of the crowd towards them, so that I can get a closer look. Are you alright to come with me?'

'Just about,' croaked Attius, 'but take it steadily.'

It was Armea, whom Victoricus first recognised. The light caught her white face and sunken eyes peering out from under her mother's cloak. He stepped towards them, abandoning Attius for the time being, and touched Anicilla lightly on the shoulder. She flinched instantly and drew back turning her face towards him. At first there was no recognition. Then Victoricus saw in her eyes that she knew him. She smiled and drew apart from Armea at the same time indicating to her daughter that here was a friend. Victoricus embraced both, with tears in his eyes, clasping Anicilla to him, having his own mother as much in his mind at this moment as any future mother-in-law. Her face registered other emotions – pleasure certainly, but pain too, which Victoricus was momentarily at a loss to understand. She felt him draw back and said:

'Don't worry, Victoricus, my back is sore from the strokes of the whip, but it will soon heal, now.'

All three were weeping freely now, Armea completely overcome. Victoricus brought Attius forward and he was introduced to Anicilla, who knew him instantly as the man who had cut her free on the ship. Tired as she was, her thanks were warm and friendly. Gathering Armea to her, she was calm now and braced ready to hear the worst news Victoricus had. She had already faced up to the fact that Arontius was dead. She'd seen the raider's knife thrust cut into her husband's body – a nightmare which had recurred throughout her captivity on the ship – and his body on the ground near the spring. The best she could hope for was that Viventia was alive and well. Victoricus' presence gave her hope for that.

She was therefore astonished and overcome once more to learn that Victoricus had located Aeternus' farm, that Arontius, though wounded, would live with careful nursing and that Viventia awaited them there. Once the truth of it all sank in, and Victoricus had to repeat much of it before it was finally understood, she was impatient to be reunited with her family. Victoricus warned them that the farm lay some distance away.

'You've both suffered much in the last two days,' he said to Anicilla, 'and Attius is still affected by smoke on the ship, so we'll only be able to make slow progress, but if we set out now and take it steadily we could be home by dawn.'

20

They moved off. Victoricus hoped that they could just slip away from the noise and excitement on the beach and find a path which would take them onto the ridge, but no sooner had they begun to move away than a horse rider intercepted them.

'You're to stay for the moment,' he ordered 'the Lord Cynan will speak to his people soon and then you can go.'

Victoricus was alert once more, fearful that they would be recognised.

'Let's get back into the crowd and stay away from the fires,' he urged. 'We mustn't be noticed.'

Skirting excited, chattering family groups on the edge of the throng they managed to make their way slowly back down the beach, Anicilla leaning heavily on Victoricus. The elation after the rescue could no longer compensate for the weariness and ache from the hours spent tied up on the ship and the beating she had received. She longed for rest. Beside her, Armea seemed much recovered, stepping out and looking around her. She has yet to realise that we are still in danger thought Victoricus. The relief of being rescued from the Scots has made her forget our other problems. Attius was still struggling to get his breath, dragging his feet through the sand and mud. Looking at them, Victoricus wondered if he would ever bring them safely back to Aeternus' farmstead.

They found themselves close to Marcus, his father and their neighbours again and took comfort in their familiar faces. Anicilla sat in the mud, oblivious to the cold and damp. Attius squatted down, coughing and retching.

'I hope Cynan gets this over with quickly,' he croaked, 'I've had enough of this beach, the river and the Scots. I need my bed.'

'Something seems to be happening near that rock at the edge of the beach,' said Marcus, pointing downriver. 'There's a group of riders moving slowly this way.'

As they all turned to look, the riders halted, one of their number only coming forward. By now the crowd had fallen silent, sensing that the night's drama was reaching its conclusion. The rider's voice, urging them to move forward to hear their lord, carried clearly in the wind and the various groups began to move. They trudged wearily past the three pirate ships, one still enough on fire to illuminate white faces and cast moving shadows onto the beach.

'Keep your hoods up,' urged Victoricus, 'and stay together.'

Cynan rode forward, flanked by riders either

187

side keeping pace with him slightly in the rear. As he halted, the crowd gathered around him, corralled into position by outriders.

A carefully managed ceremony, thought Victoricus, glancing around him, as we'd expect from Cynan, who had begun to speak.

'My people, tonight we have defeated these pirates who dared to attack our lands. We showed that we can defend ourselves. We have no need of Roman armies. You have accepted me as your leader and with my warriors and your help we gained victory. But more attacks may follow and we must be vigilant and work together. Many of you grumbled when we urged you to pay your dues, to send your sons to be trained in warfare and to labour for us at Duriarno and elsewhere. Tonight you have seen why we must work together for the good of all. I, Cynan, will protect you and your families, but in return you must give me your wholehearted support. Disperse now to your homes and from now on I will expect your full co-operation. We cannot afford quarrels or disloyalty.'

Cynan's lieutenants, clearly poised for the end of the speech, rode forward and urged the crowd to cheer their lord. Victoricus noted with some surprise a certain willingness, even eagerness on the crowd's part to do so. Cynan, for the moment had won over his people. They forget, thought Victoricus, joining in the cheering with much less enthusiasm, that but for the wind, their loved-ones would be well out to sea by now. Where was

Cynan when their families were being snatched and killed? This time Cynan was lucky.

Their ordeal was not yet over. Cynan's riders lined the route from the beach and others directed everyone towards them, so that all could be inspected and vouched for.

'We don't want any Scots escaping from the beach in the throng,' said one.

'And it will give them a chance to check up on any other undesirables,' murmured Victoricus, as despair engulfed him. He could see no way out. 'We're sure to be caught now.'

Attius could only agree, as, spluttering and coughing still, he guided the two females into line. Victoricus followed close behind Natalinus, drawing his cloak about him and pulling his hood down over his face. Armea had no cloak, only a hoodless woollen dress. She clung to her mother, who enveloped her in her cloak and together they staggered forward, Attius in the rear.

Torches had been lit on either side of the pathway and soon they were within a bright circle of light. What saved them, thought Victoricus some time after, was the fact that the guards were as weary as everyone else. They had probably had little sleep for two nights and were anxious to be away. That and help from an unexpected source.

The stocky figure of Natalinus paused. Bow legs apart and spine erect he stared straight at the guards and announced in a loud voice: 'The family of Natalinus, farmer,' before walking on. Marcus and the rest followed on automatically and no-one queried them.

Once away from the beach edge, Victoricus hurried forward to thank Natalinus.

'You have saved our lives,' he began, but was halted by the old man's outstretched hand.

'You helped to save the lives of our neighbours and friends from the valley,' grunted Natalinus, 'but I have risked the lives of my family and I will do no more. You are on your own and I will not protect you further. As soon as tonight's events are cleared up, Cynan will begin a thorough search of the area and although I will not go out of my way to inform on you, neither will I lie if asked directly if I have seen you. I advise you to leave immediately taking your companions with you. Seek the protection of another lord. I hope never to see any of you again. Farewell.'

With that, Natalinus called to his son. He was already walking fast away and probably did not hear, perhaps did not wish to hear, the murmured thanks of the small group left staring behind him.

'An honest man,' remarked Attius. 'I'd rather have him as a friend than an enemy.'

'Yes,' rejoined Victoricus, 'and he and his family know where we are staying. How long will we be safe there, now?'

Wearily, he turned his head to contemplate the hill behind them. 'We must try to reach the farm before it gets light.' Taking off his cloak he fastened it around Armea, who was shivering in the cold air.

'Attius, you and Anicilla help each other and I will assist Armea. We'll take it slowly, but we must keep going.'

Looking back the following morning, Victoricus was surprised how easy the journey was. They met no-one on the way and once on the ridge they made good progress. Each was anxious to reach their destination and to rest there. He remembered descending the little path into the farmyard and being greeted by Rufus, who had obviously been on the look-out and heard them coming. He'd stayed awake all night. Then the joy and tears of the reunion with Viventia, who ran out of the house into her mother's arms. The thrill of seeing Viventia's eyes resting on him, even while she hugged her mother and sister. But Anicilla had been torn between her daughters and the desire to see her husband. She had quickly entered the house and, leaning over Arontius' bed, had judged for herself how he was. By the candlelight Anicilla had seen that his face had a little colour and that he appeared to be sleeping normally. Tullia had re-assured her by saying that for a short time in the early evening her husband had woken up, spoken a few words and taken a drink before falling asleep once more. Attius meanwhile had collapsed onto the ground, the sound of his coughing clear even above the noise of the wind. Tullia had mixed him a thick honeyed drink with mallow syrup, which had soothed his throat.

21

Victoricus came awake with a start about the middle of the day, not clear at first where he was. Then he leaned back in the hay remembering the events of the previous days. There was no sign of anyone else, but he was not uneasy. He felt strangely at peace. He knew that he should be up and making plans yet despite the danger from Cynan and his men he was reluctant to abandon this warm place. Curiosity eventually prodded him into moving. Where was everyone?

He emerged from the barn door and surveyed the yard, which was empty. Walking slowly over to the house, he noted that the wind had dropped and patches of blue were beginning to appear in a still cloudy sky. Peering through the open door of the house, his glance took in a large metal cauldron suspended over a glowing peat fire, the smoke from which was curling into a clay hood which narrowed into a tile-built chimney. The smell of the simmering meat caused his stomach to lurch and roll and for a moment he tried to remember when he had last eaten. As his eyes grew accustomed to the gloom he noticed Anicilla, turning away from her husband's pallet and smiling at him. She moved to the door.

'Arontius has just gone to sleep again after waking and chatting to me for a while,' she said, the relief apparent in her face. 'He's growing stronger by the hour. Tullia has nursed him so well. She washed his wound this morning and the cut is not too deep and seems to be already healing. Viventia and Armea have gone down to the stream with Attius,' Anicilla volunteered, anticipating his questions. ' I told them to take great care. Rufus has walked up to the old fort. From the rampart he says he will be able to see anyone moving along the ridge. Aeternus and Tullia are about the farm somewhere. You have obviously slept well and deserved to. Come into the house.'

Victoricus did as he was bid and sat down on a three-legged stool near the fire, while Anicilla produced a chunk of bread and a lump of goat's cheese.

'I suppose we must decide what to do next,' he said aloud voicing his thoughts, 'though it seems so peaceful here I can't concentrate my mind on the future.'

'Yet, we cannot intrude on these good people much longer,' replied Anicilla. 'We put them in terrible danger and while we are on Cynan's territory we shall never feel completely safe. But, let's leave it for today,' she added, wincing with the pain in her back as she sat on the corner of the bed. 'Surely we can allow ourselves one day's peace.

Cynan will be too busy today to search for the likes of us.'

Victoricus nodded, his mouth too full to speak. Anicilla laughed as the last of the bread was devoured and moved stiffly to cut him another piece.

The trio returned, Attius supporting two wooden buckets dangling from a yoke across his shoulders. He lowered them thankfully just outside the door and the girls tipped the water into a barrel standing on a platform against the outside wall.

'So, you've managed to rouse yourself, then,' exclaimed Attius, as Victoricus joined them, finishing off his second chunk of bread.

'We've walked into the valley,' volunteered Viventia, 'but seen no-one. All is quiet. No wonder you slept on Victoricus.' She came close and touched his arm and he responded with a smile.

'At least I got out of carrying the water,' he rejoined.

Tullia and Aeternus returned to the yard just then and greeted them all. It was agreed that a watch should be kept in daylight hours from the top of the hill, so that advance warning could be made of anyone approaching the area.

'The valley approach is easy to cover,' said Aeternus, 'but we could be taken by surprise from the top of the ridge. It's time Rufus was relieved.'

Attius volunteered, but Victoricus insisted on taking his turn and started off up the path to the fort. Rufus was not in sight and it was some time before Victoricus came upon him asleep in the lee of the rampart. He determined not to hurt the old man's feelings, so withdrew and deliberately dislodging a lump of flint some feet away contriving to make such a disturbance that Rufus awoke and was alert by the time Victoricus reached him.

'Don't make so much noise, youngster,' chided the old man, 'you'll have to learn to move about more quietly than that.'

'Seen anything?' asked Victoricus, hiding a smile behind his hand.

'Nothing and nobody,' Rufus replied.

'Get on down for some food and a rest then and I'll keep watch,' said Victoricus, patting his friend on the back.

With Rufus gone, Victoricus explored the old fort, pausing from time to time to survey the horizon in each direction. He noted the high ramparts of clay and flint standing taller than a man, from the top of which he was able to see around the head of the valley, on the lower slopes of which was Aeternus' farm. Whoever built this, he thought to himself, must have had the views in mind. Beyond the valley the sea was clearly visible in the distance some three or four miles away. Inland in the far distance were the rocky pillars on the edge of the high moor, so familiar from his boyhood, yet by turning the other way the silvery water of the Isc was visible. Victoricus surveyed these lands with mixed feelings. They reminded him of his own family and happy times on their farm, but they also brought to mind that Cynan was now lord of this area and he was no longer welcome. Where did

Cynan's lordship end? Would the territory beyond the Isc give them better shelter or would they have to trek even further?

His musings were interrupted as he sensed someone's approach and dropped down into the tail of the rampart, alert now and concentrating. The fort might be a good vantage point, but it was also exposed and he shook himself for not keeping a better look-out. His eyes darted about as he tried to flatten himself into the grass close to the entrance through the rampart and ditch. Anyone making for the fort was likely to enter that way and if he was lucky they might not see him.

It was Viventia who came slowly through the opening looking about her and Victoricus relaxed, though he did not get up immediately. He waited to see what she would do. Viventia paused and turned her back on him, giving Victoricus an opportunity to approach her quietly. He was just going to reach out to her, when she ran away from him, mounting to the top of the rampart opposite. Victoricus was so taken aback that he paused before following. and she gained the top of the rampart and looked down on him.

'I saw you flat in the grass as soon as I came through the entrance,' she laughed. 'There's nowhere to hide in here. We shall have to take care not to get trapped.'

'What are you doing here, Viventia?' he enquired, joining her on the rampart top. They sat down companionably together.

'Mother said I could walk up and join you for a

196

while,' she replied, 'as long as I was careful and kept a sharp look-out,' omitting to add that she had pestered her mother for over an hour before Anicilla had reluctantly agreed to let her go.

They chattered about the events of the previous few days. Viventia questioned him about the rescue from the Taen beach, wanting to know all the details. Briginus' presence made her shudder. Was he destined to haunt them forever? Inevitably they moved to a discussion of their present dilemma. Pleasant as life might be on Aeternus' farm they could not stay there forever.

'Shall we go back to Isca?' mused Viventia.

'I'm not sure that Isca is safe any more,' replied Victoricus. 'Look how easily Briginus found us there. Cynan and Sorio may yet come to blows over Isca. We don't want to be there when they do.'

'Then, what are we to do?' asked Viventia, her gaiety gone.

'Come, we're free at the moment and all together. That's important,' said Victoricus, extending an arm around her shoulders. 'I suspect we shall have to move further east, perhaps beyond those cliffs you can see in the distance. For that we must wait for your father to regain his strength.'

'But how long have we got before Cynan's men track us down?' she queried.

Since there was no re-assuring answer Victoricus could give to this, he merely contented himself with saying that they must all meet together soon and discuss the future.

'Let's leave it until tomorrow, maybe then

Arontius will be well enough to join in the discussion,' he said hopefully. 'Come on, this grass is damp, let's take a walk round the rampart and check the area.'

Some time later, as the light began to fade, they abandoned the fort and, descending the narrow path, arrived back at the farm.

The evening meal, bowlfuls of the lamb and vegetable stew, which had been bubbling in the cauldron, was taken in the barn, with a single oil lamp suspended from a hook on the wall providing a circle of light. Only Anicilla and Arontius remained in the house. An understanding seemed to have been reached, without anyone specifically articulating it, that they would not discuss their future that night. Rufus entertained them with stories about his customers and neighbours in Isca long ago and Tullia proved equally adept at keeping the conversation going whenever it looked like flagging. Victoricus remained largely silent, content, taking pleasure from the scene but at times pre-occupied with private thoughts, the lighter mood of the morning replaced by the weight of responsibility.

Aeternus was up first, with the sun, tending to his animals and busy about the farm, but no-one slept late. Even Arontius, his strength returning, was able to sit on his bed for the first time and take a few steps across the room. With Aeternus back and breakfast over the discussion, which could no longer be avoided, began.

Rufus was all for returning to Isca, urging that

they would be safer in one of the houses there than anywhere else, his long connection with and love of the place making him passionate in his argument. Nor had he given up hope of finding Lupus again. Arontius felt that though Cynan might be vigorous in seeking out Victoricus and his own family Attius and Rufus had little to fear. Sorry though they would be to lose them he urged them to return to Isca and save themselves, but neither would agree to abandon their friends.

'I wouldn't like to find myself in the clutches of Cynan or any of his lieutenants again,' remarked Attius. 'And I wouldn't feel safe in Isca now. There's a struggle coming for control of the city and I don't want to be in the middle of it.'

'We must move eastwards as soon as we can,' said Victoricus quietly. 'That means getting over the Isc either by the bridge at Isca or by one of the ferries or perhaps by working our way further inland, though that would make our journey much longer.'

'I shall not be able to walk far, in fact no distance at all for a day or two,' remarked Arontius, 'but your lives are in greater danger with each passing day. You must leave me to take my chance and get away from here.'

A chorus of disapproval met these remarks and Anicilla said: 'We put our good friends Aeternus and Tullia in peril if any of us stay around. Wherever we make for, we must move away as soon as possible, which means as soon as you are fit enough to go, husband.'

'By today Cynan's men are likely to be searching for you in his lands,' remarked Aeternus, 'but you have perhaps a day, maybe two before they'll search this area. Even then they may not penetrate as far as our farm, though I am wary of Natalinus. I don't think he would go out of his way to betray you, but if his own family are threatened he'll trade information to save his own and who can blame him? I do have one idea, which may work, but I shall need to go off tomorrow for the whole day to look into it.'

Pressed to explain himself, Aeternus refused to give details. 'It may be of no help at all,' he said. 'Trust me. I'll want to take Attius with me, so do you think you can all manage without us tomorrow? Tullia will show you what needs doing around the farm and the rest will need to keep a sharp look-out for strangers.'

It was agreed, finally, after more discussion, that they would aim to get out of Cynan's territory by travelling into the country east of the Isc and that they would leave within three days.

22

The following day passed without incident. Aeternus and Attius were away at first light climbing up the path towards Hendinas with Rufus and Armea, who were to spend the morning in the fort. Rufus and his young companion watched the two men striding out along the track which ran eastwards from Hendinas until they were out of sight. Meanwhile the rest, under Tullia's direction, worked on the farm. It was long after the evening meal, when it had already been dark more than two hours, that Aeternus and Attius returned. Arontius had grown increasingly anxious for their safety, but Tullia remained calm and had re-assured him that her man would be back.

'We had a long wait,' said Aeternus between mouthfuls, 'the tides were wrong.' Then, sensing that most of his audience were puzzled, he embarked on an explanation.

'I wanted to see a friend of mine, Barculo, who owns a sailing boat, which he keeps in an inlet close to the mouth of the Isc. He does a bit of fishing and trading. On occasion he's taken our fleeces and hides to markets, which I could never reach overland. He's even been as far east as Durnovaria, returning with the polished shale which is found thereabouts. Tullia has a piece on that leather thong around her neck.'

His wife handed the pendant around. It appeared a dull greeny-black and glinted in the lamplight as they turned it in their fingers.

'Anyway, he'd gone out just before high tide,' continued Aeternus, 'and we had to wait for his return on the next tide. Barculo can be awkward and surly at times, but he's been a staunch friend over the years. He is interested only in his ship and the sea. He sleeps on the vessel and manages it himself with the help of a local boy. Some say that he's a rogue, that he's dishonest and would do you down, but although he drives a hard bargain, he's always treated me fairly. He's his own man and he'd certainly make a powerful enemy. Now, as you can guess, I've spoken to him about transporting you all along the coast, perhaps as far as Uxella, a port at the mouth of one of the big rivers in the country east of Isca. He was not at all keen. For one thing I think he hates the idea of passengers getting in his way, cluttering up his ship. For another he sees runaways as trouble, something he wants to avoid. However, I persuaded him in the end and he's agreed to take you aboard at high tide two hours after daybreak the day after tomorrow.'

As Aeternus finished his account, an excited babble broke out. All saw this arrangement as the solution to their problems. They would be taken speedily out of Cynan's area. But there were also reservations. Travel by sea filled some with horror. There were misgivings about the new territory. Was it controlled by a lord as powerful as Cynan? But they could see the logic of taking this chance.

Arontius especially welcomed the solution. His growing concern over the days since they had been re-united was that he would be unable to make the trek. He was still weak and had not yet walked further than across the farmyard. But one thing troubled him above all else and he voiced his concern.

'Barculo will not have agreed to make this voyage for nothing, Aeternus,' he said, 'what are we to pay him for his services?'

This thought had also occurred to Victoricus, who had been trying to think how they could compensate the boatman.

'You do not need to worry about that,' replied Aeternus, smiling. 'I have seen to it.'

Despite further questioning, Aeternus would say no more and remained silent even when Arontius persisted. Victoricus resolved that he would get the answer from Attius that night, but Attius stubbornly refused to give details of the transaction, when the three of them were alone in the barn.

'I promised Aeternus that I would say nothing of his conversation with Barculo,' he said, 'and you would not have me break my oath.' So, Rufus and Victoricus had to be content with not knowing as they settled down to sleep.

Everyone was awake early the next morning, eager to prepare for their departure. The girls helped Anicilla put a few belongings together into packs, while Victoricus took the first turn at the fort. He mounted the by now familiar path and surveyed the scene from the ramparts in the early morning light. Nothing was stirring. Marcus had been right. Local people avoided the burial mounds, which were visible as dark shapes on the horizon, and rarely came onto the ridge. Marcus had suggested the hill was used for animal grazing, but none of the watchers had seen either animals or humans during their stay at Aeternus' farm. He sat for a while on a large stone dislodged from the rampart.

Victoricus was not surprised, when Viventia joined him. She had hinted that she would get away as soon as she could and her mother's consent had been easily obtained. He studied the tall figure as she walked towards him, lifting the hem of her linen shift above the wet grass. Her plain woollen dress, secured at the waist with a wide leather belt, could not hide the movements of her graceful body beneath. She had taken some care with her hair that morning, he fancied, having pinned up the long black tresses with wooden pins, leaving her neck bare. He stared openly until she stopped close to him, planted her feet apart and stared back. He flushed and looked away and she smiled. She had known for some time the effect that she could have on men and on this man in particular.

'What are you thinking?' she said boldly, continuing to smile broadly.

Victoricus sensed that a positive move was needed if he was to make any progress in showing her his true feelings. Casting aside his usual shyness, he placed his hand on her shoulder, kissed her full on the mouth, and, sliding his other hand round to her bare neck, caressed her passionately. She did not flinch at his touch, but returned his kiss openly and joyfully. They embraced closely, kissed again and then without speaking sat together on the stone in the shadow of the rampart. Now their love had been openly expressed they did not feel the need to talk, but sat embracing in contented silence.

Finally Victoricus whispered close to her ear: 'Will you marry me, Viventia, when we reach the new land?'

Her reply, if spoken, was lost in a torrent of kisses; Viventia's hair falling out of its pins and cascading over onto his arm, where he held her fast.

The kisses seemed to Victoricus to last for a long time and he wallowed in bliss. But intruded into it were faint sounds disturbing their peace. As they registered he broke off, pushing Viventia aside. Momentarily, she was shocked, not understanding, but he motioned to her to stay still and mounting the rampart peered gingerly over the top. Three horse-riders were making their way slowly round the narrow ridge. Victoricus focussed on them and saw that they were heading in their direction.

He returned to Viventia, gave her a hurried explanation and urged her to return to the farm, keeping as low as she could once she left the shelter of the fort.

'Warn them that they may have to hide,' he said. 'I'll follow as soon as I've worked out who they are and where they're making for. They may not pose any threat to us, but we must be ready.'

So saying Viventia ran off, Victoricus following as far as the entrance. He mounted the rampart once more and saw that the riders kept their course following the path which curved round the top of the valley. He was confident that Viventia had not been seen. Studying them closely he noticed with growing alarm that the horsemen were following a man on foot, whose movements seemed jerky and unnatural. Bewildered, he continued to stare until he realised that the man was tied by a rope to the leading horse.

Now thoroughly alarmed, Victoricus decided to seize his chance to cross from Hendinas to the valley path. For a while the riders would be out of sight, but he judged that he would be in a better position to assess the situation laid in the grass at the side of the path than in the exposed fort. Moreover he would be between the strangers and the house. From his new vantage point he saw the riders come into view. Fortunately they were in no hurry. What he saw sent him flying down the path, leaping roots, ignoring the stones, in danger at every moment of breaking his ankle. Someone at the farm had seen him coming because all his friends were in the yard by the time he reached them.

Out of breath he was only able to blurt out: 'Briginus with two other men. They've got Natalinus on a rope. They must be coming here. We've only a few minutes.'

His comments didn't bring the consternation he'd expected. Forewarned by Viventia, plans had already been made.

'Go with the rest,' said Aeternus. 'Tullia and I will stay and be busy about the farm.'

'But Briginus will never believe you, especially with Natalinus in tow,' argued Victoricus. 'You'd better come with us.'

'No,' said Aeternus. 'He's no proof that you have been staying with us. We have removed all trace of you. Go with the rest now or we shall all be caught.'

Victoricus argued no longer, but with a growing sense of unease fled down the path after the others. Once they reached the spring, they turned into an adjacent valley, narrower and slighter than the one where Aeternus' farm was situated, and thickly wooded. Arontius was already suffering badly, and from the spring had to have the support of Attius and Victoricus one on each side. They sank into the grass inside the trees.

Attius urged them on. 'We don't know that they were definitely making for the farm,' he said. 'They could come down into this valley from the hill, though with these trees it's unlikely. We must find a hiding place off the path, where we can shelter in some safety.'

So saying, he moved through the trees up the side of the valley, found a natural hollow and urged everyone into it. Arontius lay on his back, sweat trickling down his cheeks, which were grey with alarm and fatigue. Anicilla tended him.

'Rufus and Viventia keep a sharp look-out,' ordered Victoricus. 'Attius and I will climb up and try to get a view of the farm.'

Bent low, the two friends climbed the slope. As the trees thinned, they dropped to the ground and crawling along on their bellies, they moved forward to obtain a view of the farm below. The back of the house was in view, but part of the farmyard was obscured. Nevertheless they could see the three horses with one of the riders near the barn. He was carrying a bucket of water across to them. Two other men came into view with Natalinus stumbling behind them, hands still tied. They were pushing a fourth figure before them.

'That's Aeternus, they're pushing,' remarked Attius, as the two observed the whole group go into the barn. It was some time before they emerged and when they did it was clear that an argument was going on in which Briginus figured prominently. Suddenly he lashed out and Aeternus fell to the ground.

Victoricus made to stand up, but Attius checked him.

'Don't be a fool, if you expose us now we shall all be caught and suffer. Keep down they're looking round. Briginus wants us to show ourselves, so that we can be caught. Somehow he knows we've been around.'

'Natalinus has betrayed us,' said Victoricus wretchedly, 'or they've found something which proves we were there.'

'It certainly appears that way,' remarked Attius. 'What will they do now? Let's risk another look.'

Aeternus continued to lie where he had fallen. Of the others there was no sign. Attius and Victoricus continued to watch with growing agitation, helpless to be other than observers. Several minutes passed with nothing happening and then Briginus and his men reappeared, mounted their horses and rode briskly down the valley.

'Where's Natalinus?' asked Attius, puzzled. 'And Tullia?'

They watched but there was no further movement. The spiral of smoke rising lazily from the flue under the eaves of the house turned from grey to a dense black mass. Then flames appeared in the thatch and smoke began puthering around the whole house.

'The house is on fire,' yelled Victoricus, standing up. Before Attius could stop him he was racing down the slope, all caution abandoned. Attius hesitated before reluctantly following at a slower pace. He caught up with his friend outside the house door. Victoricus was standing, mesmerised. By now the house was well alight and past recovery, but the bonfire, which had once been a home merely provided a bizarre backdrop to the horror at Victoricus' feet. Tullia lay in the yard, her throat cut, her blood soaked into the ground with flies already feeding on it. Close by was Natalinus, on his back, a wet stain on his leather jerkin. Attius did not consciously reason at that moment that a single sword thrust had killed him, but later, recalling the horror of that day, he knew it was so. He turned away overwhelmed, retched and vomited. Then he thought of Aeternus and with dread turned towards the barn. The old man lay seemingly peacefully asleep just outside the barn door, his knees drawn up almost to his chin. Attius felt for a moment that if he shook the man's shoulder he would wake up. But as he knelt he knew that this was everlasting sleep. The stone which had killed him and left a terrible gash in the side of his head lay nearby.

Victoricus remained standing in front of the house oblivious to everything. Attius touched his arm.

'Aeternus is also dead', he said quietly. 'But, there are things to do. We and the others are still in danger. We must act.'

'But we killed them,' whispered Victoricus, 'we used these people to save ourselves and now they are dead.'

'Nonsense,' replied Attius with some passion. 'Briginus killed them and behind him Cynan. If you doubted before that men like Cynan would kill to get what they want, to gain power, to control lands, to replace Roman authority, you know now. We will be next unless we get out of this territory. Do we know that Rufus is safe, that Viventia is safe? We've been gone some time. What if Briginus has ridden up the next valley and found them?'

This spurred Victoricus into action. He shook his head as if to shake out of it the images of violent death.

'We can easily check. I'll walk down to the spring. There's a good view as far as the sea from there. If the butchers have not turned off they'll still be in sight.' So saying, Victoricus set off, grim-faced and with thoughts of revenge forming in his mind.

Meanwhile Attius, having found a spade in the barn set about digging three graves at the edge of the yard. Victoricus was soon back and reported that the three horsemen were already well down the valley and appeared to be following the stream heading at a smart pace for the sea. Attius thought that perhaps Aeternus had done them one last service in sending Briginus in the wrong direction, but he kept his thoughts to himself. The two men worked together without speaking completing their sombre task. With all three graves occupied and back-filled the two men stood for a moment in silence. Attius wiped away tears from his cheeks but Victoricus remained dry-eyed. Finally he surprised Attius by quietly reciting a Christian prayer for the dead, remembered from his own family's funerals.

As they walked slowly up the hill behind the still smouldering ruins of the house, they discussed how much they should reveal to Arontius and his family.

'We should say only that we watched Briginus question Aeternus and that he then went away again,' said Attius. 'There's no need for them to know that Aeternus and Tullia are dead just yet.'

'They'll guess that there's more to it than that,' replied Victoricus, thinking to himself that Viventia would certainly know that he was not telling the whole truth, but saying aloud: 'perhaps they have a right to know what really happened down there so that it's clear what we are all up against.'

In the end they agreed to recount the bare facts of the deaths without embellishment, as far as they were allowed.

Rufus saw them coming, peering through the grass on the lip of the hollow. Despite a careful watch by all they had seen no-one. They sat together under the trees, the sun penetrating here and there into the hollow, dappling them all with points of bright light. Victoricus closed his eyes. Which was real? This picnic scene or the bodies lying in the yard?

Victoricus was right about Viventia. She sensed that something was profoundly wrong from the moment they re-appeared. She came over and sat with Victoricus and with a glance at Attius he recounted in outline to them all what had happened at the farm. By the time he had finished Arontius and Anicilla were weeping openly. Armea sought to hide her face in her mother's cloak.

No-one spoke for some time, each occupied with individual thoughts and fears. Rufus stood up and paced across the hollow, back and forth, his face white. Victoricus studied him idly for some time, before realising with a jolt that the old man was angry – angrier than he had ever seen him. He'll explode he thought, just like one of my father's beer flasks on a warm day. If Briginus was standing before us now Rufus would attack, with no thought for himself or the consequences.

Loath as they were to face up to their situation, it dawned on them all eventually that decisions had to be made. It was Attius, level-headed as ever, who eventually broke the silence.

'We can still meet Barculo as arranged on the riverside at tomorrow's high tide. It's still our best chance of leaving Cynan's lordship behind. It's a leap into the unknown – we don't know what's happening on the other side of the estuary – but at least we now know what may happen to us if we stay here.'

'How far is it to the ship?' asked Arontius. 'You've seen how slow I was getting just to here. I will hold you all up. Save yourselves,' he pleaded, looking directly at Victoricus, 'and take my girls with you. I know I can trust you. Anicilla and I have discussed this many times and we will take our chance in this country and wait for me to regain my strength. Then, perhaps, we will try to join you.'

'No,' said Victoricus firmly. 'This time we all go, even if we have to carry you, Arontius. You stand no chance here. We cannot leave you to suffer the same fate as Aeternus and Tullia.' The others murmured assent.

'Our situation is not too bad' said Attius, glad that they were beginning to consider the future again. 'We are travelling light. We have plenty of food and drink. The ship is only some six miles distant along a well-worn track and Barculo will not sail until well after sunrise tomorrow. The track may be patrolled in daylight so I suggest we remain here in the woods until evening and then do the walk in easy stages overnight.'

'Where do you think that butcher Briginus has gone?' asked Rufus. 'Didn't you say he was making for the coast? What if he rides along as far as the Isc?'

'That's one of the risks we have to take, I agree,' answered Victoricus. 'The valley widens below the spring and there is a scattering of farmsteads down to the sea, though many of them were burned when the Irish raiders swept up the valley. I guess Briginus will be seeking news of us from any of the settlers who have returned to their homes. We know that he won't get any. So he'll either turn back this way or work his way along the coast.'

'There may be other patrols out, too by now,' said Viventia. 'Is it such a good idea to wait? They'll only bring more men into the area.'

'But darkness is our best hope, surely,' said her mother. 'If we take care we shall be able to hear horses or men on foot coming along the track. I know it will be difficult to wait, but that's our best option.'

In the end all agreed and Attius and Victoricus

busied themselves finding coppiced shoots, which they trimmed down with the knives Aeternus had given them, into staffs to aid walking. Rufus, Viventia and Armea in the meantime kept careful watch.

23

After the sun had sunk behind the hill, casting long shadows on the woodland paths and the woods grew dim, they moved off. Attius led the way up the path which he and Victoricus had reconnoitred in the setting sun. The latter with Viventia walked either side of Arontius with Armea and Anicilla together and Rufus bringing up the rear. Within a few minutes they were on the track. This was level, some fifteen feet wide, rutted in places from cart wheels and clearly used for a long time.

'The track runs in a straight line along the side of the hill,' said Attius, 'as level as this for about a mile and then it begins to drop downhill to a river.'

'The Roman government will have been responsible for this,' remarked Rufus. 'I have heard that in the past they used soldiers to construct these roads.'

Attius doubted it. 'From what Aeternus said I think this track is older than the Romans. It goes to Hendinas and further down he showed me burial places near the track which he believed were even older. There's no surface of stones. In places it's quite uneven, so in the dark we must tread carefully. Perhaps if I scout ahead with Rufus. We won't go far, just enough to get a warning if anything happens.'

'I'll fall back a little and cover the rear' said Victoricus, 'but we must not lose touch.'

'I'll keep a regular check,' Attius assured him.

Progress was painfully slow, largely because they walked at Arontius' pace and he had to have frequent rests. But also the darkness became denser. Clouds had appeared covering the moon, so that even with eyes accustomed to the dark they could see little and frequently stumbled. Attius was keen to arrive at the shore on the Isc under cover of darkness. He had explained that there was little cover in the flat lands over the last mile or so and they would be very visible.

The track was now dropping steeply to cross a river and the incline hastened their steps. Twice Victoricus caught up with Arontius' family and paused to drop back. The third time they were all resting at the side of the track.

'Father will need to stop for a while,' said Viventia, jumping up as he approached. 'His side hurts him and he's gasping for breath.'

Victoricus walked over to have a word with the cobbler. 'We're doing fine,' he said reassuringly. 'We're well on the way – rest for a while. Viventia and I will walk on a little and meet up with Attius and Rufus. Then we'll all rest up.'

'Go carefully,' warned Anicilla. 'You mustn't pass them in the dark.'

As it was the warning was hardly needed, the pair had gone only a short way before they encountered their friends returning.

'There's a problem,' said Attius straightaway. 'We've seen the glow of a fire, somewhere near the ford ahead. We didn't approach but it could mean someone on the look-out. Let's warn the others and decide what to do.'

It was agreed that Arontius' family should draw back from the track into the woods. Rufus would stay with them, while Attius and Victoricus tried to get close to the ford to see what was happening. The clouds were beginning to break up allowing moonlight to relieve the dense blackness. The outline of trees could be seen against the sky and Viventia's face was suddenly visible as she turned towards Victoricus.

'Listen carefully for our return,' he said. 'We may not remember exactly where you are.'

'I will,' said she, kissing him briefly on the lips, 'but first I'll make sure that it is you two on the road. Don't take any risks. We need you both.'

The two friends approached the ford quietly, keeping to the grass on the side of the track. The near-full moon was now out and they kept to the shadows. Attius motioned with his hand towards the flickering light ahead. There was no need to explain to Victoricus that this was the fire he had seen earlier. They watched for a few minutes, but, hearing nothing, moved on again.

Attius stiffened and stopped abruptly. Victoricus paused, unable to see the reason. Attius put his finger to his lips and pointed ahead to the outline of a man, leaning against a tree. The movement of his body into a more comfortable position had caught Attius' attention. They moved back up the track until they could confer.

'He's on the watch for something,' said Victoricus, 'and he obviously doesn't want to be seen himself. He won't be on his own.'

'Robbers do you think, or Cynan's men on the watch for us?' asked Attius.

'Whatever, we must avoid the ford. We shall have to find a detour to take us round it. It'll be worse for Arontius, but it must be done. If necessary we shall have to carry him.'

So saying, they returned with the news to the others.

'The moonlight will help us,' said Attius, having explained the need to divert from the track. 'We shall be able to see where we're going and also make sure we're heading in the right direction. We must go downhill through the trees and aim to cross the river a little lower down, then regain the track on the other side. This time we must keep together. I'll lead and Victoricus will stay at the back.'

Attius tried to keep to paths through the trees, but it was not always possible and on occasion they found themselves pushing through undergrowth and dodging branches. Arontius soon tired and their pace slowed. Once they halted abruptly, as sounds of something moving close by reached them, but it was only a deer, which they had disturbed. Fear was replaced with relief and they smiled at each other in the gloom. The trees were thinning and soon Attius halted on the edge of the wood. Fields lay before them, running down to the river. They seemed well-kept with fences and hedges intact. Cattle grazed close by.

'Any sign of the farmhouse?' asked Victoricus, as he appeared out of the trees. 'I suppose it will be further down the slope, closer to the river,' he answered himself.

'I'll keep an eye out for it,' said Attius, 'and try to avoid it.'

He mounted the fence and set off across the field in the direction of the far corner. The rest followed. By keeping to the field boundaries, using the hurdle gates and sometimes climbing fences, they arrived at the river in a roughly straight line.

'The farm is just round that corner,' whispered Attius. 'I caught a glimpse of it from the last field.'

'How far do you think we are from the ford?' asked Rufus.

'Perhaps half a mile up-stream,' commented Attius, 'and close enough for any loud noises to carry in the still night air.'

'This doesn't look deep,' said Victoricus. 'We should be able to wade across. Sit down and get your breath back and I'll try it.'

So saying, staff in hand he started over. The water flowed fast over a sandy bottom, but it reached only to his waist and he returned to them, confident that they would be able to cross. Rufus made his way across and at the same time

Victoricus and Attius carried Anicilla and Arontius over on their backs, returning for the two girls. Viventia refused to be carried, hitched up her skirts and with the aid of a staff and Victoricus at her side moved out into the stream, Attius following with Armea.

They were more than half way over when Attius tripped over a rock and he and Armea were pitched into the water. He was quickly upright, but Armea, terrified by the shock of the cold water, screamed and struggling to gain a foothold was swept away in the stream.

Thrusting his staff at Viventia, Victoricus dived into the water. Wading and swimming by turns, Armea's shouts guiding him, he quickly overtook her. Making a grab for her clothing, he hauled her in, stood upright and held her close, his hand over her mouth. She clung to him spluttering and shivering, while he calmed her down, urging her to make no more noise.

But the damage was already done. Dogs at the farm were barking furiously. Their owners would soon be awake and alert. The watchers at the ford must have heard the commotion. Victoricus waded to the bank, Armea still clutching him tightly and they quickly re-joined the others. Anicilla took off her cloak and wrapped her daughter in it. Victoricus shook himself, smoothed back his dripping hair out of his face and looked at his friends.

'We must move on, quickly before anyone comes. We need to be out of their hearing by the time they reach this spot. Attius, lead on.'

As they turned to hurry across the marshy growth on the river bank, Victoricus sensed that the dogs were nearer and behind them men rampaging through the vegetation, deliberately, it seemed to him, making as much noise as possible. Cold, wet and fearful, he nevertheless smiled thinking of the farmer woken out of his sleep and investigating reluctantly some disturbance which had set his dogs barking. He'll be pleased to return to his bed, when he's satisfied himself that there's nothing amiss he thought. What I wouldn't give for a comfortable, safe bed at this moment, he thought.

Within a few feet of the river, the land rose steeply and they soon left fields behind and moved into rough pasture, which had never been fenced. Their pace slowed.

'We'll walk together for the moment,' said Attius, who had dropped back knowing that his flock would be struggling. 'Once at the top of this hill we can work out our best route back to the track.'

With Attius and Victoricus on either side, Arontius made better progress, although at times they were almost carrying him. Rufus was encouraging Armea, who, her fright behind her, was stepping out well. They conversed with an ease which came naturally to the old and the very young. Armea was on the threshold of womanhood and in a few years time, reflected Rufus, she'll probably make no effort to talk to someone like me. His thoughts took him back to his own daughter growing up in Isca and the arguments he'd had with her from about this age.

Having breasted the hill, they paused not on the ridge above, but just below it on Victoricus' advice.

'In this moonlight we'll be visible against the sky,' he said, uneasy about the men at the ford.

'If we go downhill in that direction,' said Attius, pointing, 'I think we should strike the road again and then an hour's steady walk on near level ground should see us close to the estuary and Barculo's inlet.'

They reached the road by making use of a farm track running into it at a right angle. Victoricus and Attius considered their position.

'We must use the track,' said Attius, 'to have any hope of reaching the river in time. We'll never make it across country.'

Victoricus agreed, but viewed the track with some disquiet.

'Let's just check it quickly in either direction,' he suggested, and they split up, leaving the others sitting at the roadside.

All was quiet until Victoricus turned to go back. Then he heard cries, quickly stifled and began to run back to the junction. As he neared the spot he slowed, and as he crept along in the shadow of the bushes he saw two men, one with a knife at Attius' throat, the other questioning Arontius. It became clear from the few words he could understand that the men were looking for valuables and were unimpressed with Arontius' denials. This is going to turn ugly once they realise that there are no pickings to be had here, thought Victoricus. He retreated back the way he had come, abandoned his pack in the ditch and grasping his staff in both hands walked towards them in the centre of the track, making as much noise as he could. He felt sure the robbers would try to ambush him, but they wouldn't abandon their existing captives altogether. The risk was that they might kill someone to reduce the odds, but he hoped they'd be too busy working out what to do.

He sensed rather than saw the man leap towards him from the side of the road as he drew parallel with him. Desperation made Victoricus quick to react and stepping back two paces and leaning to the side he caught the man a tremendous whack on the side of the head. The robber crumpled without a murmur and lay still, his knife fallen from his grasp. With that Rufus, Attius and Viventia leaped on the second man, Attius hanging on to his knife arm. Even so the struggle would have gone against them if Victoricus had not come up swiftly and pushing the end of his staff into the man's chest ordered him to drop his knife and lie still. Once disarmed, the would-be robber lost all bravado and became a pathetic wretch. His knife was the only thing which made him bold.

Even so, Victoricus took off the man's belt, cut it in half with his knife and, instructing him to turn over, tied first his hands and then his feet together, despite protests. Victoricus was conscious of having been hardened by the events of the previous few days. Responsibility for Arontius's family weighed heavily and he was taking no chances.

'How many more of you are there?' he asked,

rolling the man onto his back so that he could watch his eyes.

The robber was slow to answer, but Victoricus fingered his staff menacingly and the man replied resignedly, 'just me and my brother.'

Satisfied, Victoricus looked round, catching Viventia's eye and grinning.

'Anyone harmed?' he asked. Anicilla assured him that they were all fine.

'Let's check the other man, Attius,' he said. 'Keep a sharp look-out' to the others.

The other robber was still lying spread-eagled on the track.

'He'll live,' said Victoricus, bending over him, 'but his head will ache for a few days. Let's drag him over to his mate and they can help each other when he comes round.'

They moved off again, all anxious now to reach the end of the night's journey.

24

The sky began to lighten as the track ran alongside a marsh with a dense reed bed making faint swishing noises in the light breeze. Gradually the reeds thinned and an expanse of mud appeared, with pools of water glinting in the moonlight. Finally the mud banks, with running water pursuing a sinuous course through, opened out and the stream disgorged into the Isc. Close to its mouth several boats were settled into the mud, some leaning crazily over onto their sides.

'There's Barculo's vessel,' said Attius, pointing to a larger ship settled upright near the stream, its anchor deep in the mud beyond its prow. 'So, we're in time. The tide won't be in for some time yet. Let's find a sheltered spot to rest up until Barculo or his boy puts in an appearance.'

They sat under some trees overlooking the harbour, Barculo's ship clearly in their view. Victoricus thought the vessel looked similar to the one he had seen at Isca's quay. It was about fifty feet long he thought, but very wide, appearing almost round in the pale light. Its mast rose some twenty feet into the air and a grey-white furled sail hung from its head. A swan's head with a graceful curving neck, painted white, was visible at the prow. Near the stern, close by the steering oar, was a small cabin, the only structure on the planked decking apart from a hatch cover, presumably leading down to the hold.

Viventia broke into his thoughts. 'Are we really going to put out to sea in that?'

'Well,' said he after a pause, 'Barculo and his boy obviously do regularly, so no reason why we shouldn't be safe for a few miles down the coast.'

'Where do you think they are at the moment?' she persisted.

'I assume they're asleep in the cabin, but wait for the tide to make and we'll soon see. Why don't you have a couple of hours sleep yourself and we'll wake you when things start to happen?'

Viventia dismissed the idea that she could possibly sleep, but within a few minutes she was leaning heavily against Victoricus, supported by his arm around her shoulders, head lolling on his chest. The others also appeared to doze, too, except for Rufus, who, like Victoricus, remained alert looking around.

Water began to seep back into the creek, as the tide came back up river. Soon there was an expanse of water overpowering and disguising the flow of the stream. Their ship began to float moving slightly with the flow of the water and tugging gently at its anchor. It was now light but there was no sign of life. Attius was awake and Victoricus looked across raising his eyebrows as if to say what happens now? Attius shrugged and walked down to the water's edge. A youth appeared walking along the beach, a leather bag slung on his back. Attius went to meet him and they exchanged a few words. Attius helped him pull a small boat out of the bushes and held it while the youth climbed in. He set off across to Barculo's vessel using a paddle to propel the boat skilfully through the water.

The hills on the other side of the estuary had taken shape while they sat and were now clearly outlined against the sky. The expanse of water between looked enormous, thought Victoricus, turning slightly and causing Viventia to stir. He smoothed her hair with his hand and patted her shoulder. She would have to wake up soon. It was probably no more than one mile, he mused. Was it a mile beyond Cynan's authority? He hoped so. Down-river he could see a wide spit of sand jutting out into the water forcing the river to run through a narrow gap. We shall have to manoeuvre out through there, he surmised, although no doubt Barculo's done it hundreds of times before. Viventia stirred and opened her eyes.

'What's happening?' she said.

She received no answer for at that same moment Attius returned to his friends. All were awake and keen to hear his news.

'As you guessed, that was Barculo's boy. Apparently he sleeps at his parents' house, but it's his job to wake Barculo just before high tide. The ship can only get out around high-tide and that will be soon.

He'll wake his master and then return to ferry us over, if Barculo agrees.'

'We'd better get down to the water's edge, then,' said Rufus, seemingly eager. 'I shall be happy to leave this territory.'

The others were just as keen to leave, but some still had reservations about putting to sea. Anicilla was unhappy about the idea and Victoricus was not looking forward to the trip. Attius assured them that conditions were perfect.

'The sea's calm, there's a gentle breeze out of the south-west and we'll be there in no time.'

'It's alright for you, you've sailed before,' laughed Victoricus. 'We'll all be green before we get out of the river.'

It was some time before the boy returned and Barculo had still not appeared on deck. He was not much older than Armea, tall and thin with a shock of unruly fair hair and a permanently worried expression. He seemed overawed by their numbers and by the presence of females, the eyes of whom he avoided throughout the voyage. He singled out Victoricus and addressed all his remarks to him.

'Barculo says to bring you all aboard the *Swan* and stow you in the hold. He is not to be disturbed.'

'In the hold?' queried Victoricus. 'We can't sit on the deck?'

'There were people round yesterday afternoon asking about you. Barculo's worried. I think he'd leave you behind, if it wasn't for his promise to

Aeternus. He wants to hide you away until we are out in the river.'

'What sort of men were asking after us?' interposed Attius.

'Three men on horseback were nosing round, questioning everyone and interrupting us just as we were trying to load. They threatened everyone at the harbour and even searched our village.'

'Briginus!' exclaimed Rufus.

'Which way did they go when they left?' asked Victoricus.

'They rode on up the river bank towards Isca,' the boy replied.

The whole party seemed to wilt and shrink, clutching each other. It was obvious that they were still being pursued, that Briginus and perhaps other patrols were still hoping to intercept them.

'Why are they so determined to track us down?' asked Anicilla in a faltering voice. 'We are so little, so unimportant in Cynan's life.'

'Ah,' said her husband, sadly, 'he daren't let go of us. We have challenged his authority. If he lets us get away with it, who else might try? He rules through fear – fear instilled by men like Briginus – and the threats must be seen to work. We have seen it with Aeternus and Tullia. And with Natalinus and his family. His death may have been merciful compared with what they're suffering at Cynan's hands right now. Their neighbours won't step out of line again. Cynan is offering his people protection, but there's a price to be paid and that price is obedience.'

Anicilla shuddered. Her husband had put into words what they all knew in their hearts. But worse, the reality jarred. Arontius had expressed thoughts which each had thrust to the back of their minds. When they sailed out of Cynan's territory they were leaving behind a trail of broken lives. To keep them safe others had suffered and they were about to endanger this ungainly youth who stood quietly by the boat and his as yet unseen master.

Victoricus was now eager to get aboard and to set sail. He hurried Anicilla and Arontius into the waiting boat. The boy sensed a sudden urgency and paddled them quickly over the growing swell. The rest huddled together on the beach, glancing fearfully around them, expecting riders to appear at any moment.

Armea watched intently as her parents scaled the rope ladder which hung over the ship's side and disappeared into the hold. Within a few minutes she and Rufus were making the same trip. Victoricus insisted on being the last on shore, the boy, tiring from his exertions, ferrying him across at last. Before Victoricus reached the steps into the hold, he was already hauling the boat onto the deck, the pulley at the end of the long wooden arm over the side squeaking, as the boy worked the handle.

The hold was gloomy and it was a few seconds before his eyes were accustomed to the light, although the smell was already with him. A dank, pungent odour of fish and the sea. Not that any fish could be seen, as he soon ascertained, looking

231

round, although he supposed the barrels, running down the centre of the hold on either side of the huge wooden block supporting the mast, might have fish in them. The main cargo – fleeces and hides – were tied in bundles and piled against the sides of the ship, some as high as the deck planking. Ropes, attached to iron hooks screwed into the main timbers, held the bundles in place.

A narrow walkway down the length of the ship had been left free of cargo so that it was just possible to squeeze between the barrels and smaller piles of fleeces. It was on these that Victoricus found his companions seated, rather disconsolately and looking as if they were about to be sold in the slave market. Slavery might well be our fate, thought Victoricus grimly. We're about to take a voyage into the unknown.

He was still observing his friends, leaning on one of the barrels, when the light through the open hold was partially blotted out by a huge figure descending the steps. Barculo was almost as wide as he was tall with a coarse woollen tunic, heavily stained, reaching just below his knees. His short, muscular arms were covered in black hairs, which sprouted also from his neck and chin in strange contrast to his bald pate. He surveyed them, staring them down with unblinking red-rimmed eyes, which lingered on Viventia and Armea.

'Where's Aeternus?' he asked suddenly of Victoricus, who was nearest to him.

Victoricus did not answer immediately, but

looked anxiously at the rest of the group. Barculo sensed straightaway that something was wrong.

'Well?' he bellowed.

'Dead,' replied Victoricus, 'and Tullia with him.'

The man reacted as if he had been struck in the face. His mouth closed, his right fist clenched and he stared at Victoricus so intently that the latter felt only an explanation would relieve the tension. He described what had happened the previous day at the farm.

Barculo seemed to relax a little, though he remained angry and threatening.

'This Briginus, who favoured us with a visit yesterday, you say he was responsible?' He shifted his gaze to take in the others.

What was it Victoricus could detect in him? Surely it was not fear of Briginus. Victoricus could not imagine Barculo afraid of anyone or anything. No, he fancied rather Barculo was thinking of revenge.

'Well, I've been paid to take you to Uxella, and I'll land you there, but after that you'll be on your own. Stay in the hold. I'll put the cover over, so I hope none of you are afraid of the dark. Maybe when we're out in the river I'll let some of you onto the deck, but for the moment it's best you keep out of sight.'

'We appreciate you're taking a risk for us,' said Anicilla, stepping forward, 'and we're grateful to you. We'll trouble you no more once you've landed us safely.'

Was he deceived or did Victoricus begin to see a

slight softening in the man's attitude? As he was trying to interpret the man's mood, a shout came from the top of the steps. It was the boy warning his master that riders had appeared. Barculo turned on his heels and leapt for the steps, the whole movement accomplished so nimbly that his passengers were impressed.

Huddling together near the mast step, they sat whispering on the cargo. There was little doubt that this was Briginus returning, but surely they were safe from his clutches now. The tide seemed almost full and they were about to set sail.

'What did Barculo mean when he said he'd been paid?' asked Arontius of Attius in a low tone.

Attius at last admitted: 'Aeternus gave him his savings – coins in a leather bag. I don't know how many there were, but Barculo seemed satisfied. Aeternus and Tullia discussed it the night before we travelled to see Barculo and they agreed that they were content. They would never need such wealth. He swore me to secrecy, saying this was the last service they could render us and it made them happy to do it.'

Most were tearful after this declaration and Rufus wept openly.

'Such generosity,' he sobbed.

The ship was hailed from the shore. They fell silent and listened. Briginus was demanding to come on board. Barculo offered to send the boat for him. His voice was loud, every word carefully articulated. They heard the squeaks of the pulley, the splash of the boat as it hit the water and imagined the boy paddling it over to the shore. Barculo was about to betray them. They were going to be cornered and taken in this stinking hold.

'I'm for fighting this time,' said Victoricus. 'We've nothing to gain by being taken tamely and led away.'

He grasped his staff and looked at the others. Attius and Rufus agreed. There was nothing to lose. Even Arontius grabbed a staff, weak as he was, and prepared to fight.

Barculo appeared briefly at the top of the steps.

'Hide yourselves,' he hissed, without looking at them. 'In the darkness towards the stern. Cover yourselves with fleeces and don't move whatever happens.' With that he was gone. They heard him on deck, walking over to the rail.

'Quickly,' said Victoricus, 'take everything with you.'

They made their way between the barrels and the fleeces and in the farthest recesses, where the bolts which secured the steering oars protruded through the timbers, they hid themselves. Victoricus helped to pile the fleeces over them, making sure that nothing was visible, before concealing himself between two of the ship's ribs under a couple of fleeces.

They heard two men come onto the deck and snatches of conversation penetrated into the hold from the open hatch. Briginus was talking to Barculo. The latter's tone was reasonable, quite unlike the gruff, laconic comments, which they had been subjected to, thought Victoricus. Was the man going to betray them after all? Victoricus gripped his staff laid alongside the rib and listened intently.

'Just fleeces and hides and salted fish in barrels,' said Barculo at the top of the steps. 'Come and look for yourself, Briginus, but mind the steps. They need fixing. One of these days I'll get round to it, but you know how it is.'

'Stay on deck and keep your eyes open.' This from Briginus.

They descended, Barculo first, making remarks about the sea, about the weather, affable.

Briginus must have asked where they were bound for.

'Going along the coast to Uxella with this load,' came the reply, 'and then back with salt into the Taen for the Lord Cynan. Look for yourself. Stinks a bit from the fish, but we get used to it, Briginus. I've been thirty years at sea, fishing and moving cargoes around these waters. I'm used to some odd smells, believe me' and he laughed, a sound so ludicrous coming from this man, that Victoricus almost exclaimed aloud, but stopped himself in time.

'We don't need to bother anymore here,' he heard Briginus say. 'We'll clear off and you can set sail.'

'Watch that loose step on the way up,' they heard Barculo say in a loud voice as the two men mounted out of the hold.

There was quiet and Victoricus resisted the temptation to peer out from beneath the sheepskin.

Then came a frightened yell followed by a tremendous crash, which shook the planks. Barculo's voice came again yelling for Briginus' companion.

'Your master's fallen down the steps. I warned him to be careful. He almost took me over with him. He landed on his head. I hope his skull's thick.'

There was a pause. A strange voice said: 'He's broken his neck. He's dead.'

'Broken his neck?' This from Barculo. 'He can't have in that short distance. Let me have a look at him. You're right. Well, you heard me warn him. A death on my ship. That's unlucky. I shall have to make an offering to the sea-god. I hope this isn't going to cause trouble. I need to get this cargo to Uxella by tonight.'

'Don't worry,' said his companion. 'Briginus was always a clumsy oaf. I'll let them know what happened back at Duriarno and make sure no blame attaches to you. Perhaps your boy can bring my mate over and we'll get his carcass out of your way. Between you and me I'm not sorry to see him go. He was a pig and was beginning to get above himself.'

Victoricus listened to all this with mounting excitement. Somehow Barculo had caused Briginus to fall. Of that he was sure. He had taken revenge for Aeternus' death and looking back Victoricus realised it had been planned from the moment Briginus appeared. He couldn't wait to discuss the events with his friends. They were free of pursuit for the time being. He heard Briginus' body being removed. Barculo called down for them to stay in the hold, though each emerged from their various hiding places.

They heard the boy return and once again the creaking pulley operated as the boat was swung aboard. Immediately the anchor was pulled up and the ship began to move slowly and then gathered speed.

Victoricus found that the full details of the bizarre happenings of the previous hour were not known to all. He had been closest and heard most. Once explained however they were incredulous.

'So, Briginus is dead,' whispered Viventia, almost to herself, a curious mixture of joy and horror mingling in her face.

'Justice for Aeternus and Tullia,' said Rufus.

'Justice was given a helping hand, I think,' replied Victoricus. 'Strange that it was Briginus who missed his footing at the top of those steps and that he landed on his head.'

'What do you mean?' asked Arontius.

'I think our friend Barculo took his revenge for Aeternus' death by helping Briginus to slip,' said Victoricus. 'He's a dangerous man, our captain.'

The ship was beginning to roll slightly in the waves and they could hear the steady swish of the water as it passed along the sides. The boy appeared at the top of the steps.

'I'm to put the hatch cover on, so Barculo suggests you come up. The ladies' – this was said without once looking at them – 'may use his cabin. And he says take care on the loose step coming up.'

Anicilla and Armea disappeared into the cabin and Arontius joined them. Viventia preferred to sit outside, leaning back against the cabin with the other three. Barculo sat on a low stool his hands lightly touching the handles of the steering oars. From time to time he deftly changed the angle of the oars and bellowed at the boy to adjust the ropes attached to the great rectangular linen sail. These orders seemed more like grunts to the passengers and in any case, Attius noted, the boy was usually already busy at the ropes before Barculo shouted. They made a good team.

They were out in the main channel now sailing towards the sandy spit, sticking out into the river, which Victoricus had glimpsed from the harbour. The river flowed around it in a great curve and Victoricus imagined that beyond it would be the open sea.

25

The voyage surprised them all. They enjoyed it. It relieved the tension of the last few days. Gone were any worries about travel by sea. Instead they felt safe and strangely content. Barculo steered close enough to the land for them to see red cliffs rising high out of the water dwarfing the ship. Sometimes the land sloped down to river mouths, land divided into fields, land which was being worked. Once they had sight of a farmhouse, its red-tiled roof and white painted walls glistening in the sun. Several stone buildings nestled close to it in a hollow which ran down to a river where a ship was at anchor.

'It looks so peaceful and prosperous,' remarked Viventia.

'So might Cynan's territory appear from the sea,' re-joined Victoricus.

'No, I feel this really is going to be different. I could settle here, forget the past, and be happy.'

'How do we know that Cynan isn't lord in these parts too?' asked Victoricus, half-seriously.

'He was finding it difficult to maintain his power

in Isca,' said Attius, 'I can't see him having much say around here.'

'There, stop teasing and look on the bright side,' said Viventia, tweaking Victoricus' ear. This provoked a huge hug which had her squealing with delight.

The ship rounded a headland and made for a wide estuary. Buildings came into view on either side of the river and following a series of grunts from Barculo the boy adjusted the sail. He seemed to be everywhere at once, pulling on some ropes and slackening others off.

He gestured to them, at the same time removing the hatch cover.

'Barculo wants you in the hold as we go up-river. He doesn't want to be seen with passengers on deck. There's a harbour here with a quay where we can tie up,' vouchsafed the boy, 'so we shan't be ferrying you over by boat and you should be able to slip away easily.'

They were aware of the ship coming to rest against the quay and within a few minutes it had been secured. It was Barculo himself, who descended the steps to speak to them, the first words they had exchanged since leaving the Isc estuary.

'This is where Aeternus asked me to drop you. My part of the bargain is finished. If you take my advice you'll get away from the quayside. You're a large group and you'll attract attention. Better still split up, make your own ways up the hill out of the port and meet up on the road beyond the houses. There are officials here and they'll question any strangers they see. You'll find them a different lot to Briginus and his crowd, but they have checked much more thoroughly in the last few months.'

This was the longest speech they had ever heard from Barculo and they were momentarily taken aback. Victoricus in particular had altered his opinion of the seaman and felt he could now understand his worth. He saw why Aeternus had described him as a friend, but Victoricus was not alone. The others, too, had changed their opinion of Barculo and warmed towards him.

Arontius thanked him on their behalf and said especially: 'You mention Briginus. We are also in your debt for protecting us against him. He was a menace to me and my family and we're pleased that you rid us of him.'

Barculo's face set and his eyes grew vacant.

'The man tripped,' he said. 'I can't help it if he was clumsy. I did warn him.'

Arontius understood and just said:

'Well, at least Aeternus and Tullia are avenged. God has punished an evil man.'

'Take this and good luck,' muttered Barculo, mellowing.

So saying he thrust a leather bag into Arontius' hand and with the turn of speed they had noted earlier was half-way up the steps before Arontius had realised what he had been given.

He emptied out the contents of the bag into his wife's cupped hands to gasps as 10 gold and a similar number of silver coins appeared. The light caught the newly minted coins as they lay in

Anicilla's hands. They could pick out the name and head of the reigning Emperor, Theodosius on some of them.

'Aeternus' savings,' said Rufus. 'How did he manage to collect so much money? We can't possibly accept it.'

It was more money than any of them had had at any point in their lives.

'We shall insult Barculo, if we don't,' said Attius. 'We must accept and be grateful. Now we have all our things together, why don't we go off as Barculo suggested? Arontius and Anicilla might go first perhaps with Armea. Then Rufus and me.'

'And finally Victoricus and Viventia,' said Armea, forestalling him. 'That's a surprise!'

Despite their weariness and no small apprehension about this new territory, they all laughed.

'We'll look out for you on the main road out of the port,' said Arontius.

Barculo and his boy were already swinging bundles of fleeces over the side of the ship by the time Victoricus and Viventia left the deck via the rope ladder. Barculo managed a curt nod but no acknowledgement came from the boy, though his eyes followed them along the quayside. In truth several heads turned to watch Viventia as she accompanied her man.

The quay consisted of wooden planks supported on posts driven into the bed of the river. There was only one other ship at the quayside, but alongside it was a flat-bottomed barge full of brown crystals, which Victoricus assumed rightly was salt. Two men were using wooden shovels to fill barrels, which were then swung up by the ship's crane onto its deck. It reminded Victoricus of filling barrels with salt beef at Isca. He and Viventia had seen the salt works from the deck of the *Swan*. They were up river from the quay, shallow pools away from the water's edge. They'd seen fires alight near the pools and under large trays in which the salt water bubbled. Steam had risen continuously from the works as they watched.

The two men in the barge stopped work as they passed and Viventia blushed at the comments and clung to Victoricus. It was good-natured teasing though and Viventia was secretly pleased. Victoricus felt flattered and understood why this beautiful girl on his arm should attract so much attention. She's mine, he reminded himself and now we'll stay together. I'll find work and we'll settle down.

Piled up neatly at the side of the quay were a variety of tiles, dressed stones, and timbers. Victoricus paused to look.

'From Isca, do you think?' asked Viventia, voicing his thoughts.

'Sorio's gangs, pulling down buildings and carting the spoil away. Materials piled on the quay at Isca,' mused Victoricus aloud. 'You're right, Viventia, they could be from Isca, but what are they doing here?'

'Obviously they've been shipped in for someone,' she replied, 'but they're not going to be used much here.' She pointed to the buildings in the port, timber-framed and thatched. 'Perhaps they're waiting for a ship to take them elsewhere.'

'But why unload them here?' asked her companion. 'It makes no sense. I'm sure they're going to be re-used around here.'

The port consisted of a few houses close to the river and either side of a street leading up a hill. The few people they met showed little curiosity and they soon left the houses behind. There was no sign of the others and Victoricus suspected this was because he and Viventia had dawdled along the quay. Nor did they quicken their pace. They were enjoying themselves and in any case, Victoricus thought, Arontius will be glad of a rest having walked up this hill. There were good views of the river and the salt-workings as they ascended and they paused to look out over the scene towards the hill beyond. Victoricus put down his pack and his staff, clasped Viventia in his arms and kissed her fervently on the mouth.

'I love you so much,' he said.

'So that's why you've been hanging back,' said Viventia, returning his kiss. 'To take advantage of me. No wonder Armea laughed at us on the ship. Come on, we'd better keep going and catch up with the others.'

They'd hardly started off again before two men appeared round a bend in the track. There was nowhere to hide and in any case the lovers could see no reason to do so. They continued to walk companionably arm in arm. The first feeling of unease stirred in Victoricus as he noticed the men

245

were wearing identical black leather jerkins over their tunics. It seemed to him that they gave the men an official air. Viventia had noticed it too.

'They're not just local workers, are they?' she whispered. 'What do we do?'

'Nothing we can do,' came the reply. 'Keep walking, act naturally and hope they just pass us by.' But his alarm increased as the men approached and he saw that each had a dagger in a leather scabbard.

Victoricus greeted them more cheerfully than he felt.

'Not two more,' came the reply from the older man, his red face creased into a wry smile.

'Two more,' said the other. 'How many more are there?' he queried.

'What do you mean?' replied Viventia, hoping to brazen it out.

'Come on,' said the older man. 'you're strangers here. We've already picked up this evening a couple with a daughter, an old bent fellow with a young man and now you two. How many more are there? All strangers have to report to the assistant. That's the rule.'

'We're the last,' said Victoricus, giving in gracefully. He felt amused rather than threatened, though talk of the assistant was alarming.

'Good, we can finish this patrol, then. You'd better come with us and join your companions.'

There was no point protesting. Their friends had been taken. Victoricus and Viventia resigned themselves to joining them.

26

They were escorted up the hill and into a side track, which opened out to reveal a complex of three low stone buildings with tiled roofs. One, some way apart, had a white dome and this together with the smoke puthering from the flues suggested that it was a small bath-house. The whole site was neat with a small formal garden and a screen of trees around it. Victoricus thought that it had none of the decay so noticeable at Isca.

The younger escort walked on, but his companion turned to the largest building, a simple rectangular block of four or five rooms with a veranda. Mounting the steps onto the veranda he indicated a door and they found themselves in a small office. A clerk sat at a table in one corner.

'Two more,' said the red-faced guard succinctly.

The clerk studied them carefully.

'I need your names,' he said, reaching for a sheet of parchment already half full. They saw no point in lying and supplied them.

'How many more?' he asked.

Before Victoricus could reply, their escort

intervened to say that they were definitely the last.

'Thank the gods for that. Put them with the others and I'll inform the assistant.'

Passing through the door into an adjoining room, Victoricus and Viventia discovered their companions seated on a bench.

'So, they've taken you, too?' remarked Attius ruefully. 'I thought it was only a matter of time.'

'What is this place?' asked Victoricus, sitting down. 'It's obviously official, but who's running it and why?'

'We know as much about it as you,' answered Arontius. 'It looks like a government office, but it can't be. Is it run by the Isca council?'

'That's unlikely,' said Attius. 'They're not even running Isca any more. It could be a local lord like Cynan, in which case we might be in trouble.'

'Have you asked?' enquired Viventia.

'Rufus tried to persuade the guards to talk,' said Anicilla, 'and the clerk, but they weren't saying anything. Obviously we have to wait for this assistant, whoever he is. But we have been treated well. No-one's pushed us around and they've even given us honeyed wine.' She pointed to the beakers on a side table.

The clerk came in after a while and asked that Arontius, Attius and Victoricus follow him. They passed through an empty room before being shown into a larger office sparsely furnished. An elderly man, smartly dressed in a white linen over-tunic, was perched on one corner of a table. He looked tired, but his eyes, set deep in sockets surmounted by bushy grey eyebrows, were bright. He eyed them quizzically as they entered and motioned them to be seated on the only other piece of furniture – a bench.

'Not very often we entertain such a large number of guests,' he said. 'Where have you come from and what are you doing in Uxella?'

'First, could you tell us who you are?' said Attius, 'and by whose authority you detain us and ask questions?'

He sighed and stood up, passing his hand across his thinning hair. His actions were languid, almost weary, as if he hated carrying out his duties, but this was deceptive.

'I am Senacus. My authority was granted by the governor of the province of Britannia Prima as his representative in Uxella and through him and others I also represent Our Lord the Augustus Theodosius. Now I want to know who you are.'

He stared at them and they stared back, more from astonishment than any desire to conceal. We've only travelled about fifteen miles from the Isc and here's the Empire still working, thought Victoricus.

Arontius gave a brief outline of the events of the previous few weeks. When he mentioned Cynan they all noticed that Senacus frowned at the name. He was careful not to mention Barculo, though by now he was convinced that this official was shrewd enough to fill in the details for himself.

'So, you're runaway peasants and artisans,' he said bluntly. 'You realise it's an offence to leave your land and your jobs?'

They made to protest. He put up his hand to stop them.

'Whatever you say that's how the law sees it. However, Cynan, and others, have taken the law into their own hands. Some time soon the Empire will punish them. But in the meantime we can't blame people for trying to escape from their tyranny and return to proper authority. Can we?' said he, this after a short pause.

'But it isn't just Cynan,' said Attius. 'You may be the Empire's representative here, but just back down the road at Isca the place is emptying. The town councillors have gone. The forum is closed. What's happening at Lindinis or Durnovaria or even at Corinium? The Empire isn't in control any longer.'

'It will be again, soon, lad' said Senacus. 'I admit that its six months since I had contact with the governor and I'm running out of money to pay my staff, but we've had these interruptions before. I expect the governor will be here before the summer's out and men like Cynan will be put in their place. Some money will be spent on Isca. He'll put some officials in and the whole civitas will be up and running again.'

He's deceiving himself, thought Victoricus. Knowingly or unknowingly? I can't think he genuinely believes all of that.

'In the meantime,' continued Senacus, 'I stay at

my post. I check on ships coming in. I levy tolls. I supervise shipments of tin arriving from further west, which are carried by wagon on the great road which runs from here to Corinium and beyond. I help the farmers hereabouts to ship their products to markets along the coast.'

Senacus seemed to have forgotten them. He was striding up and down his office, lost in his own world.

Attius interrupted: 'Tin is still arriving at Uxella, then?'

Senacus stopped, looking pained. 'From time to time,' he said distractedly. 'Uxella might not be quite the bustling port it was when I first came here some twenty years ago, but there's still a fair amount of trade passing through and estates in the area use the port.'

'No Cynans round here then,' suggested Arontius.

Senacus hesitated and his confidence seemed to subside a little. He avoided their eyes, walked round the table and sat on his stool.

'One or two of our landowners are beginning to take the law into their own hands,' he admitted grudgingly. 'But then they always were masters within their own estates and their wealth always did allow them to do more or less as they liked. Just half a dozen families, marrying their daughters off to each other's sons, their wives visiting each other and gossiping over the latest hair styles. They competed with each other, but remained friendly. The difference now is that most go about with their own armed retainers, understandably since we've had problems with robbers on the roads for some years. It started with the death of one farmer's wife about seven years ago – she was robbed and killed near her home and her children seized. I remember her husband coming to see me, but I hadn't enough men to help. I reminded him that he was a member of the council and it was their job to keep the roads safe, but he laughed in my face. Since then they've take matters into their own hands, but I fear its going beyond that. Some of them are beginning to use their men against each other in fights over land.'

'But that's exactly what's happened in our area,' said Arontius ' and Cynan has come out on top at the moment.'

'Oh, we're nowhere near that point, yet,' cut in Senacus. 'A firm hand will soon sort it out. The governor will be here with his guards any day and he'll soon knock a few heads together.'

But this was said with so little conviction that Victoricus was now convinced that the official no longer truly believed this himself.

'Let's get back to you people, then,' continued Senacus, 'I do have other business to finish. Strictly as absconders I should send you all back, as I said, but I can probably find places for you locally if you're willing to work. There's a large estate on the other side of the river. Its run by a bailiff as the owner's absent from time to time on his estates elsewhere. I have sent him workers occasionally and he always seems to find places for them. I propose sending you there tomorrow. One of my men will escort you. You'll find him a fair-minded man. You'll be treated well.'

'We've swapped one form of slavery for another,' muttered Arontius.

'What do you want?' asked Senacus, showing anger for the first time. 'You're workers. What did you expect? A land grant? A villa house with bath suite and mosaic floors put at your disposal?'

'We could buy land,' said Arontius, stubbornly.

'Buy?' said Senacus, incredulously. 'With what?'

Arontius regretted his outburst and looked at the others. Senacus stared at each in turn, sensing that there was something to be told. Finally Attius admitted that they had money.

'Not stolen,' he hastened to add. 'Our friend's savings given to us to help us to a new life.'

Senacus' anger subsided. He thought for a few minutes.

'There's no market in land,' he said finally. 'Anyway you'd be better taking a tenancy on one of the large estates. At least you'd be under their protection. You couldn't survive on your own. Some landowner would be bound to interfere. Go with my escort tomorrow. Speak to the bailiff. As I said, you'll find him very fair. You won't be treated as slaves and you won't be robbed. You can stay here overnight. There's plenty of room. Will you give me your word that you won't disappear?'

'We must consult the others,' said Victoricus, conscious that they would be anxious to know what was happening, 'but I think we will do as you suggest.'

They re-joined the others. The clerk showed them to their quarters – three rooms in the block where the guards were housed. The ladies could bathe he told them if they wished. They would not be disturbed. The men would not use the bath-house until later in the day and the male visitors were welcome to join them.

Having heard what was planned for the following day and giving their assent, the women were anxious to use the bath-house and Anicilla, reminded of happier days at Isca, shepherded her daughters over to it.

The men debated the advantages of following Senacus' advice. Arontius was keen to try for work on the estate.

'But that doesn't mean you have to come with us,' he said, looking first at Rufus and then at Attius. 'Perhaps you'd sooner make your way back to Isca?'

Rufus indicated that for him there was nothing left in Isca and that he preferred to stay with Victoricus and Arontius' family.

'You are my family now,' he said, 'I'll be happy to work on the estate with you.'

Attius said that he had no desire to return to Isca.

'Work was coming to an end. I've no ties there. We've been thrown together and have survived so much in the last few weeks. I don't think I could survive without you all,' he finished with a broad grin.

'That's settled, then,' said Victoricus.

27

The next morning they set off early with the cheerful, ruddy-faced guard, Protus, they had encountered the previous day. Making their way back to the river they noted that Barculo's ship had already gone. The guard summoned a flat-bottomed barge, which conveyed them across the river mouth. Protus had warned them that it would take a large part of the day to reach the estate. Surmounting a long hill, they looked down into a deep, steep-sided valley which reminded them of the valleys near the Taen. Neat, well-managed coppices were visible on the highest parts of the hills and a pattern of fields ran down into the valley. Sheep were grazing on pasture below the woodland and cattle could be seen on meadowland near the stream. Sandwiched between the two running down the slopes were long rectangular fields of wheat and beans. They followed a track which led down between the fields into the valley.

Victoricus, as he looked about him, was impressed with the estate. It seemed well managed and in good order. As they penetrated deeper into the valley itself it was extraordinarily peaceful, but he had to remind himself that he had thought the same looking out from Aeternus' farm. Why would this estate or this owner be any different? The picture which Senacus had painted for them of life in the area had hardly inspired confidence. As the valley turned and the stream grew larger he wondered what they would find.

'How much further?' asked Viventia at his side, breaking into his thoughts.

'Nearly there,' called Protus looking back over his shoulder. He and Rufus had been sharing reminiscences about the past. Rufus had discovered that his companion had lived in Isca when he was first married and they had had several mutual acquaintances giving plenty of scope for gossip.

Protus stopped and pointed up the slope from the stream. Part-way up the hill was a long low building with its veranda towards them and at a slightly lower level an octagonal-shaped bath-house with a white dome, its lower edge stained with sooty deposits from the flue openings. In shape it was not unlike the block of rooms where Senacus worked, but it was altogether a grander and more imposing building. They could see light catching glass in the row of windows, set in a white-painted wall, above the veranda roof, which like the main roof consisted of stone tiles.

'The bailiff has his office at the back of the building,' said their escort. 'We'll follow the path round and see if we can find him.'

They passed a small stone-built gatehouse near

the path. Its thatched roof looked in need of attention and it was empty and neglected. Walls approached it on either side forcing them to keep to the path. A gate, removed from its iron hinges, stood propped against the wall. Victoricus noticed in contrast how neat and well-kept the main building was, in keeping with the rest of the estate. Even the herb garden with its low surrounding hedges was weeded and cared for. And perfectly situated for the kitchen, thought Victoricus, as a delicious smell wafted over to him.

'What a beautiful house. Who lives here?' Viventia wondered aloud. 'Whoever they are they must be rich and important. I've not seen a house as large as this outside Isca.'

'What worries me,' replied Victoricus 'is that the only villa I've seen which was anything like this was Cynan's villa near Duriarno. Let's hope the owner here isn't another Cynan.'

Rounding the corner of the house, they had time to observe a large level garden with gravel paths. No-one was about, but Attius saw movement at the far end close to the hedge. A large black dog lifted its head and looked towards them. It padded forward slowly and began to growl. They all turned to look and Armea clung to her mother's dress.

'Ignore him,' said Protus 'he's quite friendly', and he disappeared through a door leading into a small room attached to the back wall of the house. They heard greetings exchanged.

'What brings you here, Protus?' followed. 'Not

wanting to exchange that soft life you have in Uxella for some real work on the farm here, I suppose?' A loud bantering conversation followed.

'That's Lupus,' said Viventia, suddenly.

Rufus turned, looked at the dog and ran forward. The growls ceased. The dog wagged its tail furiously and rested its paws on Rufus' shoulder. By now he was weeping and laughing at the same time.

'Where have you come from, old boy?' he kept repeating, 'where have you come from?'

Victoricus, overjoyed at Rufus' good fortune, was nevertheless puzzled. They had left the dog tied up at the cattle station in Isca. How had it reached this villa thirty miles away?

As he tried to work out an answer their guide emerged from the office and joined them in the garden.

'The bailiff's out on the estate at the moment, but he's due back any time. We can have something to eat and drink while we're waiting.'

He indicated an adjoining room, where they hardly had time to settle themselves gratefully on the benches before servants brought honey cakes and a jug of beer for their refreshment. Rufus was so overjoyed that he took his refreshment into the garden and ate with one hand happily resting on the dog's head.

The doorway filled with another figure and they looked round.

'Silvius!' shouted Attius and Victoricus simultaneously.

'What are you doing here?' asked Attius.

'I might ask you the same,' said Silvius, looking round. 'I'm the bailiff.'

He sat down. 'Now, tell me all your news.'

Attius and Victoricus, with occasional interruptions and corrections from Viventia, managed to give a fairly coherent account of their recent activities, but they were much more eager to hear what had been happening to Silvius. He seemed keen to learn all he could of Cynan and questioned them closely whenever they mentioned his name.

'Silvius,' Victoricus finally blurted out, 'when we saw you last you were night-watchman in Isca. What brings you here?'

'That's easily told,' replied his friend. 'Sorio was pleased with my work, guarding his land in Isca. He knew that I'd been raised on a farm and asked me if I would transfer to his estates near Uxella. Isca was becoming a dangerous place and he said to leave its protection to his soldiers. He felt I could be of more use round here. His bailiff had just died and after a few weeks he asked if I would take over.'

'You mean this estate and house belongs to Sorio?' asked Victoricus incredulously.

'That's right,' said Silvius, 'and I might add he's a very fair-minded man. He's tough and very well organised, but he's also reasonable. He's a good listener, weighs up what you say, and comes to a decision.'

'But he's a lord, surely, just like Cynan and

wants to rule his territory and the people in it,' scoffed Victoricus.

'Sorio's not at all like Cynan, or at least the Cynan I've heard about. He doesn't demand obedience. He earns it. He doesn't allow his henchmen to kill for the pleasure of it, though they certainly have killed defending Sorio's property and rights. No-one who knows Sorio well would be afraid of him unless they had done something wrong themselves. He can be hard, he can be ruthless, but he is always fair.'

'Was it fair to turn an old man out of his house?' asked Viventia, happy that Rufus had stayed outside with his dog.

'I agree that was unfortunate,' answered Silvius, shifting his gaze and displaying slight irritation at being upbraided by a young woman. 'Rufus was the only resident left and was preventing Sorio from clearing and developing that part of town.'

'So Sorio's thugs had to clear him out, clout his dog on the head and dump all his belongings,' rejoined Viventia hotly and to Victoricus' embarrassment, for he himself had had the same thoughts.

'No, he had him moved to a house in another part of town. Admittedly not his own home and not in such good order, but it had a garden, plenty of rooms and with some work on it Rufus could have made it home. They even moved all his belongings on a cart and, yes the dog was knocked on the head, but only after it had bitten two of Sorio's men.'

'Good!' interposed Viventia, hardly softening at all. Her father motioned to her to be quiet. He did not know this quietly spoken young man, but he recognised that their future might depend upon him. Viventia was beginning to disturb what he judged had been a warm friendship between the bailiff and his former colleagues. Victoricus was torn between his love for Viventia and Rufus and his regard for Silvius.

In the event it was Silvius who softened.

'Sorio may have made a mistake, there,' he admitted, looking straight at Viventia, an amused smile on his face. 'The last few weeks in Isca were a difficult time. He was anxious to clear away unwanted properties and concentrate the inhabitants into the central and upper part of town. Sooner or later he thought he would have to defend the walls and he wanted as much open space as possible. He had this plan to produce food inside the town so that the people would not be so dependent on bringing supplies in from outside. So, as you know rubble was cleared away, foundations were pulled up and some areas were ploughed or dug over. Since you were there orchards have been planted and animals are now kept inside the town. Gradually those that remain there are feeding themselves.'

'So, he's carting away tiles, bricks and stone as well as timbers,' remarked Victoricus, thinking of the quays at Isca and Uxello.

'Yes, Sorio believes those materials can be put to much better use in the countryside,' said Silvius, 'repairing places like this and perhaps even building new farms.'

'Did Rufus tell you,' he continued, 'that the men who moved him also found his strong box below the floor with his money in it?'

'And took it, no doubt,' remarked Viventia, earning a rebuke from her mother.

'No,' said Silvius patiently, 'they left it intact with the old man.'

'How does his dog, Lupus, happen to be here?' Victoricus asked.

'I went looking for you and Attius at the cattle station and found him tied up inside one of the buildings. It must have been a couple of days after you were taken away. It took me some time to gain his confidence. If I'd let him off the leash he would have gone straightaway. Anyway, when I took this job at Sorio's villa I brought him with me. Naturally I did wonder what had happened to you all and with the dog tied up on its own I had an uneasy feeling that it was nothing good, but despite asking around I could not discover anything of you.'

'So this is Sorio's private residence and estate?' asked Victoricus.

'That's right,' answered Silvius, 'and you're very welcome. All of you,' he added glancing around.

Victoricus now stirred himself to introduce Anicilla, Arontius and their second daughter formally.

'Viventia, you already know,' said Victoricus, touching her lightly on the shoulder.

Silvius looked from one to the other, confirming what he had suspected at their evening meeting in Isca. These two are in love, he thought and they're well suited. Victoricus will have a spirited and delightful wife. Life will certainly not be dull.

Aloud he said: 'Yes, I remember, you walked over to find Rufus' house, when I was night-watchman. You are both very fond of the old man, aren't you, and I only hope that we can bury the past and that you'll all settle down here.'

'I spoke hastily, as usual,' answered Viventia, colouring. 'I was rude. We have seen such cruelty recently that perhaps Rufus' experience in Isca was not as bad as it seemed. Still,' she said, tossing her hair back and smiling broadly, 'someone has to tell Rufus whose land he is on and who may be providing the roof over his head and it won't be me.'

Victoricus took Silvius outside to introduce him to Rufus. The old man's reaction to the name Sorio was not as extreme as Victoricus expected. His delight at seeing Lupus again and his experiences of the last few weeks plus his expectations of what life could be like in the countryside near Uxella all contributed to a softening in his attitude.

'I'll judge him by his behaviour from now on,' he said, 'rather than on what he did in the past.'

That settled, Silvius sat with Attius and Victoricus in the garden reminiscing for a while. Eventually Silvius said he had work to do.

'First we must decide what's to be done with

you all. I understand Arontius is a cobbler and leather-worker. Is he any good, Victoricus?'

Victoricus was fervent in praise of Arontius' work.

'There speaks Arontius' future son-in-law,' laughed Attius.

'No,' remarked Victoricus colouring, 'I have known Arontius for some time. My father dealt with him years ago. There can be no doubt of his abilities.'

'You're right, I'm sure,' said Silvius, 'it's just that I must be seen to make the right judgement in this otherwise I'll be accused of advancing my friends at others' expense. Look, there is a cottage on the estate – its not much mind you, just three rooms, but Arontius and his family are welcome to it, so long as he's prepared to work.'

Victoricus called Arontius and his family into the garden and Silvius put the suggestion directly to them.

'The cottage is about a mile from here. It was lived in until a month ago, although the man was old and it'll probably need some work doing on it. You would come to the yard here, Arontius, to work.' Silvius gestured with his arm beyond the far side the garden. 'I know you're recovering from injury, so we'll work you lightly at first. Payment will be in produce from the estate. Not in coin.'

'Payment,' echoed Anicilla, 'that sounds a sensible arrangement. Surely we'll take up the offer,' she said, turning to her husband.

'Will you be able to employ the rest of our friends?' asked Arontius.

Silvius hesitated, looking at the ground. Victoricus wondered what was coming. Silvius almost seemed embarrassed, but finally he spoke up.

'Now don't shout me down straightaway, Victoricus. Hear me out. Sorio maintains a training area on the estate where workers learn how to use weapons – sword, spear and dagger. It's against Roman law, but despite what Senacus has been saying to you in Uxella, Sorio doesn't believe that the government will ever again enforce the law around here. I won't deny either that some of the young men from Sorio's estates have been drafted, willingly, into a war-band to defend his territory and their own families and lands. He is not aiming to extend his lands, but he is prepared to defend what he has and with your experiences you can see that men like Cynan will only be stopped if people like us stand up to them. This is what Sorio is doing. He also believes that it is sensible for all men to learn how to use weapons, whether in his war-band or not. Then they can more easily defend their families in a crisis. I'm suggesting that you get trained and then there'll be places for you to work on the estate.'

'But with all these trained men and weapons around won't all arguments easily turn to blows,' said Attius. 'Where men were content to use their fists, won't they now reach for a sword?'

'We don't believe so,' answered Silvius. 'While

the Roman government kept the peace I agree there was no need for farmers like us to use weapons, but think about your Irish raiders the other evening. Once they know the people hereabouts have the means and knowledge to defend themselves they'll think twice before they raid.'

'Who supplies the weapons?' asked Victoricus.

'Sorio has swordsmiths and weapon-makers working for him and he equips those workers who are prepared to stay with him. He feeds, clothes and arms his own war-band and even supplies mounts for some of the soldiers.'

'What happens if a worker refuses to be trained?' asked Rufus.

'Nothing,' came the reply. 'Sorio does not insist. He leads but he does not coerce. He plays fair with any man who plays fair with him. Ask around you will find he is well-liked on the estate.'

Victoricus looked at Viventia. He thought of a family and of family life. He thought over all that had happened to him over the previous months. Finally he felt what a sensible idea it was to be trained to use weapons.

'I'll go for weapon training,' he said to Silvius. Attius echoed his words.

'I wouldn't mind learning myself, ' said Rufus and all turned to look at him. 'But I might be just too old,' he added amid laughter.

'Rufus,' said Silvius, 'I might have just the place for you. The gatehouse here has not been manned while I've been bailiff, but I've been thinking lately that perhaps it's time we had another gateman.

You must have passed it as you arrived. It's not too large and we'd have to do some work on it, but it might suit you and Lupus. All you'd have to do would be to check on visitors arriving. What do you say?'

Rufus was delighted with the idea and said so. Silvius found someone to show Arontius' family to their cottage and Victoricus helped to carry their meagre belongings to it. Silvius meanwhile unlocked the gatehouse and invited Rufus to view his new home. Then, leaving Attius to assist the old man, Silvius resumed his duties around the estate.

28

Looking back, Victoricus remembered the next few months as some of the happiest of his life up to that time. He and Attius were quartered together in a room in the villa, but they saw Rufus and Arontius' family frequently. Rufus had made the two rooms of the gatehouse his own and Victoricus was frequently reminded of the rooms in his house at Isca. A small kitchen led off the main room with Rufus' bed in one corner. The roof had been replaced with red tiles, re-used from Isca. Wooden shutters were now fitted to cover the window opening at night. Rufus was as popular with the servants at the house as he was with the estate workers, so he never lacked for food and when Victoricus visited there was always some new gift on display in the house. Two stools, a small wooden table, cooking pots and a blanket for the bed had all appeared gradually to improve his life.

Not that Rufus had been idle. A small garden had been created in the shelter of the wall and was already sown with seeds supplied by his new friends and plants, including herbs and vegetables, from the same source were already growing. The new gateman had a cheerful word for all the visitors and passers-by though he stood no nonsense and he was soon well-known throughout the estate. Silvius was delighted with him.

'He knows everything that is going on,' he remarked to Victoricus, 'usually before I do. I make a point of speaking to him every day so that I don't miss out on anything.'

'Careful,' replied Victoricus, 'he'll be taking over your job soon!'

Attius and Victoricus were worked hard. They were away early each morning from the house up to the training ground a mile or so further up the hill. For the first week their muscles ached and they were glad to make use of the bath-house on their return. Sorio had managed to find a retired soldier who organised their weapon practice and in between told them stories of his army service. He'd served in forts in different parts of Britain, but had finished his time in the north close to a great wall, which he claimed ran across the country from sea to sea. So often did he tell them that it was possible to walk for 80 miles along the top of the wall without once getting down from it, that his recruits invariably finished off his sentence for him. He'd married the granddaughter of a labourer from Isca, who had come to repair the wall, bringing his family with him. Sometimes he spoke fondly of his wife, long dead and of his two sons still serving in the army. He taught them how to use a long sword, which Victoricus found heavy and awkward to wield at first. His arm continued to ache for several weeks after practising with it.

'Keep it in your hand until it becomes part of your arm,' the veteran advised. 'You should eat with it and sleep with it until it becomes part of you.' He was not amused when one of the youths remarked that he'd got better things to take to bed.

'It'll be no good grabbing hold of your woman when a raider breaks your door down one night,' he scoffed. 'Learn to defend yourself.'

On other days they were taught to use thrusting spears, jabbing them into straw figures on wooden supports. Lucius was amiable but allowed no slackness and within a few weeks his ten recruits became familiar with their weapons and confident in their abilities. At this point Lucius took each one on in single combat. Each was quickly defeated and their swords were sent spinning away out of their hands.

'You've improved' he said laconically, 'but there's still work to do. I had twenty years of this, but I still need to practice. Keep going.'

Victoricus was invariably drawn to visit Viventia after bathing each evening. Often Attius accompanied him, but sometimes he stayed chatting to Rufus. Viventia delighted in his stories of weapon training and was proud of her broad-shouldered lover. Her family had fully accepted that the pair would marry sometime soon, although it had not been openly discussed. Anicilla was happy with her daughter's choice. She sometimes feared for the future given the turmoil they had already witnessed and escaped for the moment, but she was convinced that they had a better chance than many couples of making a successful marriage. They had already survived a great deal together.

Arontius grew stronger each day. He oversaw the processing of hides from the estate and helped in the manufacture of leather jerkins and shoes in timber buildings near the stream. He often joined Victoricus at the baths in the evening, enjoying the company of Attius and his prospective son-in-law. They would sit together in the hottest alcove, sweat pouring from them, chatting and watching the steam rise into the dome. Arontius' wound was now just a long scar in his side, flaming red in the heat. Then they would plunge into the octagonal cold pool in the centre, with the water washing onto the mosaic surround with its simple designs.

Arontius' house was a meeting place. Often they were joined at the evening meal, prepared by Anicilla and her daughters, not just by Victoricus but also by Attius and Rufus. Even Silvius ate with them occasionally and passed on news of the world outside. Sorio was still in Isca and seemed to control most of the area inside the walls. When the gates were closed at night it was on his orders and the townspeople were fed by his efforts. But messages Silvius had received showed that Sorio was increasingly worried by news of Cynan's activities further west. He didn't know when the struggle would come, but he saw it now as inevitable. Silvius was to continue to ship supplies and any men willing to join him to the town. He was determined to protect the people of Isca.

They felt safe in their quiet valley, but Silvius reminded them how easy the journey was by sea, as they knew well. If Cynan took Isca then this territory east of the town might be next under Cynan's rule.

'But we'd have a chance to flee,' said Anicilla, 'disturbing as that would be. We've grown to love our life here, but we've escaped from Cynan's authority before. We can do so again.'

'Do we keep running though?' cut in her husband. 'Whose territory would Cynan take next? Better to support Sorio, stop Cynan now and live in peace.'

But Anicilla in quieter moments worried about the possibility of a long drawn-out fight, even a battle, something which was difficult to envisage given the 300 years of peace in the peninsula. Also, her experience with the Scottic raiders had taught her that Cynan and his war-band were not the only enemies to fear. Life was good and she prayed daily that nothing would disturb it.

29

Rufus strolled up the path to the villa house late one afternoon confident of a warm welcome in the kitchen, since this was a regular part of his day's timetable. The cook had no proprietor to prepare meals for, but she still catered for the servants and the bailiff and Rufus had become a firm favourite with her. He'd gone only a few steps, when Lupus began to bark and he turned, irritated that his routine was being disturbed. Horsemen were approaching from the stream, about a dozen he judged, each in long tunics and trousers with cloaks fastened around them, but insufficient to disguise the by now familiar lumps of swords and scabbards beneath.

Rufus returned to his post, noted the slow pace of the riders ascending the slope, and decided the horses had been ridden hard over some distance. He waited patiently by his door. These were not the first riders to arrive at his gate, though their number was unusually large. One man led the troop and as he approached the gatehouse he reined in.

'So the gate's manned now. Is this Silvius' doing? I must congratulate him on his forethought. I'm Sorio, the owner. Who are you and can you shut that dog up?'

Rufus quietened Lupus before giving his name. It meant nothing to Sorio, since, despite a close look at his gate-keeper there was no recognition. Rufus' stare showed him a tall man, upright in the saddle with light blue eyes in sunken sockets below thinning hair. His smile was warm, but there was an urgency about him, which fitted with his rapid speech. Everything about him proclaimed action. Sorio, once his mind was made up, would act single-mindedly and swiftly, though with compassion.

'Any idea where Silvius is?'

'Probably in the house by now,' answered Rufus. 'If you ride round I'll find him and bring him out and I'll alert the kitchen to your arrival.'

'Good man,' came the reply. 'I can see you and I are going to get on well.'

Rufus, who had rehearsed this first meeting with Sorio over and over again in his mind in the previous few weeks was completely disarmed. He hurried to make known Sorio's arrival, already well-disposed towards him.

Once he had seen that their horses were being cared for and that refreshments were being provided for the men, Sorio dragged two basket chairs onto the veranda and motioned Silvius to sit with him. He came straight to the point.

'Cynan's ships have blocked the Isc near its

mouth. They don't have many ships and it could be easily broken through even with the few vessels I have available, but it is not that which worries me. I think he's getting ready to attack Isca. Now I've come to realise that Isca is not that important in itself. I suppose the crops and foodstuffs we're raising within the walls are valuable, but with people deserting the place almost daily a case can be made out for abandoning it.'

Sorio noted the look of horror on the young man's face. Silvius had spent much of his adult life in the town and couldn't imagine it being abandoned without a fight.

'Those huge walls and gates should be easy enough to defend,' he said, 'and as you say yourself there is plenty of food inside. Cynan won't be able to raise an army to take it.'

'It's size is the problem,' said Sorio, 'it will take a lot of men to patrol the walls and gates. No, it's more of a symbol, really. If we abandon it to Cynan we shall lose face and he will grow in importance. Then it will be only a matter of time before he moves further east into these lands.' He gestured around him.

'Isca is where we make a stand against Cynan,' Sorio continued. 'If he fails to take it his power will be limited to those lands around the Taen and perhaps then he'll leave us in peace.'

'What do you need from us, then?' asked Silvius, inspired.

'I want to take Lucius back with me if he'll come to help organise the defence and as many of his trainees who'll fight with us. Then I'll need as many leather jerkins as are made up or can be made up in the next few days. The smiths have been stockpiling weapons. All this needs shifting by cart. Fortunately the road from Durnovaria to Isca is open and in good order. We used it today and I've carts from Isca following us. They should arrive tomorrow. Any wagons you can provide from the estate and the farms around will be useful. Now I'm off to see Lucius.'

By the time Silvius had risen from his chair Sorio was already striding away from the house. Capturing his mood, Silvius called for servants, who were dispatched to fetch Arontius and other estate workers to him. There was work to be done.

It was a weary Silvius who joined his friends for the evening meal at Arontius' house that evening. By then everyone knew of Sorio's arrival and his reasons for coming. The moment which Anicilla had dreaded had arrived. Attius was determined to go back with Sorio in two days' time and Victoricus was inclined to accompany him. Silvius had already said that he would be going.

'The estate can manage without me for a while,' he remarked.

Viventia remained silent, quite unlike her usual effervescent self, but the whole group was subdued that evening. When the meal had finished Victoricus and Viventia, as was their custom, strolled out into the garden. Autumn was approaching and there was a chill in the air, but it was not the cold which made Viventia shudder and pull her cloak around her. Victoricus held her tight and kissed her gently on the lips.

'You don't want me to go to Isca, do you?' he whispered.

'Of course not,' she replied, 'neither you nor any of our friends. We've not been apart now for almost a year and I've known Attius and Silvius almost as long. I'm terrified just thinking of you all fighting around Isca. But I can see that it has to be done, that a stand has to be made, and it's right that you go and help. I ask one thing only. Don't get yourself killed. Come back to me.'

'We'll be safe behind those walls,' he said. 'I won't be killed. Just a few days and we'll all be back. In the meantime look after the estate and help your father.'

'One more thing,' she whispered, as he held her close. 'I want to be married as soon as you're back. I don't want to wait any longer. I've spoken to my parents and they agree. We can live with them or perhaps Silvius could find us a home of our own.'

'Who's the lucky man, then?' retorted Victoricus and failed to stop Viventia's hand connecting with his ear. Pinning her arms to her sides, and gazing into her bright eyes he made her the solemn promise that for such a prize he would definitely return.

30

Two days later a line of wagons and men left the estate. Silvius had worked tirelessly on the preparations, urging his workers to greater and greater efforts. Arontius' stock of hides had diminished as jerkins were cut out and sewn together by all who could use the large circular needles. Anicilla and her daughters had raw patches on their hands from the threads.

Sorio was leaving some men to guard the estate. He had alerted Senacus, who had agreed to block the entrance to the port at Uxella in case Cynan's ships attempted to land, although this seemed unlikely.

'Cynan doesn't have enough ships to block the Isc,' he confided to Silvius. 'He won't venture into unknown territory this far east.'

Senacus had sent a message to the governor at Corinium requesting immediate assistance, but the port official was perhaps the only person in the area who believed his call would be heeded. Privately Sorio doubted whether the mounted messenger would ever reach Corinium.

'Even if he finds fresh horses on the way, he's likely to be robbed and killed,' he mused. 'By the time he reaches Lindinis he'll have had enough and desert.'

But Senacus did give Sorio's expedition his approval.

'You are acting on behalf of the Empire,' he said to him, 'upholding the Emperor's rights until his representative arrives from Corinium. I know you are breaking the law, but Cynan is in armed rebellion against the government and must be dealt with. You have my backing and I will speak for you when the governor arrives.'

Sorio did not argue, because he knew that Senacus was no fool. He did not think that the man was deliberately deceiving himself, but could he really still believe that the Empire's power would be restored in their peninsula?

The east gate came clearly into view as the party descended the gentle gradient towards Isca. The journey had been easy, Victoricus reflected. Sorio was right. This great stone road linking the two civitates was in good repair. Early the previous morning they had passed through a settlement at the junction with the Corinium road and Attius had speculated how far Senacus' messenger had reached. Then they had camped for the night close to a river. The wagons were slow, and Sorio had asked some of the men to stay with them, while he rode ahead with Lucius and others. He was anxious to be back in Isca. Attius and Victoricus took turns to ride an old horse, which had to be cajoled into keeping up with the wagons, but most of the men were on foot. Victoricus had ridden as a boy on his parents' farm, but preferred to walk much of the way on this journey. The effort required to urge the horse forward irritated him.

Now they were close enough to see men standing on the twin towers flanking the gateway, the gates, studded with iron bolt-heads, closed against them. For the last half-mile they had been aware of water running in a stone-capped channel at the side of the road.

'The water supply to the bath-house is still running,' remarked Attius. 'We should be able to scrape the dirt off when we arrive.'

For some of their companions, this was their first visit to Isca and they were impressed with its appearance. Victoricus noted that the gates had been repaired. New boards could clearly be seen close to one of the hinges. When they were within hailing distance the gates swung open easily on hinges thickly coated with animal fat and the party passed gratefully into the town.

Here in the northern area Victoricus detected few changes. Men had taken over deserted houses and premises. Even the forum had been opened and men were camped out in the yard and in the basilica. But when he walked into the lower part of town with Attius, after the wagons had been un-loaded and their own belongings deposited in the shed at the deserted cattle station, they found few buildings standing. There were large gaps even in the buildings flanking the main street and beyond, they could see through the gaps, all had been flattened and removed. Astonishingly Arontius' premises had survived. It was now occupied by a smith, but the building looked seedy and neglected, rather like the new owners. More surprising was the survival of the pie shop next door with the same large woman seated behind the counter. She looked more cheerful than when Victoricus had seen her last and he guessed that she saw the prospects of brisker business with all these new arrivals. Bad memories made him discourage Attius from purchasing a pie and they passed by swiftly on the other side of the street.

At the gate facing the river they found Sorio in discussion with Lucius and others. If Cynan came to attack Isca his forces would arrive from this direction, following the route which Victoricus knew so well from previous journeys.

'They'll have to make for the bridge,' Sorio was saying, 'so if we destroy it – just take out one of the middle sections – they'll be forced to make a long and tiring detour, or swim.'

'But they'll still reach here eventually,' said Lucius 'and we will still have to deal with them. Better to let them over the bridge. We're safe behind these walls. Then we'll see what Cynan will do with his forces. We'll have a clear view of the number of men in his army, what supplies they have with them and how well equipped they are.'

'Will he attack the walls,' asked Sorio 'or just wait outside hoping we will give in?'

'He may try an attack,' replied Lucius, 'but he'll

soon realise that it's hopeless. More likely he'll want to negotiate once he's had a good look round. He'll have problems feeding his men and can't afford to be away from his estates very long'

'We seem to be in a strong position,' commented one of the men.

'That's true,' smiled Lucius, 'but we also need to settle the problem. It won't help if Cynan arrives, fails to take Isca, but returns to his territory as strong as ever. It'll be a blow to his pride, but there'll be nothing to stop him attempting the same thing again next spring or summer.'

'Yes, it must come to a reckoning,' said Sorio. 'Cynan poses a threat to all of us and we must remove that threat. If it can't be done by negotiation, then it must be done by fighting. So we need to spend the next few days organising carefully so our men know their positions. We'll appoint captains – you'll know the best men to choose, Lucius – tell them their responsibilities. We'll have a meeting this evening at my house and explain their orders to them.'

The knot of men dispersed and the two friends returned up the hill to their quarters. They were hungry and soon went in search of food. Sorio had organised an open-air kitchen in the forum and men were gathering there for the evening meal. The crowd was dense, with more arriving all the time. Attius suggested to Victoricus later that altogether there must be five hundred of Sorio's men in Isca, though his friend thought this an exaggeration.

On several occasions Victoricus saw Lucius with

two assistants in the crowd. He seemed to be everywhere, talking, cajoling and giving out orders. Then he was lost from view and Victoricus settled down on the basilica steps with a bowl of stew. Attius had been swallowed up in the crowd somewhere and was temporarily out of sight. He was just finishing off, wiping out his bowl with the remains of a thick slice of bread, when Lucius approached.

'Your training's finished, now, Victoricus,' he said 'this is the real thing. You're a steady lad and handle your sword well, especially when you manage to keep it in your hand. You're being promoted to captain. You'll have twenty men under you including that friend of yours, Attius. You'll find out your duties at tonight's meeting.'

With that Lucius departed leaving Victoricus with a lump of bread poised between bowl and mouth. He had not uttered a word. When Attius caught up with him later Victoricus was so subdued that his friend wanted to know why.

'I've been promoted to captain,' he said, embarrassed, 'and you're in my troop.'

'Congratulations,' laughed Attius, 'you'll be good at giving orders. Viventia will be impressed. I'm pleased its happened to you. I couldn't cope with the responsibility.'

'That's just it,' answered Victoricus, 'what makes you so sure I can?'

Victoricus was assigned to patrol the wall close to the river gate. He and his troop took up quarters in one of the gate towers, the wooden floors of which had been repaired. Using the new ladders which had been supplied, they were able to mount from the ground floor through holes in the three floors above to the wall-walk. He separated his troop into three sections, with one man in charge of each, so that one section was always on patrol throughout the day and night. Lucius had included a small number of archers in each troop and their importance had been stressed at the meeting as being the only soldiers equipped to engage the enemy at a distance. They kept careful watch but after two days had seen nothing out of the ordinary.

On the third day Attius' section on patrol reported ships moving up river, their sails filled by a light breeze blowing from the sea. Victoricus climbed up to the wall walk to look, and then with Attius mounted to the top of the gate tower. It was a clear morning and the sunlight slanting across the river was catching four sails. They watched for some time as the vessels made steady progress towards them.

'They must be Cynan's ships,' said Victoricus at last.

'I think you're right,' replied Attius, 'and unless I'm mistaken one of them looks like the *Swan*.'

'Then they're definitely Cynan's. Barculo's ship must have been commandeered. I bet that pleased him. I'd better send one of the men for Sorio.'

Victoricus had just started down the ladder, when he encountered Sorio ascending closely followed by Lucius. News of the sighting of the ships had reached them and they had hurried to see for themselves. Sorio confirmed that they were not his ships. All stood watching the vessels closely, speculating on their destination, which was generally agreed to be the quay. But a cry from a guard alerted them to change the direction of their gaze. He had seen movement on the road, as it descended from the distant hill. They shaded their eyes against the glare of the sun. There could be no doubt that a large number of people were on the move towards them.

'Ships and men,' commented Sorio. 'Our wait is over. Cynan is on his way. We'll alert the whole garrison and make preparations to receive him'.

31

Some hours later Cynan's army streamed over the Isc bridge. It fanned out onto the river banks on either side. Victoricus estimated that they had more than twice the men under Sorio's command. Finally Cynan could be seen astride a white horse in the midst of a small group of riders, by the watchers on the gate tower. He was an impressive figure, riding easily, back straight, with a simple round metal helmet on his head and a scarlet cloak wrapped round him. He left his escort and rode up to the gate flanked by two riders only. Victoricus recognised the large figure of Gerontius, Cynan's son, but was more interested in the other rider. It was Bruscius, fit as far as he could tell, his broken limb whole again.

'He has courage,' hissed Lucius. 'We could shoot him easily from here. He's a perfect target.'

Cynan's voice carried over the still air.

'Why are the gates barred against me? Who dares deny the Lord Cynan entry into his own city?'

There was a pause before Sorio replied:

'I am no lord but Sorio, estate owner and loyal

subject of our true lord the Emperor Theodosius. This is not your city but his. You and your men are traitors and we shall continue to hold Isca for the Emperor.'

'My ancestors were kings here long before the Romans came. We are taking back what belongs to us. You are Britons. Join us and together we'll take a huge territory for ourselves.'

'And who will rule that territory?' asked Sorio.

'Naturally, given my ancestry, I shall rule it and my son after me.' Here Cynan indicated with a gesture of his hand the rider at his side. 'But you will merit an honourable and important position in the government of the land.'

Sorio appeared to be considering Cynan's offer carefully. The silence lasted so long that Victoricus glanced at Attius. It was enough to confirm what was in both their minds. Was Sorio about to make a huge mistake and surrender?

The silence was broken by Sorio voicing what was in his men's minds.

'What will happen to my comrades?'

'Most of them can join my army,' said Cynan smoothly. 'Together we will be able to protect our people. I have no quarrel with them. We can hold these lands against all enemies.'

'These are fair offers,' said Sorio, 'but I need to discuss them further and in private with my captains. I am merely their spokesman and will do nothing without consultation. Send in two representatives to speak for you and help us make a decision. We will guarantee their safe return.'

288

Cynan hesitated. He didn't welcome a fight, the outcome of which was uncertain and if he could gain Isca without it he would be delighted. On the other hand he didn't want to keep his army idle for long. Many of his men had been reluctant to march to Isca and only threats against their families had persuaded them to come. The longer they contemplated these formidable walls, the more their will to fight would be sapped.

'Send me two men out in exchange,' he shouted 'and we'll talk, but not for long. I've made a fair offer. Take it or suffer the consequences. Now open the gate.'

Lucius drew in his breath.

'Insist on using the south gate,' he whispered 'I don't trust him. His son's already looking round for help to rush the gate when it opens. The south gate and two representatives unaccompanied or I fear the fight starts now.'

So it was agreed. After a few moments' whispered discussion Cynan's son and Bruscius turned their horses to follow along the outer rim of Isca's ditch in the direction of the south gate. Meanwhile Lucius volunteered to act as hostage.

'I might learn something useful,' he said 'I can't come to harm while you hold Cynan's son. Young Victoricus can accompany me.'

Victoricus didn't relish the prospect of facing Cynan again, but he was disinclined to argue. If Lucius was prepared to risk capture then Victoricus would accompany him. After all, thought Victoricus, Sorio will be holding Cynan's son. As

Gerontius and Bruscius approached the gate with two escorts Sorio ordered one of the gates to be opened enough to allow Lucius and his companion out. As the four passed each other Bruscius looked with surprise and then astonishment at Victoricus, but said nothing. As they approached Cynan's men Lucius commented on Bruscius' stare.

'He recognised you, didn't he?'

'I know both of them,' said Victoricus. 'Bruscius pursued us when we escaped from Cynan and broke his ankle trying to grab us and Gerontius took over my family's farm when my parents died.'

'They'll be surprised to see you here,' he commented, as they prepared to be escorted formally back to Cynan.

As Victoricus suspected, Cynan was not pleased to see him.

'So Sorio harbours common criminals,' was his opening remark once he recognised Victoricus. 'If you're a sample of the men in his army I shall think twice about my offer. I should execute you now for defying me and injuring my bailiff.'

'My lord,' said Lucius 'you will bear in mind that we came freely to you as hostages and that your own son is in the same position with Sorio. Do not make threats which it would be dangerous to carry out.'

This reminder caused Cynan to shift his stare to Lucius and although he stayed silent, his anger showed in his face. Watching him carefully Lucius thought if he wins today Victoricus and I will be lucky to see the morning.

'Guard them well,' snarled Cynan at last turning away to re-cross the bridge.

Two men came forward and walked with the two hostages to the corner of the defences. There they descended a slope leading down to the river. Victoricus looked back and saw his comrades manning Isca's walls. They were watching events closely.

'Where are you taking us?' asked Lucius.

Their escorts seemed friendly enough and one replied: 'we've orders to hold you at the quay, away from our army.'

32

In Isca, meanwhile, Sorio was studying his guests closely. They were meeting in the entrance hall of the bath-house, which was deserted. Two of Sorio's captains had joined him. Gerontius looked bored and glanced frequently to the high ceiling, with its bare patches left by the peeling paint. He was over-weight, sweating slightly and his thick black hair hung limply in natural curls over his forehead and into the nape of his neck. His small eyes gleamed malevolently beneath the curls. Untrustworthy thought Sorio. By contrast Bruscius, whose limp was noticeable once he alighted from his horse, seemed to have an honest face and spoke up frankly and listened attentively. The latter did most of the talking, with Gerontius contributing only the briefest of comments.

Bruscius' main theme was to extol the benefits of Sorio and Cynan joining forces.

'You could each retain your bases, you in the east and my Lord Cynan in the west. Cynan would of course be overall leader, but I think you would find he would leave you very much to yourself. The armies could be pooled, each retaining a personal war-band for protection and the army being called upon when the territory was threatened. If the Scots raided for example, or if we faced problems from either east or west the army would be strong enough to deal with it.'

'What if the Empire sent forces against us?' asked Sorio.

'The Emperor's not interested in us any longer,' scoffed Gerontius. 'He's too busy at home.'

'But there's still a governor at Corinium,' Sorio persisted, 'and there are still soldiers in the British provinces.'

Gerontius did not like being contradicted and showed it, but Bruscius stepped in quickly to say that if the Roman government sent forces against them they would have to be prepared to negotiate, but he saw little likelihood of that happening.

'What are Cynan's plans for Isca?' asked one of the captains.

'Isca is important because of its defences. Naturally the Lord Cynan will need control of it, so that it can never again be held against him, but he'll have a residence here. He's prepared to build a church, appoint a bishop and encourage others to live within the walls. Isca will live again,' he finished enthusiastically. 'It will be the centre of our territory.'

'And no recriminations will be taken against me, my family or any of my men?' enquired Sorio.

'Not if we reach agreement,' said Bruscius 'that will be part of the undertaking.'

'Always excepting of course,' put in Gerontius lightly, 'any known criminals, deserters or runaways. You wouldn't expect my father to pardon those. It would be a sign of weakness.'

Sorio was able to disguise the shock on his face, despite the intense gaze, which Gerontius directed towards him. But not so his captains, who recognised the statement for what it was – a licence to deal with anyone who did not meet with Cynan's approval. They would never agree to that and they showed as much, although neither spoke. Bruscius looked shamefaced, almost, Sorio felt, deceived. Here is a man who has not been fully briefed, thought Sorio. It is as I suspected – Bruscius is negotiating in good faith, but without a full knowledge of what's intended. That's why he's been sent, but Cynan and Gerontius will never stick to any agreement. They'll gain access to Isca and then the killing will start and I shall probably be the first victim.

Aloud, he thanked the two for being frank with him. He now wished to consult with all his captains and he would send word to Cynan after their deliberations. They would be escorted to the gate, recover their swords, which had been left there, and released through it only when his own representatives were in sight. He walked with them to the entrance and thanked them again courteously.

'We're running out of patience,' called Gerontius from the steps, 'surrender within the hour or we attack.'

Surrender to you thought Sorio. Never. I shall be signing my own death warrant and that of many of my men. Inside the building he turned to his colleagues.

'I think we've heard enough. Agreed? Alert the rest of the army. We may be defending Isca within the hour.'

33

Once at the quay Lucius and Victoricus were allowed to wander freely. Their guards sat on a heap of tiles, keeping a general eye along the quayside, but they saw no reason to stay close to their charges, once they had separated them from Cynan's army. They were unarmed, their swords left with the guards. Men were loitering on the decks of the four vessels, which had come up river earlier. Others lounged on the quayside close-by. They all looked as if they were waiting for something to happen.

'Let's stroll along to the *Swan*,' said Victoricus 'and see if we can learn anything.'

The vessel was third in the line and it took them well away from their guards. They expected any minute to be re-called, but no shout came. Once they were abreast of the vessel Victoricus looked about him.

'I want to try and get into that cabin on the deck,' he muttered to Lucius. 'Can you keep that fellow talking for a few minutes?' He gestured towards a man on the quayside.

Close to the stern Victoricus swung himself over the rail and made for the cabin. He swung the door open and stepped inside. It was nearly the last step he took. Barculo was poised, club in hand and about to strike.

'You!' he said. 'You're lucky not to have had your skull split.' He grabbed Victoricus arm. 'Tell me, quick what you're doing here.'

Victoricus explained in a few words what had brought him to the quay. Barculo relaxed.

'Two days ago,' he said, 'wagons full of food and weapons arrived at the harbour. Cynan's men of course. We were ordered to transport them up to Isca. These other ships joined us later fully loaded out of the Taen. At first I refused. I was already full of cargo and about to sail for Uxella. To be honest I'd had enough and I was planning to stay at Uxella, but I didn't tell them that. Anyway they got hold of my boy and said if I didn't do as ordered it would be the worse for him. They put that fool out there on board to help out, but he's been green, throwing up his guts all the way up river and no help at all. I was tempted to pitch him overboard, but the other ships kept close and I didn't know then how loyal they were. I know now that we've all been treated the same. Cynan's men are on board every ship and we've all been threatened. You watch out. Cynan's not to be trusted. You tell them that when you get back inside Isca. Whatever you do, don't surrender and don't worry about these ships, Cynan will never get them unloaded; we'll see to that.'

At this point someone clattered noisily over the deck and Barculo said in a loud voice 'She sails true, even in a heavy swell. I keep busy working for my Lord Cynan. He's a good master.' At the same time winking broadly at Victoricus.

'She looks a trim vessel' said Victoricus, keeping up the deception, 'Thank you for showing me around,' just as the cabin door opened to reveal one of the guards.

'This young man is interested in ships' remarked Barculo.

'Come on,' said the guard. 'You're wanted.'

He and Lucius were escorted up towards the south gate. Their swords were returned to them and they were sent ahead alone. On the other side of the gate Gerontius fumed at the delay. He was already mounted and impatient to be off. His horse stamped and swerved and was rewarded with savage tugs at the reins.

'What's the delay?' he snarled, 'We're ready, open the gate!' His hand crept to the hilt of his sword, but his temper was not so out of control that he drew it. He knew that there were archers on the wall above him and that the captain and his men, well armed, were watching him closely. Bruscius sat quietly to one side, apparently lost in thought, his horse still and contented.

When the gate was opened, Gerontius rushed forward, squeezed through the smallest of gaps and galloped away. Bruscius followed at a sedate pace, as if reluctant to leave. His companion thundered over the wooden bridge carrying the road over the ditch and keeping to the centre of the road sped towards Lucius and Victoricus. They were walking at a fair pace along the edge of the road discussing Barculo's revelations. Lucius looked up and paused.

'Gerontius is in a hurry,' said Victoricus, amused, 'perhaps things haven't gone all his way.'

But as Gerontius came up to them he drew his sword. Victoricus, after a second's hesitation, realised that he was under attack but in the act of drawing his own sword heard Lucius shouting at him to move fast. The next moment he found himself on his back in the ditch. A sharp, stinging pain in his upper sword arm made him wince and he became aware of blood trickling freely down his arm. He raised himself up and stood, shakily, trying to clear his head. Then he scrambled up the side of the ditch.

Lucius had side-stepped Gerontius' assault, which in any case had been largely directed at Victoricus. As he did so he drew his sword and in one graceful but deadly thrust cut open Gerontius' thigh to the bone. The latter's high-pitched scream echoed against Isca's wall. His horse reared and he fell in a heap on the roadway, silent, his cloak spread-eagled across his body. Lucius, still with sword in hand, turned to face Bruscius. Victoricus, now on the edge of the road, was too weak to help and could only watch as Bruscius rode up, sword in hand.

'You saw what happened here,' said Lucius. 'Gerontius broke faith and deliberately attacked us.

We have no quarrel with you. If you allow us to pass, you are free to go and take this' – he indicated Gerontius' body by a slight turn of his head – 'with you. But I warn you that if attacked I will fight and I have some skill in that trade as your companion has just discovered to his cost.'

Bruscius wearily sheathed his sword.

'I saw all that happened. I saw Gerontius break his word. He was always a hot-headed fool. You are free to return to Isca and I will go on and explain these events to Lord Cynan.'

Victoricus, dragging his feet across the road towards the horseman and fighting a wave of nausea, which was threatening to overwhelm him, begged Bruscius to return with them inside the walls and to join Sorio.

'No,' said Bruscius gently. 'I have pledged my loyalty to Cynan and been deceived by him. I know now what his true nature is and that he does not deserve to lead our people. I have excused some of his excesses and those of his son in the belief that what they were striving to do was for the good of all. I deceived myself and put my fears to one side. No, I must go back and see if I can restrain him, although I am fearful of what he will do when he sees his son dead.'

Victoricus became dimly aware of movement. Men were crossing the bridge towards them and shouting. At the same time Lucius turned to see a group of Cynan's men advancing up the slope towards the road. He grabbed Victoricus and urged him on. They had little time to get back to safety.

Stumbling, weak and only faintly aware of his surroundings, Victoricus was half-dragged, half-carried back by the veteran. They reached their own companions with little time to spare. Victoricus was seized and carried back to the gate, while Lucius and others provided a safety screen. The archers on the wall fired over their heads towards Cynan's men, who were now on the road and they slowed and stopped. The gate closed with a thud. The bar was slid into place and all were safe.

Victoricus had fainted away. Lucius, having removed his jerkin, looked at the wound.

'Not deep,' he said. 'Fetch someone to dress it and bind it up and then see that he's comfortable. He's lost a lot of blood. I'd better report to Sorio, quickly. And the rest of you stay alert. Get to your posts. This won't be the last blood to be shed today.'

34

Victoricus awoke to find Attius bending over him. He felt weak and listless and took a few moments to adjust to his surroundings. He was lying on a pallet in a small room. Sunlight shining through a window high in the wall created a bright circle on the ceiling, but the rest of the room was in shadow. Then he remembered the morning's events and looked quickly at Attius.

'What's happening?' he croaked.

'Have a mouthful of water first,' said Attius, reaching for a beaker, 'and then try not to talk. You need to rest. Your wound is not bleeding any longer, but you must stay still.'

Refreshed, Victoricus sank back onto his pillow and looked at Attius enquiringly.

'It's all over,' his friend said.

Lifting his head from the pillow, Victoricus looked as if he had failed to understand.

'What do you mean?' he asked.

'Just what I say, it's all over. Cynan's army has gone. His ships have gone. Isca is ours and we're all safe.'

'But what about Bruscius, and Cynan and all their men? What's happened?'

'Don't excite yourself, Victoricus,' said his friend 'and I'll tell you everything from the beginning.'

'But . . .'

'And if you try to talk I'll go away and leave you to guess.' Here Attius paused, but the interruptions had finished and he continued.

'You'll remember being attacked by Gerontius and falling into the ditch. You're aware that Gerontius was then killed by Lucius and I think you had a conversation with Bruscius about changing sides, once you'd dragged yourself out of the ditch. Lucius brought you back into Isca and eventually you were brought to this room in Sorio's house where they found a doctor to look at your wound. The men at the gate had made a good job of binding up your arm, but he dressed it properly and gave you poppy syrup to make you sleep. And it worked you've slept for about five hours and missed all the fun.'

Seeing that Victoricus was becoming impatient, he hurried on.

'Bruscius tied Gerontius' body to his horse and led it back to Cynan. We were at the bridge gate and knew nothing of this until Lucius arrived to warn Sorio what had happened. Cynan was still on the far side of the river with the bulk of his army but he must have got wind of something happening because he returned on horseback with his men streaming over the bridge behind him. Bruscius appeared from the quay leading Gerontius' horse.

He rode slowly towards Cynan, his face grim and set. Cynan made no attempt to meet him but sat absolutely still, slightly forward of a small group of horsemen. Bruscius rode right up to Cynan through a crowd of men. We had a full account of the meeting later from Cynan's own men. Bruscius said: 'My lord I have tragic news. Your son is dead. He broke his word, attacked one of Sorio's envoys and was in turn cut down himself.' There was a silence. Cynan sat absolutely still, his face a mask. He did not look at his son's body, but kept his eyes fixed on Bruscius' face.

Finally he spat out 'And where were you, Bruscius, when my son died? Did you kill his murderer. Where are your wounds? Why are you not dead in his defence?' 'Your son raced ahead,' replied Bruscius evenly 'and took matters into his own hands. He broke his oath to keep the peace, drew his sword and attempted to kill Sorio's envoy.'

'Liar,' shouted Cynan suddenly, 'liar. My son would never have broken his word. He must have been provoked. Those scoundrels drew first and my son died defending himself while you looked on and did nothing. You deserve to die for this and I'll see that you do.'

'My lord I have spoken only the truth,' said Bruscius quietly seemingly unperturbed by his master's ire. 'Gerontius was hot-headed and angry and attacked even before his intended victim had time to draw his own sword.'

'Take those words back or die now,' shouted

Cynan so suddenly that even Bruscius was jolted out of his calm to find Cynan's sword out of its scabbard and poised ready to strike him. Instead of retreating he spurred his horse forward, at the same time grasping his own sword and as Cynan's blade flashed down he thrust his own point first into his lord's chest. Cynan's sword flew from his hand and landed harmlessly on the ground. His bailiff withdrew his blade and Cynan slithered down the flank of his horse to the ground.'

Victoricus was so startled that he was not sure that he had really understood. Was he fully awake and was Cynan really dead?

But Attius was continuing, confirming everything that Victoricus had heard.

'We saw all this from the town walls,' he said. 'We saw Cynan's body fall from his horse. It lay on the ground and all the men around were so shocked that nobody moved or spoke. Then Cynan's bodyguard moved forward. They drew their swords and surrounded Bruscius. He stood no chance. He fought them, but they hacked him down. Then the onlookers gave a great cry and the horsemen found themselves surrounded. It was just as if Cynan's death had unblocked a swollen river. Their anger surged around the bodyguard. They were pulled from their horses, trampled on, beaten and killed. Most of the men are farmers. It was fear that made them fight, fear of the threats made against them and their families by Cynan, Gerontius and their cronies. Gerontius in particular was hated. Many were pleased to see him dead.'

'So its ended then,' said Victoricus 'and Sorio has won?'

'Yes, Isca's gates are open once more. Some of Cynan's men have come into the town and been well-received, but most of them have departed back to their own homes. If anything Sorio's rather embarrassed by all the fuss. He says he can't wait to return home to his estate and become a farmer once more. He's shocked Silvius by saying that he proposes to divide up the estate into separate farms, keeping only a small estate for himself. The families can work their own land and feed themselves from the produce. He's giving up this house. I think he realises that Isca has had its day. He'll abandon it to those few people who want to continue living in it.'

'Did Lucius mention that I'd seen Barculo?' asked Victoricus.

'Yes, I heard all about it. All four ships sailed down river after Cynan was killed, leaving their guards behind. We're not sure where they've gone, but I should think Barculo will show up in Uxella one of these days.'

'Speaking of Uxella, when can we travel back home and has the news been sent on to our friends?'

'Don't worry, Viventia will hear of your exploits soon. Sorio is sending messengers out at first light tomorrow. But you've got to regain your strength, before you make the journey. Viventia won't want to see you like this. You'll need the use of both your arms when you meet up with her again. Go back to sleep and I'll see you again in the morning. Lucius and Sorio want to see you and Silvius begged to come with me, but the doctor said one visitor only and not too much excitement, so we got it half right.'

35

As Attius slipped away Victoricus dozed. He was hardly aware of the doctor at his bedside, but drank a further draught of the sweet poppy syrup as the doctor raised his head from the pillow.

When he awoke again he was aware before he opened his eyes that the room was full of light. It penetrated his eyelids creating a warm rosy glow. Next he was aware of someone bending over him.

'You here again, Attius,' he murmured without opening his eyes. 'Give me a drink.'

A beaker touched his lips and he drank the cold water gratefully. Gently his pillow was smoothed and his head laid back at rest. No-one had spoken but the thought came into Victoricus' head that if this was Attius he was wearing perfume. He almost giggled at the idea, but then focussed.

'Viventia!' he said, without opening his eyes, 'it's not possible.'

'You don't believe it then,' whispered a familiar voice and he opened his eyes to stare in disbelief at the face which had swum in and out of his dreams all night, the dear face of his beloved Viventia. She bent over and kissed him gently on the lips.

'Not a dream,' she said, echoing his thoughts, 'I'm really here.'

'How is it possible?' he asked.

'Ask Barculo that,' came the reply. 'He made the voyage to Uxella in record time, even though he stopped to pick up his boy on the way. He was the first to bring the news to Uxella and while Barculo's ship was unloaded Senacus himself rode over to Sorio's estate to let us all know. He was relieved that Sorio had been successful, especially as he had had a message back from Corinium to say the governor could not help and instructing him to take charge. When Senacus told us that Barculo was planning to return overnight to Isca I persuaded father to let me go with him. Eventually he relented on condition that Rufus accompanied me. We borrowed horses and returned with Senacus. Somehow Barculo did not seem surprised when we turned up. And do you know, Victoricus? . . .'

Here she kissed him again, as he closed his eyes, enjoying the sensation, but wishing he didn't feel quite so weak.

. . . 'Barculo's boy said he was pleased you were recovering from your wound and then looked me straight in the face.'

Derek and The Mint Press would like to thank Derek Acton, Esmé Acton, Sandra & Mark Acton, Am Afifi, Rob Alexander, L. Allison, Jenny Andrews, Peter Paul Anthony, Mary Avent, Avril Avery, Dr & Mrs David Badcott, Althea Bailey, David Baker, Philip Banks, Adèle Beale, Ethel Bennett, Camilla Blackman, Eileen Bloor, Michael Bloor, Barbara Bone, Pam Boreham, Margaret Braddon, Anthony Bradfield, Bruce Bradley, Mark Bray, Mary Bray, Lydia Breeze-Chilcott, Alison, Neil & Luke Brown, Jeanne Brown, Olivia Brown, Peter Brown, Sheila Brown, Bob Bruce, Jonathan Bryant, Pauline Bryant, Timothy Bryant, the Bullivant family, Hazel Bunyan, Mary Burleigh, Dorothy Butler, Christine Caldwell, Janet Cambridge, Marion & Robert Cannon, J. Carter, Jane Casey, Chris Chapman, Joyce Cherry, Tim Clarke, J. Clatworthy, Ann Claxton, Roger Claxton, Yvonne Cleave, Jill Cobley, Bill Coldridge, Peter & Annet Coles, Jenny Collins, Jean Cowls, Sue & Norman Crampton, Pauline Crean, Oliver Creighton, Jacqueline Cummins, Marion Curtis, Christena Custons-Cole, Daphne Dance, Ursula Davey, Anne Davies, Valerie Davieson, Richard Davin, Stuart Dawson, Val Dawson, Kevin Dixon, Ena Doak, Sheila Drew, Sarah

Dunn, Jan Dunning, Yasmin Durrant, Sally Ealey, Pam Eames, Roy & Mary East, Deyman Eastmond, Stefan Edwards, Heather Ellor, Matthew Ellor, Sue Farrell, Mary Faulkner, Jenny Fennell, Malcolm Fletcher, Arthur Force, David Force, Barbara French, Diana E. Friendship-Taylor, Denise Fry, Oliver Gardener, Sheila Gibbons, John & Alison Gibson, Bernice & Daniel Golberg, Barbara Goody, Edward Gore, Helen & Martin Gore, Olivia Gore, Geoff Graham, Kate Grayshan, Stephen & Karen Gregory, Rosemary Griffiths, Christine Hall, Nellie Hall, Brian Hammond, Jennifer Harries, Hazel Harvey, Sean Hawken, Michael Head, Peggie Head, James Henderson, Pat Henham, John Henley, Mr & Mrs Graham Hessé, F. Roy Hewlett, Kenneth Hibberd, Geoffrey Hickley, M. Hicks, Robert Higham, Margaret Hill, Peter J. Hill, Anne Hine, Edward Hitchings, Rebecca Hodge, Anne Holmes, George Holmes, John Holmes, Edna Honour, David Howell, J. M. Hughes, Linda Hurcombe, Rachel & Derek Jackson, Jo James, Margaret James, Marion Johnson, Susan Johnson, Andrew Jones, Bernard Jones, Harold Jones, Gill Juleff, Barbara Keene, Jean Keevill, Sue Kennedy, Joan King, Lewis King, Lottie King, Abi Kirk-Walker, Rachel Kitcherside, M. Knight, Tanya Krott, Rod Lane, Margaret Lawrence, Iris Liddicoat, Stephanie Linnell, Patricia Lomax, Iris Long, David Luckhurst, Peter Luckhurst, Stanley Luckhurst, Norah & Henry Luxton, Barbara Lyall, Neil Macaulay, Lesley Marchant, Jane Marley, Vaneeta Martin, Helena & Peter Mathew, Kelly May, Elizabeth Maycock, David McCann, Anna Katerina McKinnon, Carla Miller, Joyce Mills, Ann Mitchell, Margaret Morgan, Morwen Morris, Paul Moynagh, Helen Muirden, Margaret Murch, Jean Nankervis, Maureen Naudé, Joan Norman,

Joy Nottidge, Richard O'Neill, Richard Osborne, Alan Outram, Liz Palmer, Roz Pardee, P. Parkins, Mr & Mrs D. L. Parnall, Nancie Parr, Jim Partridge, John E. P. Passmore, Don Paterson, Michael Patrick, R. I. Payton, Hilary Perry, Sam Phillips, Rosemary Rankin, William Rankin, Rosaleen Rashley, Margaret Reed, Alan & Amèlia Redding, Stella Redgrave, Margherita Rendel, Pam Reynolds, Beryl Richards, Sandra Richards, Isabel Richardson, Jean Riley, Stephen Rippon, Barbara Roberts, Heather Ross, Iain Rowe, Sheila Rowe, Chris Ruse, Shirley Ryan, Clive Samuel, Dora Searle, David Shipstone, Philippa Shipstone, Heather Simons, Jill & Frank Sisson, Elizabeth Sparkes, Matthew Spriggs, John Stebbing, the Stephens family, Nann Stimpson, Sarah & Derek Stoddart, Donald Stone, Mavis Stuckey, Sylvia Suddaby, Iris Sutton, Esmee Sykes, Philippa Szymusik, Robert Thompson, Audrey Thorp, Janet Thorp, Margaret Toole, Pauline Tregaskis, Roger Trengrove, Mavis Tucker, Brian Tugwell, Colin & Sue Tugwell, Robert Van de Noort, Peter Vance, Sheila Wain, Christine Wallace, Philip Ward-Green, Rachel Ware, Jenny Watling, Sue & Martin Watts, Helena Wayment, Jeremy W.E. White, M. E. White, Patricia Whiteaway, Margaret Wigg, Betty Wilkins, Howard Williams, Beverley Williams, Diana Williams, Sam Williams, Susan Willmott, Marilyn Wills, Kathleen Wright, Duncan Wright, Tom & Rosie Wrigley and Pat & Stuart Yates for their support in the publication of this book.